About the autho

The author was a parish priest for over forty years in Derbyshire and Suffolk. Born in the Anchor Inn, Maulden, he was brought up in Ampthill, Bedfordshire.

He failed the "11+", having turned up for the exam, in Bedford, at the wrong school. At Luton Technical School he went on to fail religious education at O level.

The author trained for ordination at Kelham Theological College, run by the Society of the Sacred Mission, a religious order of the Anglican Church.

Before the five-year course he was literally sent to Coventry, to work as a labourer in the carpenters' shop at an aircraft factory, during which time he was in digs with a family that included six daughters at home - an ideal preparation for living in a monastery.

He has no degree. But he was awarded the Territorial Decoration, with two bars and rose, for service in the Territorial Army.

The author has been married to Barbara for forty-nine years. They live in retirement, in Suffolk.

WITH CLOUDS DESCENDING

THE HUMOROUS AND SOMEWHAT NAUGHTY STORY OF A CLERIC'S ANCESTORS

David Charles Lowe

WITH CLOUDS DESCENDING

Illustrations and cover design by Simon Merrett

Vanguard Press

A CIP catalogue record for this title is
available from the British Library.

ISBN 978 1 784658 76 2

*Vanguard Press is an imprint of
Pegasus Elliot MacKenzie Publishers Ltd.*
www.pegasuspublishers.com

First Published in 2020

**Vanguard Press
Sheraton House Castle Park
Cambridge England**

Printed & Bound in Great Britain

Dedication

These chronicles are dedicated
to Barbara;
to Penny, Sally and Emily;
to Jonathan, Dean and Mark;
to Megan, Charlie, Tilly, Harrison,
Oliver and Oscar.

Contents

PREFACE 11

PART I Betsey and Bill 13

   Another and Another and Another by James Henry 15

   CHAPTER 1 PAINFUL ENCOUNTER 17

   CHAPTER 2 EARLY YEARS OF ELIZABETH 20

   CHAPTER 3 MY STAMPING GROUND 26

   CHAPTER 4 MISDEMEANOURS OF WILLIAM 33

   CHAPTER 5 MY STINTS IN DERBYSHIRE AND
   SUFFOLK 42

   CHAPTER 6 ON THE RIVER AND RAILWAY 51

   CHAPTER 7 AT THE BAR 62

   CHAPTER 8 ON THE LAND 75

   CHAPTER 9 BETSEY AND BILL'S WEDDING 85

   CHAPTER 10 THE RECTOR IN CLINK 93

   CHAPTER 11 FOREIGN AND HOME AFFAIRS 102

   CHAPTER 12 ENTER ANN 115

INTERLUDE 119

   Poem by Anthony Thwaite 121

   LUCY LOW IS DONE FOR MURDER 123

PART 2 Eliza and Pop 125

   Stanza XVIII (final) of Verses written on the Alameda by
   Jeremiah Holmes Wiffen 127

   CHAPTER 13 DELIVERY OF POP 129

   CHAPTER 14 THE RECTOR'S MATCH 132

   CHAPTER 15 JOSIAH'S HATCH 143

   CHAPTER 16 POP DELIVERS 149

   CHAPTER 17 FATHER CHRISTMAS 155

   CHAPTER 18 MISTRESS ELIZA 164

   CHAPTER 19 AT WAR 172

   CHAPTER 20 ORIGINS 181

   CHAPTER 21 UP THE HATTERS 187

   CHAPTER 22 ELIZA DELIVERS 191

   CHAPTER 23 DISPATCH BOX 197

   CHAPTER 24 MY RETIREMENT 206

POSTSCRIPT 216

   END OF A CENTURY 216

APPENDICES 219

   1. A map of villages close to Ampthill that are mentioned in the text.. 221

   2. The LOW family tree 222

   3.The ROBINSON family tree............................... 223

   4. The BURGESS family tree 224

   5. The BRIDGE family tree 225

   6. The THOROGOOD family tree........................ 226

   7. Time line of background events......................... 227

   8. Time line of Low family events 229

   9. Time line of the rector's events......................... 232

   10. Time line of the author's life.......................... 234

   11. List of illustrations by Simon Merrett.............. 237

   12. Acknowledgements 238

   13. Bibliography.. 240

PREFACE

WITH CLOUDS DESCENDING is an autobiography. But it is one with differences. The differences are, first, that I write about myself 130 years in the past. Secondly I alter some of the areas where events take place.

The book is also more than an autobiography. It is a story of some of my ancestors of the nineteenth century. Writing about myself as if I lived 130 years ago means that I can interact with those ancestors.

For this reason, I have needed to make adaptations to my life. For example, I could not have been a 53-seater coach driver in the 19th century. But I could transport people by coach and horses.

The book is written in the context of local historical events. There is a little family history, a little social history, a little ecclesiastical history, and a great deal of fanciful embroidery.

My family name is LOWE. Some time ago in the family's history it was lengthened from LOW. For the purpose of the book's title I have further shortened the name to LO, thus making a pun of the opening line of the Advent hymn, "Lo, he comes WITH CLOUDS DESCENDING." There is a further pun in "descending", which refers to both clouds and descendants.

These memoirs tell the story of a real family. The main characters are Bill Low (1821-1875) and Betsey Robinson (1824-1866); and Josiah "Pop" Burgess (1833-1915) and Eliza Low (1843-1928). Some incidents related below (such as floods, riots, murders, suicides, diseases, crimes, wars, etcetera) are based on fact, but details are elaborated and not necessarily true.

I am a retired parish priest. I carried out my ministry in Derbyshire and Suffolk, where I now live. But to allow me to mingle with my ancestors I have translocated my ministry to the Bedfordshire town of Ampthill where I was brought up and where, in my imagination, I become the rector of that town. Thus I become the parish priest of my forebears!

I am aware that my ancestors are also other people's ancestors. I hope that no offence will be taken by my often imaginary descriptions of and stories about them.

In other words, I look at myself from now to then, and hence use contemporary colloquialisms rather than the language of the nineteenth century.

I was born in Maulden supposedly in 1813. After curacies in Derbyshire and Suffolk I was, as I say, notionally, instituted into the living of Ampthill in 1841. I continued to live in Ampthill following retirement in 1890 at the early age of 77. The year of my death is at the time of writing unknown.

It is said that most families have a skeleton hidden somewhere in their cupboard. This family appears to have a few skeletons in their own cupboard. But they are not too well hidden.

The book is also inspired by private diaries that I have kept from 1984-2019. They are about experiences as vicar of three Suffolk parishes and, latterly, in retirement, but adapted to fit another time and place.

It remains for another book to tell of my 'proper' story. This will be related in the sequel, *Lo He Comes*.

The clouds, as we will discover, are now stormy and cheerless; now letting through sunshine; now and then dark and dismal; now sometimes hopeful and blissful. The fabric of life comprises clouds black and white, representing crisis and calm.

PART I
Betsey and Bill

Let us now sing the praises of… our ancestors in their
generations.
Sirach 44.1

Another and Another and Another

by James Henry

(written at the time between Betsey's and Bill's final sunsets)

Another and another and another
And still another sunset and sunrise,
The same yet different, different yet the same,
Seen by me now in my declining years
As in my early childhood, youth and manhood;
And by my parents and my parents' parents,
And by the parents of my parents' parents,
And by their parents counted back for ever,
Seen, all their lives long, even as now by me;
And by my children and my children's children
And by the children of my children's children
And by their children counted on for ever
Still to be seen as even now seen by me;
Clear and bright sometimes, sometimes dark and clouded
But still the same sunsetting and sunrise;
The same for ever to the never ending
Line of observers, to the same observer
Through all the changes of his life the same:
Sunsetting and sunrising and sunsetting,
And then again sunrising and sunsetting,
Sunrising and sunsetting evermore.

CHAPTER 1
PAINFUL ENCOUNTER

It happened on a piece of grassy wasteland in the tiny Nottinghamshire village of Kelham. Messing around with a hard ball with others of my age I was stood erect between two coats serving as goalposts when Billy Beaumont cannoned the ball from short range into what were at the time my very private parts. The save put me out of action for some considerable time.

Some fourteen years later, by now long recovered, an incident occurred in the small Bedfordshire town of Ampthill. The incident was altogether different but it had a similar effect

Never mind precisely what I said. It takes something to make me swear. But curse her I did. She had kneed me hard in the crotch. Even for a mild-mannered and easy-going parish priest this sudden violent action that brought tears to my eyes more than any humble onion had previously accomplished triggered a verbal reaction that is rarely heard from the lips of a respected canon. But hold on - I must wait a further twenty years before being fired up, or canonised. So perhaps my blasphemies were not that serious after all.

What had I done to deserve such an assault from a dainty eighteen-year-old girl? And what swear words did I use? The answer to the first will become apparent shortly. As for the second, we will let it go. It was the rector's warden's fault. He had told the girl that I was not available to be seen at that moment. He knew that I had had a few too many in the Queen's Head and imagined that I was not up to meeting parishioners so late in the evening, though the church clock had not yet registered nine-thirty. The warden had called at the rectory earlier in the evening about a problem he was having with the architect. So he decided to answer the door when it was thumped loudly and impatiently. His reply was not what fiery Elizabeth wanted to hear, especially when she had seen me wobble up the rectory path seconds earlier.

She called him a bloody nuisance and punched him on the nose, though not sufficiently hard to cause bleeding. He may have been a bloody nuisance but at least he did not have a bloody nose. Naturally, hearing the rumpus, I wanted to hide. Yet I thought it expedient to follow up the event by searching her out and to proffer a stern rebuke for her attack. So I called after her as she made off angrily down the driveway. She turned about and confronted me. Hence the encounter between her knee and my balls.

Moreover, I had not long recovered from a debilitating spell of mumps. My precious nuts had survived a double dosage of danger. The walnuts might have withered into ineffectual peanuts, but I remained fortunate enough to retain my prized potency. Proof of the pudding established itself in the years ahead.

Not, then, suffering permanent damage, or so I hoped, there I wanted to let sleeping dogs lie, at least after recovering breath. But churchwarden Charles Moore insisted on making a formal charge, which resulted in young Elizabeth being committed to Bedford New House of Correction for two months. Charles was not satisfied. This penitentiary was intended for light offenders. He thought Betsey should have spent time in the County Gaol itself.

CHAPTER 2
EARLY YEARS OF ELIZABETH

Bill's mother, Frances, and father, John

John was already earning a little money by working on the land when Frances was first born. (She was born only once, but she was the first-born.) She was born at the beginning of the new century. John was born fourteen years before the old century finished.

My predecessor, the Reverend Mr Knapp, had married Elizabeth's mother, Frances. That is to say, he did not actually marry her. She was one of several scores of brides he had hitched together with a man. This particular man who scored with the bride was called John Robinson. He it was who in reality married Frances. All the rector did was to recite the words of the ceremony of matrimony and cement Frances' right hand with John's, and his with hers. Thus were they pronounced Man and Wife, no just impediment having been declared, and, of course, after warning them that their marriage must not be enterprised to satisfy men's carnal lusts and appetites, like brute beasts which have no understanding, as the Prayer Book puts it.

Frances' clothing for her wedding, or lack of it, caused some controversy. For one thing she wore a white dress. Gossipers who came to view her arrival at Saint Andrew's parish church said she ought not to be wearing white. "Tut-tut!" For another thing, with so many family and friends being employed in the town's hat business, Frances was undiplomatic, in that she married hatless, showing off her golden-brown hair, done up in a pretty bun. Talking of which, Elizabeth was already rising in the oven on the wedding day. Frances already was a Fanny of some experience, even at her tender age. Before the wedding John had wondered whether he was too old to father children, but he proved himself five times wrong.

Black-bearded John was as easy-going a man as one could find. He was as capable and competent at practical jobs as he was at siring children. His technical skill was useful both at work and at home. But more importantly, soft-spoken John was tolerant and, above all, loving towards Frances.

At their wedding Frances was, if hatless, otherwise respectably clothed and well corseted. Much of what was beneath the dress was held up by elastic. It had recently been invented, so she was giving it a try. I see from my diary that four years ago, when I was a curate in Wingerworth, I had experienced a rather wicked wedding. Lack of headdress was nothing to the seventeen-year-old's attire. She had no use for elastic. I cannot for the life of me now recall her name. But I do vividly visualise her body:

June 1837 *At today's wedding the seventeen-year-old bride wore a low-cut and see-through wedding dress. Some of the church ladies were mortified, especially since this contradicted current fashion, but I was not going to object. In fact it was observed that I hardly needed to read from the Prayer Book. My eyes were raised well above book level so that I could do a meditation on her body generously endowed with freckles, especially her barely-covered bust. Two of the freckles were more prominent than the rest. The lady verger reported me to the rector.*

At another unusual ceremony in my second curacy in Bury St Edmunds I wrote of a situation I had not encountered before:

May 1839 *I married two brothers to two sisters. The four had come to book a double wedding. This turned out to be a bigger job than I first imagined. Both sisters had a bun in the oven, according to a reliable source. One brother is a chauffeur for the funeral director. So we had undertakers and bearers in church for the wedding, by which time the sisters had become most plump. I needed to be cautious so as not to marry the wrong brother to the right sister, or the right brother to the wrong pudding.*

My little sister Elizabeth, by the way, was staying with me at the time. She was my reliable source. And, although they never met, the two Elizabeths (my sister and my assailant) happened to be born on the same day. I also officiated at the wedding of both Elizabeths - not on the same day. Having already related something of Frances and John's wedding, their daughter Elizabeth's marriage ceremony as well as my sister's were pleasures still to come.

Elizabeth (by this name was she baptised but we will now call her Betsey, lest she be confused with my little sister) was born seventeen years before I was instituted as rector of Ampthill. She had been baptised in Lidlington. Frances and John had taken her back there to be christened but not until she was eight. The eldest of six children, Betsey had moved with her parents and sisters, Ruth, Lydia and Mary, and her brothers, James and John (sons of Boanerges, as I later called them), to Duck End in Maulden.

Much later in life Betsey's brother John worked on Mr Street's farm in Maulden. His only illness during his working life was in his late forties when he suffered a severe throat ulceration. He was not the only one on the farm to go down with the illness. The doctor believed it was due to pollution in the atmosphere caused by sewerage from the people not of Maulden but of Ampthill. There was a sewage farm on the boundary with Ampthill, and the shit had got into a stream that flowed into a reservoir on Mr Street's land. The sanitary authority had recently turned down plans to install a sewer and drains, in spite of a residents' petition. They said it was unnecessary. Instead they illogically advised people not to throw soap suds into the street.

Returning to Betsey, she was indeed a hot-tempered girl. Possibly she needed to be, to draw attention to herself, being three inches shy of five feet. She was a good-looker, despite the prominent scar on her left cheek. How she came by this she never admitted, not to me, anyway. She had brown hair, bright grey eyes and a good, if pale, complexion. She was not without curvaceous contours, and, when not on the attack, delicate.

Almost two decades after her parents' wedding, when Betsey was in gaol, I summoned up courage to visit her during her two months in Bedford New House of Correction. It was an easier call than I expected for she was full of remorse. Ashamed to find herself under lock and key, she gave me the impression that she felt rather embarrassed by what she had done, first to the churchwarden, then to me.

I asked her why she had come to visit me that eventful evening. Until now I never knew the reason. It transpired that she had been sent by her father to bring a bag of onions for the garden fete. She also had a message from John that he would call around with a marrow on the morrow.

This explained why I spotted several balls, as they at first seemed next morning, spread across the rectory garden. They were the gift of onions. In her temper she had tipped out the onions and kicked them over the garden, just as she had kicked my own onions. This realisation again brought tears to my eyes.

Betsey, as she now asked me to call her, since everyone else did, she explained, told me when I visited her in gaol that she was made to work in the laundry. She also said that they had tried to put her on the treadmill but she could not manage it. So instead they gave her the portable hand-crank mill to work on. I suggested that, in addition to going to these areas, she might also use the chapel sometimes. She did not reply.

But she did ask if I could visit her again and perhaps take her some books. She was capable of reading, if imperfectly. That is what the warden (the prison warden, not the churchwarden) told me. I decided to gift her my copy of John Bunyan's Pilgrim's Progress and see what she might make of it. This was over-hopeful, not to say unrealistic. My thinking was that she would be encouraged to see what Bunyan could achieve in the same Bedford Gaol some one hundred and eighty years earlier. In fact, on my second visit, I tried to console Betsey by telling her that John Bunyan was imprisoned for *twelve* years, not two months. Her sentence in comparison was a doddle. This information did not seem to provide any consolation whatsoever. I did get a smile from her, however, when I said that preacher Bunyan had taken up his father's trade. He was a tinker. "You're a tinker of a different kind," I joked.

Before his imprisonment John Bunyan had walked, so it has been said, from Bedford to Luton. His journey was a particular trial as he climbed up Hazelwood Lane, the steep hill leading up to Ampthill. That is romantic surmise. But let us stick with the romance and go along with his description of the "Hill of Difficulty" in his book as being this approach into Ampthill.

As a thirteen-year-old I had walked the fourteen miles from Luton to Ampthill. That is no surmise. The whole journey was a "hill" of difficulty, not least because of having to egg on two lagging and flagging younger brothers for whom I was responsible that day.

As far as my precious book by John Bunyan was concerned, I never set eyes on the volume again, even when later I scanned the shelves in Betsey's home. If she had not made good progress as a pilgrim, she had at least proved to be an orderly inmate, her conduct being exemplary while under lock and key. For Betsey the hill of difficulty, as she returned from Bedford after her sentence, became the hill of delight. She had a card that told her that she was out of gaol free.

If Betsey was orderly, not so was William, who was detained at Her Majesty Victoria's pleasure in the County House of Correction at the same time. Before coming to William I should describe something of my upbringing.

CHAPTER 3
MY STAMPING GROUND

My parents were both twenty-one when they made their overture into marriage in 1812. I was born, eight months after the wedding, at the Anchor Inn on George Street in Maulden.

The day I was born the chimney fell off, so I am told. Apparently I picked up a few swear words at an early age when toddling into the forbidden tap room. My grandmother Maud would chase after me in the bar and scoop me up in her arms to carry me off to the more uninteresting private rooms in which I was permitted to wander freely. I never use those bad words now. Well, I only do so when someone kicks me in Baldock. They come in useful when dealing with bad-tempered girls like Betsey. My great-grandfather, another William, was landlord of the Anchor. He was, as I remember him, a gentle man, if not a gentleman, not like the roguish William whom we will shortly meet.

Grandfather William had been a farmer for a couple of years at Street's Farm before Betsey's brother John worked there. But most of his working life had been spent as a driver of horse-drawn trams in London. Then he took on the Anchor pub.

William retired from the pub while I was still only three and lived with my great-grandmother Clara on the Knoll, around the corner from the Anchor. I would go to Clara's to be looked after while William was out, gardening or drinking I have no inkling, and while both my mother and grandmother were somewhere or other too. The very aged Clara walked one morning into the pantry. I thought it would be fun to close the pantry door from the outside. I gave it a push. Unfortunately for her the door did not open from the inside. Nor was I tall enough to reach the latch. Clara was imprisoned inside the dark pantry until my mother returned to collect me some hours later. What mischief I got up to under my own auspices I no longer recall. I know that in future my great-grandmother never again went into the pantry without ensuring that I was with her.

My mother Elizabeth had moved from her home in Brighton after her father George died when he was thirty-seven. She was thirteen and moved with her mother Maud to Maulden to be with her maternal grandparents. Elizabeth's mother was known in the family as the Maulden Maud. Elizabeth was then fourteen and her great sadness at leaving her home town had nothing to do with being separated from her many aunts and uncles and cousins, or even her best friends. Her sorrow was due to having to leave behind the country's very first pleasure pier. It had been built when my mother was two and had given her so much enjoyment throughout her childhood. She was bitterly disappointed when she found that Maulden had no pier. Nor was there opportunity ever to go to the seaside, not at least for many years to come.

My mother had only one sibling. Her sister May was younger than she. She and John, her husband, lived in Westoning. We occasionally went over as a family and my two brothers and I enjoyed playing with our two cousins Elizabeth and Mary. It was a tradition that we made the long journey every Boxing Day, usually ploughing our way through deep snow.

My father had only one sibling too. His brother Francis was much younger than he. He was a confirmed bachelor - almost. He did marry at long last. Then his wife left him. Then he married again. His second wife left him. Then he reverted to his life as a confirmed bachelor, except that he was two sons to the good. Frances had the Low characteristic of rubbing the side of his nose, protruding his chin and staring vacantly into distant clouds. What was going through his mind nobody knew.

I was present many moons later for the reading of uncle Francis' will. Naturally he left nearly everything to his sons. But he generously left me his ashes, which he instructed to be scattered in Ampthill Park.

At the age of four I moved with my parents, Arthur and Elizabeth, to Ampthill. We had a downstairs living room-cum-kitchen (in which the tin bath was brought out on Friday evenings) and two bedrooms upstairs, one of which I shared with my one brother and before long with my two brothers. The other bedroom was presumably shared by my parents. We also had a little boxroom where my sister slept when she arrived. I was aware that something was afoot when my mother was giving birth for the fourth time. I asked my uncle about it. "Your mother's in a bit of pain. She's swallowed a fish bone and it needs taking out," he said with a hint of embarrassment. Many years later I realised that the fish bone was a euphemism for my sea-urchin sister. The problem was what to do now that there were six of us in the house. It was solved by shipping me back to Maulden to my grandmother's, where I could have my own bedroom (and poached eggs every night for supper).

Even though we lived in Maulden until I was four, and Roy until he was one, we were both baptised at Saint Andrew's in Ampthill. The Reverend John Hawkins' name is on our certificates. Our brother John was the last baby to be baptised by him. His ministry in the parish had come to an end after fifty years. Our sister Elizabeth was baptised by the Reverend Mr Knapp.

My father worked in a butcher's shop and slaughter house. Roy my younger brother took up the trade after leaving school. As a young teenager I worked for my father on Saturdays and sometimes other days (for next to nothing). The Christmas holiday was murder, with hundreds of turkeys' feathers to pluck. It was pluck, pluck and pluck recurring. At least this was a job that I could manage. But, try as I might, I could not cut the right joints that customers asked for, so I was always in trouble. Even the sausages came out unevenly with many a burst skin. They would have looked like faulty condoms had anyone seen a condom in those distant days of my youth. One hot summer's afternoon I had forgotten to wash the mincing machine. When I put the mince through the next day it came out full of maggots. One lady I served was not delighted by the outcome when she arrived home to unwrap her crawling pound of best mince.

Years later at college we students would occasionally make our own Saturday evening entertainment. One event full of merriment was the "hat night". Pieces of paper were folded into a hat. In turn we took out from the hat a paper on which was written a subject about which we had to speak off the cuff for two minutes. My subject was "the life of a maggot". It was a gift handed to me on a plate. I related the above story.

My grandfather Walter (Arthur's father) used to call at the shop on Saturday afternoons and cross the palm of my hand with money as I cleaned the bloody butcher blocks with elbow grease and soap. He had been widowed for a couple of years when I worked as a Saturday boy.

As a young lad I visited my grandparents on the Crescent, where I eventually retired. My recollection is of a dingy, dark and sombre living room, and an equally gloomy elderly couple who did nothing but sit and talk of the world's ills and how much better life was in the 1700s. My grandmother, Alice, sat in a rocking chair in the corner of the room. She seemed incredibly old. Dressed in black she was hardly visible. I was ten when she died. Much later I discovered that she was only fifty-three when she went to lie in the grave. So the sense of someone's age to a young person is unreliable. How ancient, therefore, must my grandchildren view me! My grandfather died when I was a curate in Suffolk. But I have no memory of hearing the news of his death let alone of making the journey to be at his funeral.

My final Saturday afternoon task was to scrub the benches and sweep the shop floor. The rubbish I would collect in an upside-down dustbin lid. To get to the dustbin at the back of the shop I needed to manoeuvre past my father as he sat "doing the books". As I squeezed behind his back one sabbath I tripped. The lid was no longer upside down. The contents, mostly bloody sawdust, had dropped onto the ledger books and, even worse, down the old man's neck. I learnt some more swear words (in addition to "bloody sawdust") that day. They were stronger words than pluck, pluck, pluck.

So I did not make it as a butcher but became a priest.

In this as in so many other ways I was considered the odd man out in the family. I was not the black sheep. Perhaps I was seen as the white sheep among an otherwise black fold. I was too quiet, never forward at taking part in serious discussions, and certainly not on political themes like my father, who was ever ready to hold forth on the country's ills.

However, if only they had known the truth. Deep down, black sheep I really was. I suppose the sleepy tranquillity hid a decadent streak, though I am sure that nobody spotted it.

I did hold some attributes in common with other Lows. For instance, I was obstinate, wanting my own way. By no means was I usually allowed my own way, which served to make me sulky, touchy, tetchy and easily hurt.

My mother Elizabeth was brought up a Methodist and, after our move to Ampthill, would go with my grandmother Maud to the Wesleyan chapel on Woburn Street for the Sunday evening service, and when I was about nine I started to go with them. My father, though, was firmly "Church of England", not that he went much. But his influence meant that my mother would take me from the age of four to the parish church, where I worshipped every Sunday. The rector Mr Hawkins I barely remember but he (after fifty years in the parish) was replaced by Mr Knapp, who was my mentor as I grew up. I went to St Andrew's in the morning with my mother. In the afternoon I went to Sunday School, while my parents presumably went to bed. And in the evening I would often go to the Methodist Church with either my mother or grandmother or both.

Elizabeth was a mild, calm influence on the family, a good mother. She took a pride in our simple home, keeping the house spick-and-span. She was the protector. She needed to be. My father Arthur, forthright in his socialist opinions and ever ready to talk politics, was kind and generous, occasionally tender, but could also be easily riled. In other words he had a brutal temper, albeit recovering composure quickly and repenting of his bursts of rage. I, no doubt, fully deserved to be the object of his wrath due to the unthinking and silly things I did, caused more often than not by my day-dreaming, aloofness and living up in the clouds. As I grew up I believe that he understood me less and less. His questions about my activities I resented and responded to with moody silence. This worked him up into a stew, and his voice would become more and more voluminous.

I only recall two occasions when he boxed me hard (other than by his voice box). One was as a little boy when I fell over in the back yard and badly grazed my leg. My mother sympathised and tended me, washing away the blood. My father saw this not as an accident but as carelessness. Instead of offering sympathy he struck me for being stupid enough to fall over.

The other time was a few years later when he gave me his last shillings to buy provisions from the corner shop. I dropped the money down a hole, so returned home without food. Soon enough I had a sore backside.

Perhaps I got my own back. Apart from dropping his money I once dropped his dinner. He was home from the shop for a lunch break. My mother had asked me to take his meal from the stove and put it on the table. Not realising how hot the plate would be, I dropped the dinner over the kitchen floor. Nobody saw me. I scooped it back onto the plate and he was none the wiser. The dustbin lid, then, was not the only thing I dropped.

However, Arthur later admired my progress and achievements at college, my passing exams, my vocation. He told people proudly, "This is my eldest. He's going into the Church." Not only was I the eldest child but, "He's one of the best I have". At that stage he had, to the best of my knowledge, only the four of us. Sadly I did not appreciate my father's many good sides until after his death at the age of seventy-six. He had a heart attack, probably caused by eating too much beef and chocolates.

My mother, whose benevolent and benignant breasts I had sucked as a baby, had died of malignant breast cancer when she was forty-four. Helplessly I watched her suffering when home on holiday. Returning for the new term and faced with more examinations, this time my concentration wavered and I failed them. Luckily they were merely mocks. My ordination was just a year away when she died. I scraped through the finals and scraped through my interview with the bishop, mainly because it was he who did all the talking. It was a cause of regret that she (my mother, not the bishop) did not see the day of ordination.

Then my father married Crystal the same year. Almost a year later I had a twin half-brother and half-sister, Arthur and Beryl. Crystal stepped into my mother's shoes, which I recall rather resenting. But two half siblings made a whole, and it was a wholesome and satisfying feeling to have such a tiny sister and brother, not that I ever saw much of them. I remember returning home on new year's day, soon after their birth. Crystal told me that she had just had Arthur circumcised. (I am sure she meant the new baby, not my father.) She must have been unaware that she was informing me of this on the feast day of Jesus' circumcision.

CHAPTER 4
MISDEMEANOURS OF WILLIAM

Bill's father, Philip, and mother, Mary

Mary fell for Philip when he boasted that he had met the famous painter William Turner. He was still a young man but even at twenty-six was well-known for his landscape watercolours. She did not believe Philip to start with. He assured her that he had stumbled on the painter by chance on the roadside. He literally stumbled upon him. Daydreaming, Philip was looking up at the gathering and threatening clouds when he collided with the great artist, who was himself concentrating on the clouds. He was in the middle of painting a view of the sun setting over the Bedford bridge.

"Look whar yer gwine, yo' soddin' fool! Yo' 'aff nearly destroyed me next masterpiece," shouted the painter in his best cockney accent. "An' you've made me splash oil over my bloody waistcoa'."

Philip apologised embarassingly.

"Can yo' afford ter buy me paintin' to compensate for puttin' me off, yer bugger?" asked the eccentric.

"No, I'm sorry, sir."

"In thet case, 'aff yo' got enny snuff for me?"

Since Philip had neither money nor snuff the two men parted the worst of enemies.

Mary suggested that Philip might search out the artist, apologise again and perhaps offer to buy a picture.

"That's a stupid suggestion," said Philip. "Where on earth do you think I could find the sort of money to buy a painting of his, even if I wanted one?"

It was the first and last time that he called Mary stupid, for they were shortly married. Then it would have been more than his life was worth to be so daring.

At their wedding it was questionable whether William's mother Mary, like Frances, should have been married in white. For she was no blessed virgin. Unlike Frances' wedding it did not matter whether she wore a headdress for the ceremony, since in the end they decided not to have the service in Ampthill after all. So there were no sensitivities about offending local workers in the hat industry to be considered. And unlike my young almost topless bride years later Mary wore considerably more undergarments beneath the wedding dress, not that I was there to witness it. She was therefore doubly plump.

Mary had wanted to marry at the new Wesleyan Methodist church on Woburn Street. It was not quite three years old. When the idea of building a Methodist Church had been mooted it was objected that the chosen site was in a part of Woburn Street called Slutts' End. The objections were countered by accusations that the protesters could not spell. The residents were not sluts because they lacked an extra "t"; so that is where the church ended up. Mary fancied a modern wedding and what could better provide a modern wedding than a new building? But Philip insisted that they marry in the parish church. He had always been Church of England. Not that he ever went to church. Well, he did sometimes go at Christmas, and usually went at Harvest, the latter being the more important to him. This was the first and last argument with Mary that Philip won. But he did not win the argument altogether. Mary said that if it had to be in an ancient church then so be it but it would not be in Ampthill.

"My village church in Stoke Goldington is just as good as Ampthill's. If you must have an old church mine's older. We'll get wed at Stoke."

And so they did. They had to see the archdeacon of Buckingham to get a licence. Mary, although she knew her mind, was still sixteen and sweet.

My great-grandfather William died making way for another (Mary's) William to be born. I was nine. I have no recollection of his funeral, so perhaps I did not go. But then, I have no recollection of anything whatever while being nine. I suppose I was asleep most of the time. I do remember, though, that William was a thoroughly good man. His name was Thorogood, which the registrar of deaths spelt

"Thoroughgood". So the thoroughly good William died; and long live not-so-good William.

William was born of Mary three years before Betsey was to emerge. He was taken back to Wootton to be baptised. His father hailed from the village. Philip was an agricultural labourer, or when he wanted to create a good impression he liked to promote and describe himself as a market gardener, as if he owned the fields, which he certainly did not. However, he conned the rector into describing him thus in the register where the marriage was recorded.

William had no schooling. Had he had he would have left school in disgrace. He earned himself a reputation, and it undoubtedly was justified, as a rebel. He learned practically nothing as a young boy. He was certainly incapable of reading or even writing his own name. At least Betsey *said* she could. To compensate, William was blessed with a fascinating face, beguiling in appearance. He was by no means tall. In fact he was downright short. But he was stocky and strong. He made a first class labourer on the land. William at first began working with his father, who had rather stupidly, in hindsight, put in a good word to the landowner. Philip attempted to teach his son the ropes. But what others could not accomplish, William's own father had no chance of doing. Would William take advice? Would he hell! His rebellious nature was still alive and kicking. This caused heated arguments between father and son. It caused friction between father and employer, Mr Burgoyne. And it caused downright hostility between son and boss. In fact it led to William's first spell in prison.

Philip was as strong as an ox. This did not mean that he could control his wayward son, least of all physically, because William was as strong as two oxen. He demonstrated his strength to his emasculated father whenever there happened a clash of violent tempers. This the son accomplished even without the aid of strong drink. However, a few jars of ale always served to add further venom to his tantrums.

William was tough but wayward. He was unscrupulous, without principle. He did not seem to care about others, either their feelings or their welfare. Yet he was prepared to live off the generosity of those around him. He would suck all he could from his family, and anybody else who was silly enough to give him what he wanted. Perhaps some of them were scared of his potential violent reaction should they cross him.

After getting himself the sack William spent some time without employment. The scope for finding mischief increased manifold. The scope for mischief magnified when William found himself an accomplice. He was one William Neal, who also held a grudge against the unfortunate Mr Burgoyne. Not only did they visit the farm premises by night doing wilful damage to property, but together they stole what they found lying around, not because of the value but solely to get one over on this gentleman farmer and market gardener (a proper one).

Mr Burgoyne had had a tree felled. It happened to be Philip who had felled it. William and William took a saw and made away with some branches. On this occasion the Bills were not so fortunate. They were chased and caught by Mr Burgoyne's terriers, with Mr Burgoyne tearing along behind. The snappy dogs, tails wagging proudly, went for their ankles and brought them to the ground pleading for pity, as if the hounds were likely to relinquish their enjoyment. Mr Burgoyne eventually caught up, breathless, and brought a halt to the dogs' fun, showing the mercy that the youths had begged for. The constables were called and the two Williams ended up in court and then in gaol. In their defence they had pleaded, again, for pity and mercy. They claimed that the wood was needed for keeping their desperately poor families warm in the winter. It was indeed mid-February, but the claim did not wash with the magistrate, who sentenced each young man to six weeks hard labour for stealing part of a tree. The only consolation was that both William and William had committed offences far worse and got off scot-free.

Two years later William was back in Bedford prison for disturbing the peace by starting a fight in the Old Sun pub. The pub belonged to John and Joseph Morris, the Ampthill brewers. As we mentioned, William could flare up without aid of drink. But he did drink heavily. Frequently would he have one over the seven. Then disaster struck, as on the occasion when he offended even his friend William Neal. It was an argument between the Wills that led to malicious damage in the Old Sun public bar and consequently, once again, to the whistle of the constables. It took several to restrain the loud and troublesome louts - several whistles and several constables.

William never returned to the Old Sun. He was banned for evermore. But he continued to go on the rampage in other places.

After serving his next sentence and somewhat calmed down, William found another job, still labouring in the fields. But he was in and out of jobs. He tried his hand at dealing. A general dealer he called himself. For a while wheeling and dealing seemed to be what he was cut out for. He became an accomplished haggler, or higgler as he would call himself. But his longest spell of work other than labouring on the land was as a carter on the farm where his youngest brother George worked with horses as a groom in nearby clip-clop Clophill. In my younger days I wrote a poem about the sound of horses' hooves clomping and clumping through Clophill. "Clip-clop Clophill" is all I remember of it. It must have been a commendable poem.

Neither he nor his father nor Betsey's father John, when both fathers were in their forties, created a good impression with the law. They joined a hundred and fifty or so other labourers, together with four hundred paupers from all over, who had come into Ampthill to demonstrate against the new Poor Law. They gathered at the workhouse, the House of Industry, on Park Hill to protest against the injustice of paupers who would no longer be paid for their work in cash. They would in future be paid in kind. This caused massive resentment. The crowd were threatening and violent, especially against the workhouse's three elected Guardians.

"We want work and to be paid in money, not in bread," was their demand. They remonstrated about the hardship of workers having to leave their families.

"Impossible," responded the Guardians.

Serious rioting was the result. This took place six years before I came to the parish. The disturbance was still vivid in the mind of the Methodist minister, also a County Magistrate, who related to me how he had tried to disperse the gathering, by this time a mob. They did anything but go home quietly, as he had begged them to. Rather, they threw stones and pebbles, any missile they could find, even cabbage stalks, at the building where the Guardians had been meeting. Many windows were smashed and broken glass caused cuts in one of the Guardians' eyes. Another Guardian braved the crowd and went outside to read the Riot Act. He held an umbrella to defend himself.

It was indeed a riot. The revolt spread into the Market Square, with the crowd carrying sticks and clubs. There was a frightful fight between the mob and special constables. As well as John and Philip, William also joined in the battle. This happened before William had been sacked. He was always, even at fourteen, up for a good fisticuffs. But on this occasion he held a heavy club between his fists. And he used it.

Police were brought in from the metropolis, all twenty-two of them, there being not yet a proper force in Bedfordshire. London was no mean distance. As the town pump indicated, "To London, XLV miles". Police on horseback attempted to arrest ringleaders, which they did. However, as soon as they were taken into custody and some placed in the town cage and others in the stocks they were rescued by the rabble. The local authorities were unable to cope. They wanted to use the whipping post in the Market Square but were unable to tie up the culprits before the mob set them free. The government promised that Household Troops from Windsor, as many as needed, could be sent out at short notice. Four troops of yeomanry were transported to Luton and held in readiness. But the police managed to capture the main trouble-makers. This time William escaped arrest, not that he deserved to.

The crowd held banners, "Money or blood"; "Blood and Bread, or Work and Money". Shouts were heard, "We'll have either the money out of your pocket or the blood out of your veins." Sadly the paupers did not win. Life became harsher.

But the disturbance accelerated the demise of the House of Industry. There was no further trouble there. There could not be. It was pulled down. No longer would people have a great dread of "going to the Industry". Instead they would have an equally great dread of "going to the Union", for a new Union workhouse was built at Cowfair End, ironically next door to the Lows' and Robinsons' households. Whether it was ever full is unsure but it was big enough to take in 469 inmates (the workhouse, that is to say, not the Lows' and Robinsons').

Regular church services were held in the new workhouse. They were conducted by different churches, the ministers usually taking along a few of their congregations. I did more than my share.

The regime was no less disciplined, no less strict than the previous. It split families due to its policy of segregation. No wonder people feared lest they ended up in such a frightful hell-hole. The hell-hole was otherwise known as the Spike.

Bill's sister, Lucy

Mary and Philip lost their first two children. Both had been vaccinated, although at the time they were too poor to pay. The doctor still received two shillings and six pence for each child he pricked, being under contract by the vestry. But the needle was no prevention for either kind of death. Lucy was two when she died of tuberculosis, not that it was called by that name for another twenty years. They were told that Lucy had consumption. It was no comfort that so many children of friends and acquaintances in the vicinity and beyond were struck down by the same disease. It was so distressing to watch helplessly as she suffered. All they could do was sit by her, hold her hand, wipe her fevered brow, clean up the bloody phlegm, and weep. The doctor wrote the cause of Lucy's death as phthisis on the certificate, which would have baffled her parents had they been able to read. In any case the doctor's writing was not legible even to those who could have read it. And had they been able to read it they would not have understood it anyway. Not only was the little girl Philip and Mary's precious and beloved daughter but their firstborn to boot. It was at the funeral and burial that the real weeping and wailing began. And vaccination was no help for James either, as we will shortly discover.

Before we make the discovery we will trace my journey from boy at Sunday School to rector.

CHAPTER 5
MY STINTS IN DERBYSHIRE
AND SUFFOLK

At Sunday School I got by with a basic learning of reading, 'riting and 'rithmatic, doing well particularly with the latter. But I did hopelessly with the fourth "r", religion. My teacher told me that I would never make it as a Sunday School teacher when I grew up. I could not even make it in the parish church choir. My friends were being asked left, right and centre to join the choir. Why was I always left out? I felt unwanted, rather as I did when the captains at sports chose their teams. I was ever the last to be selected. Yet I was good at sports. So I thought. Years later I came to understand that I was not good at singing. The truth began to dawn when the headmaster during singing lessons would come up to me and put his hairy ear to my mouth. I considered giving it a hard bite but thought better of it. Perhaps he was a spy for the choirmaster. But I did continue to worship, even though I made rude signs to the choir when they were not looking.

Having failed miserably in religion (as well as singing), I passed my interviews to enter St Michael and All Angels' College, Oxford.[1] To be honest, I failed the initial interview. However, that was but a mock carried out as a hoax by students. They pretended to be lecturers and gave me a grilling. In my naivety I fell for their prank. The following morning when the real interviews happened I was that little bit more experienced as an interviewee. I was asked about my school reports and admitted that I had failed every religious exam that I had ever sat. They seemed to like

---

[1]There is no such college. But it fits my training by the Society of the Sacred Mission, whose college at Kelham, Nottinghamshire, did not exist 130 years earlier. The dream described below is a picture of life at Kelham Theological College at which monastic community I was trained for the ordained ministry.

the answer and I was accepted. Either they appreciated my honesty or they thought that I would be their greatest challenge so far.

I thought that I was going there to study theology. To my surprise there were no religious studies, let alone theology - not yet. To begin with there was a lot of mathematics, to my delight; there was English literature, ancient history, logic, Latin and Greek, and ... sport. I was soon made captain of sports, so now it was I who could do the selecting.

At last I had made it into the choir, not because my singing had improved but because everyone who worshipped in the chapel without exception was in the College choir. It was suggested that I mime rather than attempt to sing and mess up the beautiful sounds that all other students seemed capable of producing.

After a particularly lovely choral service which touched me deeply I retired to bed and spent, so it seemed, the entire night in a long and vivid dream. I am never able to recall my dreams the following day. This one was an exception. I remember every detail of this dream.

***

The dream began in the austere and awesome but stupendous and sublimely beautiful chapel. I looked up to an imposing life-size rood screen, then down to a highly-polished black floor. Surrounding me standing on the jet black floor were millions and millions of monks dressed in black cassocks and sky-blue scapulars. Filmy smoke was descending like clouds as they sang the most perfect plainsong, and in the dream I was permitted to join in the singing, which I did without disrupting the beauteous melody.

The dream changed gear abruptly. I was standing not in a beautiful chapel but shivering in a cold shower. The shower woke me and told me that I was in desperate need of a pee. I think I woke other students as I stumbled over bedroom furniture. Whether they got back to sleep I am unsure. I certainly did, for the fantasy continued. I was now in the lecture room being lectured by a monk in habit rather than a don in academicals. The dream was uncannily realistic in that I was understanding nothing of the lecture. Before lunch I joined the monks for the short midday office of sext. I clearly heard the prior tell me to be careful to pronounce the

43

final vowel of words, especially words ending with the letter t. I was not permitted to pronounce any vowels at lunch, for this was a silent meal. There was a problem getting someone to pass me the milk. It was the beginning of my drinking black tea. After lunch I saw that my name was on the notice board to let me know what job I had been allocated for the afternoon. It could have been in the printing works. It could have been in the pigsties. It could have been driving the tractor. It could have been tending the gardens. It could have been scrubbing floors, or, in the case of the chapel, polishing them. As the dream progressed I wondered how all this related to training to be a priest. It turned out that most of the jobs were indeed a sound training for ministry in an agricultural parish - not that I was allowed to drive tractors or feed the pigs on any of my parishioners' farms. But scrubbing floors at the rectory - yes, that was permitted.

***

At last I woke up and was back in Oxford. I was in Oxford when my great-grandmother Clara died. The last time I saw her she had been ill in bed at my parents' home and I had not bothered to say goodbye to the frail old lady. When I heard of her death I felt sad, but not only sad. I felt guilty that I had not made a final farewell gesture. Nor did I return to Maulden for her funeral, for which lack of respect I later reproached myself. But when I heard that the minister had signed the burial register "according to the Rites and Ceremonies of Protestant Dissenters" my sense of guilt dissipated.

Having related my ever-so-real monastic dream, I assure readers that my meeting with Archie Tate was no dream. I had attended a lecture at Balliol College where Archie was a fellow and tutor. This was before his and my ordination a few years later. He was made deacon the year after I was, and he was ordained priest two years after I was. The difference between him and me was that he was elevated to archbishop of Canterbury and I was not. He deserved it. There is no doubt that I did not. Nobody knew him later as Archie. He was henceforth called Archibald. He was the Most Reverend Archibald Campbell Tait. He was enjoying a cushy post as archbishop while I was slogging it, as we will discover, in the small parish that hardly anyone I spoke to seemed to have heard of - at Ampthill - as its rector.

A fellow student at Oxford was called Barrymore Trout. He was a white South African. We became sort of friends. He was totally outgoing and I was totally retiring. Our complementarity was beneficial in some social circumstances. Trout later became Dean of Texas.

We had a free day every so often. My father's auntie Susannah had gone to live near Oxford in Kidlington. She had married at the turn of the century one Richard Bridge from that village. He was, believe it or not, another agricultural labourer. For some strange reason he was unwilling to move to Bedfordshire, so Susannah had to go to Oxford. This worked for me because it meant that I had a bolt-hole to escape to. And, my God, I did need to get away now and again from the university environment. The Bridges were not at all close to me other than geographically. But over the five long years during my student life I did become closely attached to the family. There were Susannah and Richard and, in Lower Kidlington, their son and daughter-in-law, John and Sarah. John, a millwright, had three sisters who lived locally, one of them married to William Hutt. What relation they all were to me I never worked out. My fellow students thought that I was joking when I told them that I was going to spend the day at the Hutt. The truth is that I never did. I had better things to do than chase all over the place visiting distant relations. But I often saw the sisters Elizabeth, Mary and Maria at John's or Richard's.

I enjoyed being with John and Sarah and their family. Sarah as I picture her wore pretty dresses with puffed sleeves. Abraham was eight when I first went up to Oxford. Charles would have been four had he not died when six months old, so of course I never saw him. Isaac was one year old. Jacob was born two years after I arrived. I went to his baptism. It was late September and I recall admiring the pleasant manner in which the rector, the Reverend Mr Harrington, officiated. I also observed Mr Harrington conduct a funeral. It, too, was Jacob's. He died when he was seven months. Every now and then I walked into the large churchyard and brooded at Jacob's grave.

Why did Sarah and John name their children after the three patriarchs, with Charles an odd one out in between? I should have asked but it was too touchy a subject. I simply reflect that this Charles, the author, is often the odd one out, or simply just the odd one.

Lodging in the home was one Frank Padbury Bloss. He too worked on the land. He worked for farmer Baker at the far end of the village. A hard worker, Frank laboured on the farm and in his little spare time looked after the land of the Bridges with whom he boarded. I got to know Frank really well. He was honest and reliable and loyal. And he was a most amenable great character. His heart was made of gold. In fact he was worth gold dust to the Bridges.

I visited my long lost relatives in Kidlington the day after an almighty storm, which had brought down numerous trees and created devastation in the garden. There was not a fence left standing.

"Frank," I asked, "how on earth will you cope with all this mess?"

"There's allus anower day tomorrer, govner."

I never recall him using my name. Both John Bridges and I were always the "govner". He stood back to consider problems, fag in mouth and ash about to drop off but somehow rarely falling to earth. Big difficulties he would ponder overnight, I imagine without the fag. He always came up with a practical solution. The garden, of course, took time to put right. But he did it, including the removal of hefty trees. Frank was a little man. That does not mean that he was not powerful. His strength combined with his practical brainpower made him a formidable labourer.

Although Frank was gold dust he was not paid in gold dust. He told me that his wage packet one week had been a groat short. He told Mr Baker, who rectified the apparent mistake. But the next week Frank received a groat too much. He returned it to the farmer. There was no recognition of Frank's honesty but Mr Baker took the groat and put it in his own pocket. This was just a single instance of Mr B's meanness. The other Mr B (John Bridge) was not stingy but neither did he pay Frank for his work. Frank was willing to tend the grounds for love, and of course in return for his board.

Back at the university, later in the course, of course, we progressed to the study of theology, via philosophy, church history, liturgics, dogmatics and biblical studies. Although I no longer failed exams my essays were often marked (in red) "on the edge". So I scraped through the course, despite once being almost given the push because of a girl. It happened like this:

I was deputed to show a group of young lady teachers-in-training around the limited parts of the college where females were allowed, which included the chapel and not much more. I took quite a liking to one of the girls and we arranged to meet secretly outside the hall of residence one evening later that week. I walked through the gates undetected (so I thought), took off my gown and tied it to a tree, then went off with the girl into the bushes. The Dean must have seen me leave from his well-positioned first-floor window, for when I returned to the tree there was a note pinned to the gown. It read, "When you return, see me - whatever time this is." I was sussed and I was hanging on to my studenthood by a narrow thread. Fortunately the thread held and I breathed another day. Another student, Henry, who became a lifelong friend, suggested that I must have blue eyes, but I insisted that they are clearly dark brown. Possibly in a metaphorical sense he was correct.

On the football field (not that there were yet any laid down rules to the game and we got by perfectly well without a referee), playing in goal, I spotted a strange clergyman standing behind the posts. Unbeknown to me at the time he had come to observe me as a potential curate. Luckily he spectated during that part of the game when I let in no goals. Possibly because he thought that I had safe hands he offered me the title (as a first curacy is called) at Wingerworth, near Chesterfield. I was the parish's first ever curate, which meant that I had no act to follow.

So it was that I came to be ordained (or "made", as the Prayer Book puts it) deacon in Lichfield cathedral. Twelve months later I was ordained (indeed "ordained" as the Prayer Book puts it) priest. The second ordination took place more locally, in Chesterfield parish church. This is the church with the iconic crooked spire. Some say that the spire will straighten only when a virgin bride walks down the aisle. To be sure, it did not become uncrooked by my ordination. Perhaps it leant over a little further.

Paul and Patricia were instrumental in building up a thriving youth group in the parish. As a curate I was almost young enough to relate to the youngsters. There was such cohesion that many of the group met up fifty years later for a reunion in a Chesterfield hotel. They looked so much older that I recognised nobody at the party. First to arrive, I kissed Pat, who had rushed up to warmly welcome Mary and me and helpfully said, "Hello. I'm Pat." Mary and I chatted with people as if we did recognise them and, of course, drank all that was on offer. After an hour's bluffing it dawned on me that we were at the wrong party. It was someone's fiftieth *birthday* party. No wonder we did not know anybody. We sped a hasty retreat and found the youth group (plus fifty years) in another part of the hotel, where we met up with Paul and the correct Pat. (The lady whom I kissed earlier was also called Pat by a chance fluke.) I therefore kissed two Patricias in one evening.

Our next close friends after my ordination were professor William and his wife Gwendoline. Shortly after their first baby was born I visited them. William was out. The midwife was in. But she was not the midwife who had delivered the baby. This was her first call to check on Gwen. She saw me through the window and beckoned me in. "Your wife is having a bath," she said. It was a big tin bath placed in the centre of their kitchen. "Get him out!" Gwen shrieked. The midwife was by now aware that I was not her husband. We were close friends, but not that close. (William, years later, was himself ordained and canonised.)

My friend Henry Baker with whom I studied theology at Oxford was appointed to a curacy in Sheffield, so we would meet up from time to time. In fact he suggested that we went away together for a break. Henry asked me to arrange a stay in Ireland. I agreed. When we next met I informed him that I had made all arrangements. But it was in ... Spain. He was displeased. However, it was in Spain that he met a Scottish lass, Christine, whom he wasted no time marrying. As far as I know he was displeased no longer. The four of us enjoyed spending time together, sometimes in Dunwich, sometimes at Loweswater (not that it was really mine).

Forty years later both Baker and Trout were present at Oxford with me and another dozen by now ancient clergymen at an Old Sods' reunion. I had pre-arranged with the college to have a room with an extra bed so that I could hide Mary away. We were planning to spend a few days exploring the countryside after the reunion before returning to Bedfordshire. Mary successfully remained unnoticed, spending the three days enjoying Oxford. She was unobserved, that is, until the final night.

Bells were ringing furiously. Hooters were sounding. The night porter was shouting his head off. The commotion was a warning that a fire was raging. We all scampered down to the quadrangle in various states of undress, some in pyjamas, some not. I was not, but I did have a small towel to cover essentials. Now Mary was visible even in the dark. She was assumed by the other old students to be a loose woman whom I had picked up in Oxford.

Back in the parish I was more respectable. I wore quite ordinary clothes, no different from what other men were wearing - except that as a curate I had little money to dress as I would like. For dressing up in church the parish bought me a white surplice. It was pure white when they bought it but did not remain spotless for long. They also bought me a preacher's scarf. I took it from that that they expected me to preach, which is what I tried so hard to do.

The bishop told me that I should serve a second curacy. Then he told me that he did not have one available. I wondered if I should give butchery another try. But then in the end I was offered a further curacy in Bury St Edmunds. In Derbyshire the Suffolk part of the larger Ely diocese was known as the Dead See, and so it seemed to me. I did not last long in the job. With one curacy already under my belt I felt ready to convert Suffolk if not the world. However, a few parishioners vetoed all my sublime suggestions, disagreeing with everything I proposed. But I soon learned that that was part and parcel of a priest's job. That was the case in Suffolk anyway. There was no harm in having ideas and projects as long as they were not expected to be put into practice.

Perhaps I was unpopular due to my tactless remarks. One lady whom I had not seen before shook hands with me after the service and commented that she had not at all enjoyed the service. I replied, "Good. You don't come here to enjoy yourself." She did turn up for further punishment the following week. Over the years I came to realise that services were indeed to be enjoyed.

I was in Bury St Edmunds long enough to make a lifelong friendship with Edward and Ann. They, like us, had three beautiful daughters, Ann, Ellen and Eileen, and we kept in touch, distance notwithstanding. Their hospitality was worth accepting, not least because of Ann's cooking and Edward's ever-flowing supply of beer.

It was here in Bury that I tried to look like a cleric by wearing a white cravat. Then I noticed that the tradesmen and farmers were wearing one too. I wore a second-hand black frock coat to look like a priest. Then I noticed that so did the Quakers.

When I received an offer of a living back in Ampthill, to replace my predecessor, George Maule, I snapped it up. Bedfordshire was also in the Ely diocese, having been transferred from the Lincoln diocese only two years earlier. The bishop was either impressed with me to offer such a good living, or perhaps he had simply not even heard of me. I was now twenty-eight and all set to meet some Bedfordshire Bulldogs, among them the Lows.

CHAPTER 6
ON THE RIVER AND RAILWAY

August 1851 *Our friend Fred has a boat moored at the river. He let us use it for the morning. I'm not a skilled rower but confidently set out with Mary and our three young children determined to prove my oarsmanship. I lost the key to the boat shed. I lost a wellington stuck in the mud. And, not having access to the shed, I left the rowlocks behind. Bowlocks! We flowed down the river, the wind in our favour. But it was impossible to row back. It took three hours to punt back through the mud along the bank. The outing was a disaster.*

On the next trip Fred and his wife Sue (whose wedding I had blessed in a marquee in their garden) accompanied us. This time we were well equipped, with sunshine, picnic and beer and even rowlocks. On our return and having almost completed a perfect afternoon, the otherwise splendid day did not prevent my falling into the mud as I attempted to hoist the boat ashore. Fred hosed me down and suggested that our next outing might include some women's mud wrestling.

Bill's brother, James
They lost James in a tragic accident. Philip and Mary had been married eight years. They took a trip to Bedford with William, who was two, and James, who was now five. Mary was pregnant with her second Lucy. They assuredly would not have ventured there had they known about the storm that was to brew. Although it was late November the Sunday was mild and calm, so they decided to treat themselves and get away. The park was their usual option for a Sunday walk. Or they would take a stroll along the Alameda, a lovely line of lime trees given to the town by Lord and Lady Holland. This led into the Firs, a pine plantation much visited by locals, for a peaceful stroll. Mary loved to walk with Philip to the park

through these Darkenings. But this Sunday was different. If only they had had foresight the fatal catastrophe would not have happened.

They ventured on this occasion all the way to Bedford using a borrowed horse and cart. Their neighbour's coachman had prepared a mare and a colt from the stables and off they set. The glorious day turned dark. A remarkably heavy storm brewed. It rained. It hailed. Eventually many streets within the vicinity of the Ouse were flooded. Some late morning church services were interrupted by torrential rain and heavy hail beating against windows. Not a few were broken. The terrific storm persisted, with lightning more vivid than had ever been seen in people's lifetime. The river burst its banks. This turned out to be a major flood, as devastating as Bedford had known. Water rose to six feet. It was talked about for many years to come as "the great flood of 1823".

Before the devastation when all was still peaceful Philip and Mary were carefully watching young William as they ambled along the water's edge. He was liable to shoot off suddenly, so Philip held him particularly tightly. Without warning the sky turned dark, the clouds turned black and a gale started to howl. Windswept they continued walking along the embankment. A surge of water drenched them. Out of breath they struggled away from the side. Philip was now even more tightly and desperately holding on to William. At the same time he was attempting to steady Mary, badly beaten and weakened by the gusts. It did not help that Mary was with child.

"Where's James? Oh, my dear God. Where's he gone? He's gone. James! My darling James! Where are you?" she screamed.

James was being swept away by the current. They were helpless. For long seconds they stood looking, staring ahead, incapable of taking in what had happened and so quickly. Mary was in a frenzy.

Hysterically they both yelled for help. Nobody heard. Anyone who had heard would have been powerless to affect a rescue in any case. The body was recovered from the water some days later.

Vaccination, then, had done James no good either. The incident put a blight on his parents' future married life. They would never forgive themselves.

Both Mary and Philip already knew what it was to lose a child. But nothing could prepare them for such a poignant tragedy as this.

Bill's sister, Lucy

They had another Lucy, with whom Mary was pregnant during that fateful excursion. She died, as we will find out, aged twenty-four. The parents felt that they needed to replace their first beloved child, so they gave her the same name. But shortly before the baptism Mary felt uneasy about the idea of replacement. The second Lucy was utterly different from the first. She wondered about changing the name. Philip suggested other names beginning with L, like Louisa. Mary ignored all his propositions. In the end she settled for another Lucy after all.

As she grew up she went through boyfriends like a dose of salts but was unable to sustain relationships. She even fell out with her mother. Nevertheless, she was friendly enough with most people, and generally vivacious. She was alert and sensitive to others' needs. She had a youthful yet strong conscience and sense of morality.

Louisa's, I mean Lucy's, brother William, the third child, was to become a cause of despair for different reasons, some of which we have already seen. As a toddler he lived up to the reputation of being terrible in his twos. But he never lost the notoriety of being a terror, at least not until he married Betsey. Then his life changed direction.

Bill's brother, Thomas, and Mary

Thomas was taken to Bedford too. As a boy newly entering his teens he never forgot being taken by his mother to see the much publicised presence of George Stephenson, who had come to look at the feasibility of opening a new railway line from Bletchley. The authorities wished that they had kept the visit secret because spectators gathered in their thousands. There was excitement, exhilaration, even intoxication among the invasion of masses gathered along the streets, squashed and jostled in the densest parts of town. They were interested not in the purpose of the visit but simply to glimpse the great man. Such arousal of interest was unheard of in Bedford. For Tom, though, it really was the railway that mattered, not the man.

His fascination for trains grew. Two years later the line opened and he persuaded his older sister-in-law Betsey to take him to visit Betsey's new-born nephew Charles, who lived in Bletchley. Cunning Tom knew exactly what he was doing. He was not bothered about seeing baby

Charles at all. He did want to have a train ride. Tom had a great day out with Charley's aunt. She paid as well.

When it was known that a line was to be built from London to Bedford a number of Ampthill conservationists were worried about the tracks being laid through part of the park. They were specially concerned that some of the famous stout old oak trees, the very oaks that King Henry Vlll himself loved, might now be at risk. But the oaks were spared (which is more than can be said of Henry's Katherine, who also knew those oaks). The construction of a deep cutting and tunnel beneath the park was of considerable interest to the locals.

Tom was thirty-seven when Ampthill station opened, looking rather pretty with its red brickwork, white stone facings and wrought iron canopies. He still had a fascination for trains and would now walk the long couple of miles from Maulden where he lived on the Moor into town and out the other side to the station to watch the trains puff past proceeding through and into the mysterious tunnel. Tom would chat with Joe Minney, the stationmaster, who would usually have time to talk to Tom about his job. The platform was very long, ideal for the lines of rifle volunteers of the 3rd Battalion Bedfordshire Regiment alighting to march on to the annual camps in the park for field training and exercises over the next ten years. "If only I was a bit younger", he mused. "I could be joining them."

Another of his dreams, which also required an "if only", was to travel to London for the day. He was old enough but the ambition was unfulfilled. "If only I had the money to pay the fare plus a day let loose in the capital." And, more to the point, "If only my Mary would let me"!

Mary was a wayward, giddy and flirtatious character, not helped by her addictive drinking. Whereas she kept a keen and jealous eye on her husband, Tom was quite incapable of controlling the life-style of his wife. Mary would think nothing of making attachments with other men, sometimes younger, usually older. Nor did she attempt to hide her dalliances. Mary was angular, thin (in fact, too thin), hardly beautiful. Yet she seemed skilful at attracting men friends. Tom, then, led a progressively difficult life. But he suffered patiently and passively, finding relief in his hobby of steam engines. He might have left his wife but did not even consider the possibility. All he did was watch his acquisitive spouse spend his money like water, which she did partly on her clothes and partly on allowing their children to have whatever they wanted whenever they wanted it.

Later in life Mary was afflicted by illness and became severely handicapped. Her children had given up on their mother due to her loud behaviour caused by tipple. Even when it had been confiscated she found a way to find some alcohol from somewhere. Tom did not give up on Mary. He uncomplainingly looked after her. She was reliant on him but never appreciative. At least, she would not admit it to his face.

We look back for a moment to Mary and Tom's wedding. On the same day as their wedding there was by coincidence another marriage taking place. The bride, whose name we do not know, but who deserves a mention in passing because she was a workmate of Mary, had been one of many who relied on the town clock on her way to work at the hat factory as she passed the Moot Hall each morning. The clock was mounted on top of the hall for all to see, and its time-keeping was reliable. She did not believe rumours when she heard it mooted that the hall was to be demolished. One day she had a blow. The Moot Hall really was being pulled down. Now her time-keeping was liable to be up the spout. The iconic clock was no more.

It was only a matter of weeks after the demolition that our anonymous bride was married in St Andrew's. As she passed through the town centre in her carriage, with a few inquisitive onlookers wanting to catch a glimpse of the bride en route to church, she exclaimed to her father, "O, look, Dad. There's Nora; and there's Pru; oh! And Mabel; gosh, there's Flo as well - all the girls from work." Then louder: "O Dad, look. Look! There's the *clock*!"

It had a new home to sit on. They had built a clock house and the clock was even more prominent than it was before. Today she was going to pass it, though not on her way to work. But at least she was able to tell that she was rather late for her wedding. The work on the clock had been carried out by Bill's next wife Ann's father George, whom we will be introduced to all in good time. (I buried George in due course - when his time was up.)

In the meantime Tom and Mary were being married in the parish church at Maulden, where Mary had been brought up. The rector was the chubby-faced, white bushy-bearded, bald-headed Mr Ward. The Reverend Charles Ward, MA, had recently built Maulden's first school. He now had plans to enlarge the church's nave and chancel, but on their wedding day Mary and Tom had to settle for the smaller church as it was.

It was Mary's uncle whom Bill had badly offended when young Bill worked for Mr Burgoyne. It was the very same Mr Burgoyne whose mother I had delivered meat to many years earlier. Tom used to travel by foot all the way to the station, boasting that he could leg it from Maulden to Ampthill in nine minutes, and through the town and down Station Road to the railway in twenty.

Most passengers did not have to go by shanks's pony from the station. They had Mr Manton's eight-seater horse bus. Mr Manton was landlord of the White Hart. He drove the "bus" to meet all the passenger trains for fifty years.

Joe had been poorly when he was five. His skin changed colour. Tom came to visit his parents when he was *twenty*-five with his skin having come out in brown blotches. Being accustomed to illness by now, Mary and Philip were sure that Tom was ailing for something serious. They questioned him about how he was feeling, trying to persuade him to take things easy.

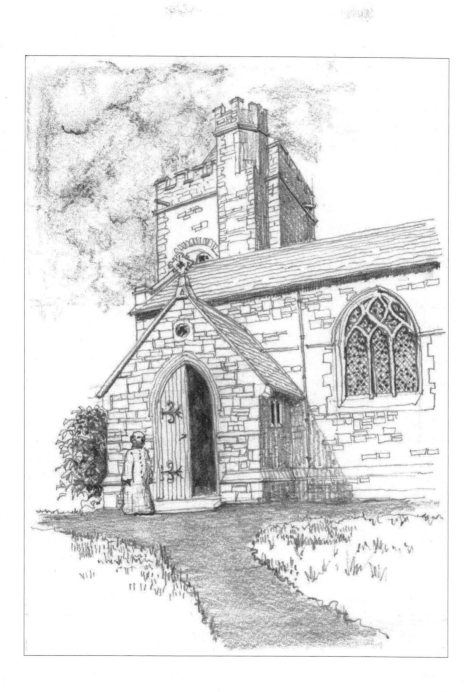

Tom could not understand the fuss. He was more concerned about telling his parents that he had visited the new police station. Ampthill had just been made an independent division. Not managing to make it home after a few pints at the pub Tom had been observed taking a piss behind a neighbour's bush and was reported. He was proud to be one of the first to be asked to call in at the newly opened station, especially since he was merely admonished and not charged for exposing his staff. It was a little thing (the incident, I mean).

But his parents accused him of avoiding the issue. What about his blotches? Tom assured them that he was on top of the world. Four years of marriage had done him the world of good. Life was treating him well. (Little did he know that life was not to deal him a good hand much longer.) They all had a laugh when it transpired that he was not at all off colour, despite his blotchy face. He had been outside painting his fence brown and his face had caught the splashes! "It's just as well," he thought, "my neighbour didn't catch my splashes when I was behind her bush."

It was not so funny two years later when Tom did indeed fall ill and suffered blotches as a result of the epidemic that seemed to have been imported into the town but which, nonetheless, had a devastating effect on many of the population. Most recovered and so did Tom.

Joe and Mary were childless. Tom and his Mary, however, did have their fair share of children, as did Daniel and Jane, twelve between them. Tom beat Dan by seven to five. One of Tom's did not survive. Their first child, Philip, was born prematurely and died five weeks after the birth. There was no medical attendant, but Mary, naturally, was there when Philip died.

Most of the male cousins grew up to be, unsurprisingly, agricultural workers. The female cousins were, in the main, bonnet sewers and straw plaiters. The women, especially those who had learnt their skills in plait schools, could earn more money than their men earned from labouring on the land. It tended to make some of them, Joe included, rather lazy.

Not everyone worked on the land or plaiting hats or making lace. Some worked at harvesting lavender and various medicinal herbs that the pharmacists grew. The brewery employed many others. Yet others were employed at the foundry. Some had jobs at the gas works. A few worked in the candle factory. Girls were taught dressmaking. Boys learned boot making. There were wheelwrights and umbella makers. Generations of locals were rope makers. Their factory was, naturally, on Rope Walk. There was the horse mill on, of course, Mill Street. Some worked in the pubs. Some were builders. Many worked in trade (the most important, in my opinion, being the butchers). Peck's the draper and furniture store was an important employer. After all, they made butchers' requisites. Then there were the solicitors, and auctioneers like George Greene, later succeeded by Swaffield and Son. There was a printing works. I narrowly escaped having my work cut out when a gas engine, newly installed to work the presses, exploded and nearly destroyed the whole works. However, apart from Pop and his pop business, most of the family were occupied in agricultural labour or the hat and lace industries.

Tom's Ada and Esther, both spoilt children while growing up, were exceptions to the rule. They branched out in different directions from the norm. Ada, the second daughter, became a school teacher, and her aunt and uncle, as well as her parents, were most proud of their grown-up little angel. She taught at the National School on Bedford Street, which had been open nearly thirty years when she began her career. Ada worshipped at St Andrew's parish church rather than at her village church, which was no closer to her home, being on the far side of Maulden. She was thrilled when she secured a position in the school, since hers was a church school, supported by the parish church. The headmaster was almost a pillar of St Andrew's. So Ada would see her head every Sunday as well as every weekday. She hoped not to bump into him on Saturdays.

The British School was built on the "Sands" a year earlier than the National. Its purpose was to provide education for children of parents connected to the chapels. They were not in competition, but the National School was the better school. I thought so because, like most of the Lows, my children went there too. No doubt those who attended the Sands school were convinced that theirs was superior. However, as I say, they were not in competition. But the National was definitely bigger! The Sands school, on the other hand, had an added attraction for the children. The smithy was just across the road opposite and some of the children went after school to watch horses being shod by the blacksmith.

Esther, their eldest child, went to Bedford to assist a photographer. Part of her assistance was to do some modelling for him, of which the said parents would have been less proud, had they but known. They did not know. It brought good business to the photographer and extra pocket money for Esther. Photography was born just over a decade before Esther was born. The photographer had to visually estimate exposure according to his experience. But his main experience of exposure was Esther herself.

The boss carefully explained to Esther that the purpose of the nude photographs was purely for artistic and aesthetic studies. In other words the pictures were simply being taken as an aid to painters and sculptors. Esther, however, cottoned on to the surmise that the nude photos were being used for more lucrative aims. So the photographer's use of the word "pure" she regarded with suspicion. Nevertheless, she kept quiet because she was benefitting financially too.

Mary and Tom never saw any of their daughter's photographs, not the nude prints at least. Neither, I am sad to say, did I.

Esther was assertive like her mother and was tireless and steely like her father. Unlike her mother she was a true beauty, friendly, even lusty.

Yet she found it hard to retain relationships with men for long periods. Her partners were various even if she did not choose it to be so.

Mary was Tom and Mary's third of five daughters, poor molly-coddled Arthur being the only son, Philip having died. With so many Marys (Dan and Jane had a Mary as well, though they always called her Mary Jane), this Mary was known as Polly. Being close in age Polly and Arthur got on well, rarely quarrelling. Perhaps he was given sisterly affection most of all by Polly, which meant he was Polly-coddled. In adult life he had had enough of female company with five sisters and tried to avoid finding a wife. In this he was successful.

No child had been naughtier than Arthur. But when grown-up he turned out respectful towards other people. To compensate, perhaps, for his lack of family he took up sport and excelled as a boxer. Even his opponents, though, Arthur always respected.

Tom himself was more than a little excited when, on the Midland railway line through Ampthill, the world speed record was broken. A train travelled at ninety miles per hour on over two miles of track at Ampthill. The record was broken six years later. Tom died soon after, of disappointment. Mary, now recognising that life was going to be unmanageable without a husband to care for her, said that he died still at heart a little boy.

CHAPTER 7
AT THE BAR

Bill's brother, Daniel, and Jane

Daniel was the only Low to become a Friend. Most of the family had friends as well as enemies. But Daniel became a Quaker. He went to meetings at Ampthill Hall on Dunstable Street and enjoyed the silent and spontaneous worship. The Quakers were a strong community in Ampthill. The Morrises, the Mays, the Allens, families we will meet in good time, were all among them.

So perhaps it was no accident that Daniel was a quiet one, just like his brother George. The two, youngest of all the siblings, were not only brothers but close friends (or to avoid confusion should we say mates?). This was true as they grew up and also throughout their adult lives. Dan had been unforthcoming as a boy. Things hardly altered when he grew up. You never knew what he was thinking. He hardly spoke. Yet he made relationships easily, some deep. His chums were many. They respected him and admired him because he had a pleasant, likeable character, and because of his good humour and good sense of humour. His female friends were fond of him perhaps because he was dark in complexion, handsome in looks, muscular in physique. And he was chivalrous.

Unfortunately Dan was somewhat gullible too. He had an early relationship with a girl who later told him that she was expecting a kid. Dan accepted responsibility, even when the couple drifted apart. But some in the family believed that Dan had been kidded. The child, they said, bore no resemblance to Dan. He had ginger hair for a start. Dan, however, believed that the little girl was his own daughter and he felt bitter that he was not permitted by the mother to visit her. Dan was honest about the relationship and this somewhat jeopardised his chances with other girls. But in due course he met a maid who fell for him lock, stock and barrel.

Meanwhile, like his brother Joe, Dan eventually turned from the land to the building trade. But, again like Joe, he had not the capacity to progress from being a labourer. He was now labouring for bricklayers rather than market gardeners.

Jane was the maid he fell for, or more precisely the barmaid at the Queen's Head. She too was extremely quiet and rather unattractive, two qualities unusual in a barmaid. Dan first met her when he started drinking there, instead of going out to the King's Head (which had at one time been known as the Swan) with Tom, first just for a change of scenery. The scenery change took the form of this attractive barmaid. That is to say, if to nobody else, she was indeed attractive to Dan. Some men at the Queen's Head said that Jane's breath reeked, especially any who had dared to try to kiss her. However, Dan would not have said so. He would not have noticed. Or had he noticed it would not have mattered. Such was his captivation once she had stolen his heart.

In any case Dan soon discovered the reason for her bad breath. He caught her popping the odd picked onion into her mouth from a jar that she kept on a shelf behind the bar.

Dan was enamoured but nevertheless slow to say much to her. His speech came out tangled, and it became worse after his second pint. He continued, though, to drink at the Queen's just to catch sight of his goddess. It took a long time before he dared engage her in a longer conversation, or to put it bluntly, to chat her up. The fact that anyone could get Dan to chat at all was a massive achievement. But it turned out to be not so hard in the end. So he practised becoming less tongue-tied by claiming a stool at the bar, close to the sink where Jane would wash the glasses. Then he could try to make small talk in between her serving other customers.

As rector, I would try to visit all the Ampthill pubs every now and again. The Old Red Lion (conveniently closest to the rectory), the White Hart (which brewed its own ale until the brewery stopped it), the George, the Rose and Crown, the Compasses (one of the town's oldest and smallest pubs, once called the Three Compasses and, in medieval times, the Bell or Snowe's Place), the Cross Keys (the Commercial Inn, where John Webb was landlord when I first began to drink there but demolished shortly before I retired), the Crown and Sceptre (I have no idea why they changed the name of this coaching inn to the King's Arms - I suppose to cause confusion or perhaps competition with the King's Head, another of the coaching inns). It was here that I witnessed old Sam as he entered the pub; he fell down the step and broke his wrist. He had not even yet been drinking. Immediately after the fall he looked up and noticed the sign, "Mind the step down". This pub was particularly busy on market day.

All these welcomed a clerical customer. But perhaps I felt more at home in the Queen's Head than the others. It was here that I had a little too many the night I returned home and had my first unfortunate encounter with young Betsey.

All this drinking kept me fairly busy, so there was little time for church meetings in the evenings, though some took place in the King's Arms, where they gave us a private room. There was no charge. All we had to do was buy a pint.

Next to the pub was the King's Arms archway, where offices were built in the fifties. The Post Office there was popular. It was popular for another thirty years, when another, bigger PO, was opened in Bedford Street. The Inland Revenue office was also in the Arms archway. But that office was not so popular.

Another place I called in later in my ministry, if less frequently, was the Drum and Monkey. I was keen to try this new place with such an attractive name. The first time I walked inside I discovered that it was not, after all, a pub but the Church Army Social Centre.

Anyway, back at the Queen's Head, Jack the landlord took me on one side while Dan was occupied chatting to Jane. In a hushed tone he told me that his inn had a ghost. The pub was hardly a hundred years old. But unexplained shadows were seen by customers in the lounge bar. They did not appear to have had too much drink when they told their story. Several unconnected clients had said and seen the same. They did not appear to be in cahoots. They did not appear to be hoaxing. On the contrary, the presence did seem to appear with some frequency. I spoke to several customers to try to form a picture of what the presence was like. There was one leg-puller who assured me that he heard howling hounds and heavy breathing; he told of a haunted airing cupboard; he saw a girl who played death ring games who was pushed downstairs, a grinning baby, a monster with evil eyes, fangs and claws and a see-through head, and a mother with a constant headache.

Even Jane believed some of it. She told the owner that she had had her legs slightly slapped by something unseen while she was working behind the bar. She first thought it might be Dan playing a trick or even becoming flirtatious. But that was impossible. For one thing he was too shy to try that. For another, he was out in the latrines at the time. Then she wondered if it was Victoria, the Queen's cat. But the cat was nowhere to be seen all that evening. In any case, the temperature would suddenly fall, and a few sensitive drinkers would shiver in harmony. Stories spread. The ghost was heard upstairs, along the corridor. There were phantom footsteps, and these were certainly not made by a cat's paws. It was assumed that the pub had the spirit of a former landlord, perhaps. One guest said that he actually got a glimpse. He looked rather like a seventeenth century chap. At least (so far) he had appeared friendly. (Perhaps he was a Friend too, like Dan).

This is where I came in. Jack the landlord asked me if there was anything I could do about it.

"Exactly what, Jack?" I asked. "I'll be a hundred years ahead of myself if I attempt an exorcism."

I told him that it would not be appropriate to exorcise it, especially if the spirit were harmless and, indeed, amicable. I would be willing, though, to come in and say some prayers when the pub was empty, apart, that is, from the friendly ghost. This is what I did. I considered a sprinkling of holy water, but Church of England clerics by law established were not permitted the use of holy water. I considered sprinkling beer. But that would have been a waste. In any case, the sprinkling even of water would be frowned upon by a number of my congregation, claiming that I was popish. It would probably be more than frowned upon. It would stir up considerable controversy. The main reason, though, was that if my beloved flock got to hear of my asperges they would readily and gladly report me to the bishop. This I could do without. So I did not even mention to the landlord that it was even a possibility.

Nevertheless I seemed to have a reputation for this kind of thing. People came to regard me as having a gift to banish unwanted presences. One was a farmer. He sent one of his labourers to ask me to come to attend to his pigs. "And bring your boots," he added. I had already gone to bed, so my reply to the farm worker was, "Tell him I'm the rector, not the bloody vet." But it was indeed I who was required rather than the vet. The farmer was convinced that a ghost was running amuck in the farrowing pig sheds. I went and said some prayers. The farmer was satisfied that it had done the trick, even though the pigs did not charge off like the swine of Gadarenes.

My divinity professor at Oxford had once been challenged to prove the existence of God. He walked the prober to a pigsty that he happened to have handy and said, "There is your proof of God's existence. I love pigs. They are so delightfully ugly, and so blissfully self-satisfied about it. Is there a God who understands that bundle of incompetence and commonplace, ugliness and self-satisfaction, which makes the most obvious "experiences" of the sublime thing I call my personality? Can he make any use or sense of it, even if he smiles a bit over its funny absurdities as I like to think he did over the pigs?" [2] I was not so sure that I agreed while standing in a muddy pig shed on a cold night when I should have been tucked up in bed.

---

[2] This is a quote from Fr Herbert Kelly, founder of the Society of the Sacred Mission.

Then, as I was drinking a glass of port, there was the late night message from a man who wanted a priest because he had a deranged wife in bed. I went to find the home. Knocking at the door I was met by a lady who did not seem in the slightest bit deranged. This was because I had called at the wrong house. At the second attempt I found her. The husband led me upstairs to the bedroom. I was greeted at the top by an unfriendly alsatian dog. Having overcome that obstacle I was greeting by an even more unfriendly fuzzy-haired woman with long red claw-like nails held out as if to attack. She was bare-breasted, fixing me with a fierce-eyed glare. It was the husband who spoke first. "Here's the priest."

Then it was her turn. "Fuck off," she hissed in reply. The husband was going to do so and leave us but I persuaded him to stay. An hour later I said prayers as her shrieking eventually died down. I returned home and drank another port.

It must be time to find out how Dan was coping with Jane. He took every opportunity to engage her in conversation. Eventually they were engaged full stop. Jane left the pub and took on a job as a straw plaiter. Then they married. The Queen's Head employed a new barmaid. Jane continued plaiting. The ghost never returned. (He had not at the time of writing, anyway.)

Dan and Jane's daughter Mary Jane went into service for a doctor in Luton. She did nearly every domestic job in the house, all the chores except cooking, for which they employed an older woman who earned much more than Mary Jane. She had sufficient money to survive but this did not run to the expense of travelling back to her family on her precious days off. At least she got free pills when feeling off colour.

Willie their middle son lost a hand in an accident on a farm. Jane never got over the accident, even though Willie recovered, at least mentally. Jane's own mental state suffered. It was not easy for Willie, either. He could compensate for the loss of the hand, but not sufficiently to hold down a job. He felt himself a burden on his parents, as indeed he was.

On the Sunday following the ghostly incident I wrote in the diary:

April 1857 *I was in church kneeling down during prayers at evensong, the service being conducted by the curate. I felt my left leg being gently stroked. My mind was asking questions about who was in the pew behind me. A lady? A young lady who fancies me? I turned and was disappointed to find it was a cat.*

Perhaps it was Victoria who had followed me from the Queen's Head.

Daniel died aged fifty-two. I never discovered what he died of - his family did not seem to want me to know. He might have wished to have his funeral in the Quaker Meeting House. But he had no say-so. The Friends had a small burial plot, with no more than thirty gravestones, at the back where other Quakers were buried. But the family did not wish him to be in the limited company of a small number of Quakers for the rest of eternity. So I took his funeral at St Andrew's and buried him where he would have a considerably vaster assembly of deceased friends, whether he was aware of them or not.

I remember the date because the same evening was one of the rare occasions when I went to a Nonconformist service. A new cathedral had been built. At least, that is what some people sarcastically called the new huge Methodist chapel on Dunstable Road. If the Primitives could have a new chapel the Wesleyans were not going to be outdone, although they were thirteen years behind. It replaced the little chapel on Woburn Street. They took most of the furnishings from the old chapel. They were unable, however, to take with them the few gravestones at the back. I was invited to the dedication, but was not asked to take part. Some Church of England clergy had begun to wear the new-fangled dog collar. Not me - I turned up in the white neckcloth that I always wore. It was 13th August. It was also Friday.

Bill's sister, Elizabeth

Elizabeth survived two years longer than her elder sister Lucy, dying six days short of making it to the age of twenty-six. Unlike Lucy she did not marry. Unlike Lucy she seemed somewhat unbalanced. In her late teens Lizzie was a charwoman and chambermaid at the White Hart hotel, another old coaching inn, which, she told me, was once the Red Hart, though the reason for the change of colour she did not know. No doubt the new landlord wanted to give the hotel an improved image. Or perhaps it was to avoid confusion with the Red Lion, which had a reputation, according to court cases reported in the newspapers, for attracting more disorderly and abusive clientele.

Despite its reputation men would drink beer to the accompaniment of a game of dominoes. For a change I suggested a game of chess. Only one man ever took up the challenge, I suppose because they thought that I must be a good player. (Their supposition was correct.) The old crony who took up the challenge had often referred to me as "mate", a form of address I did not particularly relish. Anyway, our meeting over the chessboard attracted several serious spectators. It was not long before I was able to say "mate" to him, after a few times putting him in check.

May 1868 *I am staying two nights at a hotel in Limerick. I forgot to bring a nightshirt but did bring a travel chess set. After my morning wash I decided to play with myself (chess) before getting dressed. Unexpectedly a chambermaid walked into the room while I was sat at the table naked. She took fright and fled, clearly not wishing to be mated.*

Although the White Hart was a respectable, indeed quite high-class hotel, where the gentry would spend a night on their way to and from London, arriving not by horse and cart but by horses and carriage, it was not unknown for the White Hart itself to have to sort out a rowdy customer. One such incident was unfortunately witnessed by Lizzie, whose nerves were on edge at the time of the incident. The barman refused to serve the man, a dealer from Bedford. He kicked up a lot of fuss. Fuss was not the only thing he kicked. He knocked over chairs in his excitable state. The manager was called and attempted to eject him. I say attempted because the dealer was unwilling to leave the premises as requested. The constable was summoned. He arrived and his cuffs proved to be more persuasive than the manager. The incident had a detrimental affect on Lizzie. However, it was nothing compared to the event that followed.

One of Lizzie's jobs was to prepare the lounge every first and third Thursdays for Ampthill's Petty Sessions that were held in the hotel. The inn was used too for inquests, and Elizabeth was actually called to give evidence for a suicide that had occurred in the White Hart itself. A resident had cut his wrists in his room. For a time, then, with so much blood around, the White Hart reverted to being the Red Hart once more. Lizzie was expected to clean it up. The experience did not help to improve her mental state of mind. On the contrary, Lizzie was adversely affected by the trauma. Nor did she receive any help other than talking to me, which I prayed would give her a modicum of relief, if only she could get it off her chest. But it was not so simple to get off her chest. She needed more counselling than I was capable of providing.

Lizzie had been asked at the inquest if she had witnessed the character who had taken his life and to describe his state of mind. She testified that she had seen the unfortunate man on a few occasions. He always appeared miserable, never smiling, but there was nothing she was able to pin-point to indicate that he was disturbed enough to take his life.

Lizzie's own state of mind was in turmoil. The previous detrimental affect had now crescendoed to have a major mental affect. She was on the brink of being taken into Bedford asylum on Ampthill Road. Her brother Tom would threaten, unkindly in retrospect, "It'll be the lunatic asylum for you, the way you're carrying on, my love."

It was in fact Lizzie's youngest brother James who ended up there. There was little wrong with his mental health, not until, that is, he caught syphilis. The doctor told him that it might just be possible to get rid of it if he took a course of mercury. But one of the side effects, he was told, was the possibility of his teeth falling out. He decided against mercury poisoning, even though he was aware that the disease could prove fatal if left untreated. It was not fatal for James. But he did slowly go mad. That is why he ended up in the asylum for lunatics. He was one of the last inmates at Ampthill Road before the asylum closed. Some patients were lucky enough to be sent home. James was transferred to the new Three Counties Asylum at Stotfold.

My sense of humour failed me. I lacked the tactlessness to say to the family that I might be able to help James with my special VD fund. It might have cruelly raised false hopes. After all, the fund had nothing to do with venereal diseases. It was a small fund called "vicar's discretionary". Anyway, I decided not to attempt the bad joke. (About the same time I spotted the letters vd in my diary, which perplexed me. Was I due for a check at the doctor's? No. It was a relief when I realised that it simply referred to "various dates".)

To tell the truth, Elizabeth really should have been in the hospital herself, whether mental or otherwise. She was taken home from the White Hart, unable to complete her task of sorting out the seating for the next round of sessions. It was considered by the family that she was likely to get worse and worse before she would return to some sort of normality. She never did improve.

Her head was not only in a spin mentally but she suffered acute headaches and felt drained and lifeless. She had felt unusually tired at work in recent weeks. She was not eating much at home. The girl was very poorly. She was eventually put to bed and her body began to quickly waste away. The nights were long as she felt chilled one moment, then lay in heavy sweats the next. Her chest was in pain and the constant coughing aggravated it. Her father thought that she had some dreadful plague, so awful was her condition. The doctor did not take long to realise that Elizabeth was suffering from consumption, tuberculosis, the same disease that Lucy had died of years earlier. John Bunyan of local fame had once called the illness "the captain of all these men of death". Death was not far away. Lizzie died at home, with her mother looking after her as best she could at the end.

Needless to say her mother Mary, herself having been besieged by one tragedy after another, was at her wits' end.

The landlord of the Queen's Head had not kept reticent about the good job I had done in keeping his ghost at bay. On the contrary, he recommended me when he heard that the White Hart had its own spook. I forget the landlord's name. It was well before the popular landlord John Gray took over. I was informed that unlucky residents of room thirteen were especially susceptible. The management said they could solve the problem by changing the room number. But, when their landlord heard from Jack about my skills to encourage phantoms to bugger off, he agreed to give it a try. This apparition was female. She strongly disapproved when guests tried to shut the room door, which, of course, they occasionally needed to do. One man attempted to close the door and it flung back hitting him hard on the bonce.

I was tempted this time to have a go with holy water. But I did not know how, having never tried it. Nor was I supposed to. It would be fun chasing after and splashing a female ghost. However, I resisted the urge and suggested that the landlord get in touch with the Roman Catholic priest. He would do the job better than I could. I stayed well clear when he turned up with his equipment. Sprinkle. Sprinkle. Sprinkle. The rite, I gather, was to no effect. The carpenter met with more success after he changed the hinges and, for good measure, screwed onto the door number twelve A and put thirteen into the bin.

Betsey's brothers James and John both worked for John and Joseph Morris, who operated a brewery on Bedford Street, next to the Crown and Sceptre yard. They established the firm in 1820. It was a huge and impressive pile, with its tall chimney erect behind. The business prospered and local people benefited from employment there. Ampthill House was built for Joseph a few years later. The House was sold to the Wingfield family some thirty years on. Anthony did not remember coming to the House. He was one year old. Sir Anthony, as he was to become, became an established figure in the town.

One of the first pubs that the Morrises purchased was the Old Sun, where Bill had once caused such a rumpus. James and John were among the locals who benefited from being employed at the brewery and started work there in the fifties. They were still there when the business became a limited company in 1877. The brothers remembered the year for the pay rise that they were awarded and for the barrel of beer that they were given, partly to celebrate the firm's becoming a company and partly to thank them for twenty-five years' loyal service. They did not turn up the following day. They were legless.

CHAPTER 8
ON THE LAND

Thomas Gibbs was well-known as a seedsman who worked for the Board of Agriculture. He lived in Church Square in a large house built specially for him. In stark contrast to the army of agricultural labourers who worked long hours for little money Thomas grew rich from the experimental work that he did on grasses. He was respected by some for his achievements and looked up to by many for having earned a position in society. But neither the some nor the many included the agricultural labourers. They resented him and his nameless bosses, especially because of his high income that allowed him to live in a big house well beyond the dreams of the ordinary worker.

It was not so with Charles May the herb grower. He was equally notable in the community. He produced drugs for medicines. He started to manufacture chemicals in Ampthill. Large amounts of drugs were brought into Ampthill by road. He grew and processed plants (lavender, rosemary, gentian, foxgloves, peppermint, to name a few) behind his premises on Church Street. His home was more modest than Thomas' on Church Square. It was also more central in the town and more accessible to people. Moreover, he was approachable. He was popular, even though he demanded hard work and long hours from his workforce.

However popular Charles may have been, he had stirred up some interesting memories in the family many years later when Bill and Betsey's eldest great-grandson married Thomas Manton's great-granddaughter. It happened like this:

Not long after Charles set up his business he prosecuted the Manton brothers, James and Thomas and their sister Ann, for not delivering several hundredweight of bones that he had ordered and paid for. They said that they had delivered them on two carts drawn by ponies. The steam engine, they claimed in their defence in court, was going at the time, so the delivery had not been heard. The men in the yard assured the court that no bones had been delivered that day. The magistrate did not believe the Mantons (or the steam engine) and the three Mantons got done. The great-grandchildren were amused by the tale about their ancestors. This is the reason it caused a bone of contention between the families.

Thomas Gibbs and Charles May were hardly the chief providers of agricultural work in the town. They were both specialist operators. No Low worked for either. Most male Lows worked in less glamorous areas in the fields and on the farms. Some Lows did, however, have a reputation for experimenting with their seeds, sometimes known as wild oats, which they scattered and sowed wherever they found opportunity.

We have yet to be introduced to Josiah. But Josiah's brother-in-law George Allen continued the business after Charles May retired. George carried it on for nearly forty years until he died at the end of the century. The firm moved to Suffolk. There were no more drugs in Ampthill. Or rather, no longer were they manufactured there.

It is time we were introduced to another George.

Bill's brother, George

Of the eleven brothers and sisters only five married, including Lucy who tasted married life for only two years. William, of course, married. He made up for the others a little by having two wives, though not simultaneously. William's baby brother George, fifteen years his junior, was one of those who never wedded. At least he managed to attain marriageable age, which several did not achieve. These two brothers worked for the same employer for a time.

George was intensely shy and not easy to get to know. He was so shy that we can confidently assume that he sowed no wild oats. Yet he had some bosom friends who thought highly of him. He hardly spoke in company but was nevertheless respected greatly as a warm, kindly, mild man. Probably it was his friendly face, his easy smile, that attracted people's esteem. George was happy to please, amiable and easy-going. It is difficult to see how George and William were brothers, so diverse were they in personality. We might compare or contrast them with another George and William.

George IV was king when William (Low) was born. William IV was king when George (Low) was born. King William was King George's younger brother. Yet they were so different. George, though charming and cultured, was extravagant and wasteful in lifestyle, concerned for leisure and pleasure. He lived mainly for himself and was rather irresponsible and certainly unreliable. King George's brother William, on the other hand, was popular, unassuming, conscientious, and concerned for others, especially the poor and unfortunate. He reformed society as best he could, being particularly concerned about child labour and slavery. What brother monarchs could be more diverse than these two? And what Bedfordshire brothers could be more different from these two too? Our William and George were in no sense regal. They were almost on the bottom rung of society's ladder and they were highly unlikely to do any climbing.

George looked after the draught horses and drove them delivering wheat, straw and haulm, as well as working the horses in the fields. It had taken him a while to learn how to put the harnesses on. At first he had been allowed to do little more than muck out the stables. But he progressed swiftly and was even able to plait the horses properly. He received several kicks for his trouble and once a stallion bit his chin. But he persevered. If he was shy of people he was not shy of his beloved horses. He used to tell people that his horses could actually speak to him. They did not talk in public, he would explain. But they spoke to him when they were alone in the stables. No doubt George needed to compensate for his inability to articulate with his fellows, so he imagined conversations in the stables. One day a fellow worker decided to test out whether one of the horses could indeed speak. In front of George, he enquired of the horse, "Dobbin, canst thou really talk?"

George was equally as astounded as his mate when the horse replied, "Nay"!

The business on the farm was thriving, so, when William started to work with George, another pair of strong hands was a useful asset. Moreover, William actually enjoyed the work and began to settle down.

George lived for a while with Daniel and Jane during the early days of their married life. So did their mother Mary after Philip's death.

Although the farm where George worked was doing well for a while, things started to go downhill. Life had always been hard for agricultural workers. It was not an idyllic life. Labourers were poorly paid. The situation worsened during the six months of the agricultural strike. The workhouse filled up. Deterioration in the agricultural industry was due not only to a series of seasons of bad weather. There was an abundance of wheat being imported from America. Work was just not there. Agricultural labourers went on strike first in Suffolk. It soon spread to Norfolk and then all over, and so to Bedfordshire. This all took place two years before George died. Had these events led to his death? We will never know.

George died when he was forty. He went down with chronic bronchitis and was taken for a spell into Bedford Infirmary. Although the Bedford hospital was to be home from home for so many of the family in years to come, George was the first member of the family to be a patient, despite its seventy years of operation. Dan and Jane visited George often. On one visit they found a religious pamphlet by his bed, which caused Jane to make a fuss, or more precisely a vociferous complaint to the matron. It was hardly in Jane's character to stir up trouble, usually being so slow in coming forward. However, this is what she did. It turned out that there was a Mormon on the ward who was responsible. Shortly after the Mormons' first missionaries arrived in England a mission was set up in Bedford. The Mormon patient was sternly rebuked by the ward sister, under orders from the matron. Whether he took any notice neither Jane nor Dan discovered, for George (who, due to his illness, cared little about the leaflet) was discharged soon after. The hospital could do nothing to relieve his distress. Four months later the bronchitis became acute and after three breathless days he died. Daniel was with his brother at the end.

October 1876 *I am addressed in all sorts of peculiar ways when people write me letters. I received details of George's funeral from the funeral director. He usually calls me Reverend", which infuriates me but there is nothing I can do about it. Today his pen had slipped. He wrote, "Dear Reverended ..." I wanted to reply to "My dear Neverended ..."*

I dreaded officiating at the funerals of farm labourers. They were a most unfriendly breed. After a service many would hardly look at me let alone return my smile. A few would even refuse to shake my hand. The reason eventually dawned on me. They resented the difference in lifestyle. Apart from the disparity between their modest shacks and my large rectory they compared their weekly income of a little below seven shillings (when I first arrived in the parish) with my annual income of £495. They knew that I had extra money coming in from glebe land. So I was receiving, they reckoned, about £11 per week. Moreover, they were earning their wages by very hard work. They did not consider that my occupation was even work, let alone hard. Yet they were charged one shilling and five pence for a loaf of bread, no less than my wife paid for it. To tell the truth, a loaf of bread did not cost us even that much because Mary made ours herself. But the labourers were not to know that.

Owning glebe land was not without its problems. All the rabbit warrens proved a nuisance. Had my father been still alive, though, he would not have found them a problem. The rabbits would have been a bonus for his butcher's shop. They would provide extra meat for his customers' tables and extra money in his pocket.

Anyway, unfriendly mugs and hands in pockets notwithstanding, I officiated at George's funeral. He was brought in a coffin to church on the carriage pulled by his horses for the final clip-clop.

Bill's brother, Benjamin

Benjamin was Joseph's twin. He was born minutes after his brother. Benjamin died as soon as he was born. It was difficult to ascertain whether Mary was experiencing joy at his brother Joseph's birth or whether the devastation of her younger twin son's death had diminished, if not totally wiped out, the exhilaration. Her emotions were mixed. There was a loving bond between her and Joseph. But there was also always sadness and the deep depression that went with it, the sense that Joseph was not complete.

Bill's brother, Joseph, and Mary

Joe became ill when he was five. His parents were anxious, to put it mildly. Joe had a fishy-smelling diarrhea. He was constantly being sick. He was lethargic, unusual for Joe, who was normally bouncy. When his skin began to turn bluish they called in the doctor. The doctor was normally in his local in the evenings. That was the reputation he had, anyway. On the evening that Philip knocked on his door he was at home, albeit making short work of a bottle of whisky. The doctor came out straight away and was most concerned that Joe might have contracted cholera. He did not express his fears to the family. On his second visit Joe was finding it difficult to breathe. He had even gone into a coma for a while. The doctor was more convinced than ever that he had the big "c" (or more correctly the big "C"). Still he did not say so to the boy's parents. But Mary had suspected the same. She was aware that cholera had now found its way to Bedford and even closer to home.

Nevertheless, Joe made a good recovery. He was soon back to his normal playful self.

Joe did not turn out like his older brother. His temperament was altogether different. He was more gentle, softer. He was quieter and had lost much of the bounce he displayed as a child. He was more talented. But his drawback, again unlike William, was that he was lazy. The only aspect of his childhood illness that remained was his lethargy. For a lengthy spell, therefore, he found himself unemployed. He decided to change jobs from agricultural labouring. He sought work as a bricklayer. Or rather, although he might have applied himself to learn the skills of a bricklayer had he put a mind to it, he was merely a bricklayer's labourer. Unhappily he did not have the appetite for the hard work that the job demanded. So he went back to labouring on the land. That, of course, was hard work too. But at least the land was in his blood.

Although Joe was not physically strong he was keen. Having had an affair with the building trade he discovered that the grass was not necessarily greener on the other side. Once he returned to his former love he embraced the land more than ever. He even got himself involved in the Bedfordshire Agricultural Society, once their annual show began to be held in Ampthill Park. In working to support the show Joe was unwittingly involved in improving the system of agriculture. He was not to know, and would never know, that in another sixty years the show would be attended by the Prince of Wales.

One day through lack of concentration he (Joe, not the Prince) fell in front of a horse. The horse trod on him and broke his leg (not the horse's) and caused profuse bleeding from his buttock. Now not only was the land in his blood but his blood was in the land.

Joe's marriage caused division in the family at first. Mary was a staunch Baptist. "What could be worse than that?" thought Joe's brothers and sisters. Some of them not only thought it but said it openly. The ones who said it loudest were those who never went to church at all. But it was a family scandal until they got to know Mary better and she won them over. It took a long time. Ten years after their marriage she asked the family to join her at a special evening service when a harmonium was to be played to accompany the singing. This was an innovation. One or two accepted the invitation. Joe was not one of them. He had never been inside the Union chapel (and indeed rarely inside St Andrew's, where despite Mary's disapproval they had been married) and he did not intend starting to attend there now.

Joe was married for over forty years. He never looked for greener grass to lie on. However, he and Mary had no offspring. They craved for a baby but fortune did not favour them with a longed-for pregnancy. Perhaps he was as lazy in bed as he was at work.

Joe and Mary, being childless, were specially close to their nephews and nieces, not least Tom's and Dan's little ones. The children often called to visit them. They went to their aunt and uncle's not only for the love and affection always shown to them but perhaps also for the penny pieces they each always received from Mary before returning home. The regular visitations proved expensive but they were always truly delighted to receive the youngsters and supplied them with drinks, sweets, biscuits, cakes, kisses and cuddles in plenty.

Joe was a regular at the King's Head. Whenever he could skive off work, as well as going for a drink he would call in to listen to the auctions that took place there. Interested as he was, he never dared make a bid. Neither could he afford to do so.

Speaking of the King's Head, I read in my diary:

30th January 1849 *Today is my 36th birthday and the 200th anniversary of the death of King Charles. Perhaps because I was born on this day is the reason that I am so named. So far I have kept my head.*

23rd April 1849 *On Saint George's Day we acquire a puppy to replace the labrador. This one is a King Charles spaniel. So we pray she will not* *bark her head off. We have to name her, of course, George. (If we named her Charles, I wouldn't know whether Mary was calling the dog or me.)*

I came home one evening after taking George for a walk, stopping first to lock up the church. "Where's George?" asked Mary. I had come in without her, having locked George in the church. I was ordered to return immediately but took a long time to retreive her. She had become stuck beneath the organ pedals.

Word got around that our dog had died. It was no more than a misunderstanding. I had told people that I had lost our dear dog George and it was taken as a euphemism.

Bill and Joe's brother George would have been delighted to have a dog named after him, but perhaps not have approved that it was a name given to a bitch. We will meet another dog, the mad labrador, in due course.

Joe's apparent laziness was due, in hindsight, to a dibilitating illness. At the age of five he had recovered spectacularly from the big "C". But he succumbed at the age of sixty-eight to another "c", cancer or, as the doctor put it, carcinoma. This was big enough to do him in. He had lost his strength for some considerable time and this was unacceptable for a labourer. Now we know and understand the reason for his apparent laziness.

Bill's brother, James

Philip did not need to go to work the day James, their last child, was born. It was Christmas Day. But for Mary the celebration of the birth of our Lord was a day of hard work indeed. It was the day when she gave birth to James. It was far from an easy birth despite the practice that she had had. She was a mother of some experience. Yet the pain was still intense. The arrival of James took place at four o'clock in the afternoon, so Philip was detailed to put the kettle on for the excited family. Even Mary was glad to sip a cup of tea, not so much by way of celebration but from exhaustion following her hard labour. Nobody mentioned it but, after all the children Mary and Philip had lost, everyone was relieved that the baby lived, and prayed that their wonderful Christmas present would continue to do so for a very long time.

Christmas was not especially important in Philip and Mary's home. This year they had not written or given a single card. Neither had they a cracker to pull. There was not even a Christmas tree in the home.

In this they were not so different from many other families. The festivities had not yet become out of hand. The difference in this household was that with a baby about to be born they had not even given Christmas a thought. What Mary had given plenty of thought to was putting a stop to Philip's lovemaking. He could go and do his philandering elsewhere for all she cared.

It was not yet new year when Mary told him that enough was enough. She would have no more children. And she kept her determined resolution. No more children did she bear, to the disappointment of Philip. It was not that he wanted more babies so much as the blighted hopes of joining Mary in bed. The poor chap was henceforth banished from sleeping with his wife, unless he kept his trousers on.

Philip now found a new interest. He would put his trousers on and walk down to the newsagent's to buy the Bedford Mercury before setting off to work. The paper was first published the year after James was born. It was a novelty for Philip to read a daily. But Mary chided him daily for keeping his head stuck in a paper after the evening meal when there were jobs to do in the house, not least the washing-up.

Admonitions came thicker and faster when eight years later Philip started taking the newly founded Bedfordshire Times. The washing-up was sorely neglected.

CHAPTER 9
BETSEY AND BILL'S WEDDING

William had known Betsey since the swish family Robinson moved in next door to the Lows at Cowfair End. He could hardly believe his luck when he found that a comely girl, apart that is from her ugly scar, should be living cheek by jowl. Brutish though he was, William was nevertheless shy of the other sex. The shyness was not reciprocated. Possibly subconsciously Betsey set out to entrap her neighbour. After their first few tentative encounters they got around to giving each other a quick kiss. That is to say, Betsey egged him on to do so. It was soon discovered that both had been neighbours during an enforced absence from Dunstable Street. Although they never actually met there, they had been close neighbours in Bedford prison, or more correctly the House of Correction. Now they had at least one thing in common.

One day the chit-chat got around to clothes. "You always wear good clothes. What do you do to afford dressing so smart, Liz?"

"Don't call me that. My name's Elizabeth. So my mum says. But she does sometimes call me Betsey. Dad always does."

"OK, Betsey, so what do you do?"

"I said my parents call me that. I didn't say you could."

"Well, I'm damned if I'm going to say Elizabeth all the time, Liz."

"I said I'm not Liz. Be told. Well, all right. Call me Betsey then, if you must."

"My sister is called Lizzie. She likes it. Anyway, Liz, you didn't answer the question."

"I work in lace making, with my mum," she informed him. "We make lace pillows. But clothes and other things as well. What about you, Willy?"

"Willy! I hate that. I'm Will to my mates. You can call me Bill if you like. On East End Farm, Liz. I used to work with my father on another farm. But we didn't get on."

"That's a shame, Will. I always get on with my dad. He's lovely. But I've never worked with him. I wonder how he'd get on in the lace factory surrounded by giggly girls. Anyway, I'd like to see the farm where you work. Can you show me around sometime? But only if you stop calling me Liz. "

"OK. If you like I'll take you on Sunday afternoon. There shouldn't be anyone around, Li..., er, Betsey."

The trap was set. The spider had made her web. They found themselves in a barn. Still William was slow to take any initiative. Betsey showed off her lace underskirt. More interested than what was underneath, he wondered how she came to be wearing such la-di-da stuff.

"It's a perk of the job," she assured him. "We're entitled to buy seconds for next to nothing."

Betsey unhooked her corset. She pulled up her petticoats. She loosened her laces. She loosened his braces. He knew he ought to react in some way. William's hand, trembling, crept slowly and nervously up her leg. She put her hand over his to prevent it going further up the thigh. And he was quietly pleased to be stopped in his tracks.

"Am I wearing lace drawers or cotton ones, do you think, Bill?" She asked him to guess. "If you say right, I'll take them off for you."

(Betsey had begun to call him Bill. He no longer objected. She was the first to do so. Others had got as far as calling him Will. So now we will recognise him as Bill too.)

"I'm dead sure they'll be cotton ones," Bill replied, shyly half hoping that he would be wrong.

"Sorry, you're badly mistaken, Billy boy."

She lifted her slip and revealed that she was wearing no drawers, neither lace nor cotton nor anything else.

But nothing too dramatic seemed to take place other than some hesitant and awkward groping.

"Oh, you're a Willy, after all," she giggled.

It turned out to be a fruitful fumbling though, for in due course the apparent lack of anything significant happening did not prevent Betsey realising within a period of a few weeks that her period had not occurred. They feared the worst. The worst happened. They did not see how. But a baby was on the way. I officiated at their wedding, some thirteen months after their baby Eliza was born.

An idea struck me. What if I drastically shortened my surplice to introduce a new style ecclesiastical robe? What if I added a strip of lace at the bottom, created for me by Betsey the lace maker? Perhaps, if only I could persuade her to embroider and sew it on, I could wear it for the very first time at her marriage ceremony. Would it ever catch on? No. On reflection I considered it a daft idea. No sane priest would ever be seen dead in such a garment. I decided to discard the plan, at least for a few decades.

Anyway, before the wedding all hell had been let loose in two households next door to each other. After initial rows had died down the Robinsons insisted that their beloved Betsey marry the father forthwith. The Lows were more cautious. They laid into Bill something chronic, yet they counselled their boy to take time, to see if it turned out that the couple could make a go of it. Betsey gave birth before any decision was reached. Then they decided to marry forthwith and plans were speedily made. It was Betsey's mother, Frances, who first called on me to ask for my services. It was a tentative visit, she wondering what would be the rector's reaction to her daughter seeking marriage in church when already a mother.

When I told her that I would be delighted to perform she said that I would in due course receive an invitation to the reception. I wondered whether I would be invited to say the grace. I was mindful of a recent wedding at which I was asked to go to the reception to say the grace but was not invited to stay on for the meal. (I would much prefer to stay for the meal but not say the grace.)

Bill's sister, Lucy the second

My reaction was one of acute embarrassment. I go back three years. Bill's sister Lucy, the sibling we have not yet met, had encountered me when I first arrived in the parish. She asked to meet me in church with her sixteen year-old friend Susanna. Both were keen to join the choir, so they said. That was not the real motive. It was a ruse. Lucy excused herself saying that she had to get home for tea. Susanna took me unawares and kissed me in the vestry. She kissed me again. I reluctantly responded. We petted. What a sticky mess I then got myself into.

The following week Susanna sent me a note. Could she please meet me in church to apologise? It should never have happened. Yes, she could. I felt not a little relief. I suggested tomorrow after choir practice. Susanna was full of verbal apology but had turned her back on me as she proclaimed how sorry she was. I told her not to let it happen again. She promised she would not, then turned around. She had undone her shirt buttons and exposed bare bubbies. It was a delight: at first to gawp at her ripening melons; then to dare to touch them. It was hard to resist. I did not resist. But I felt it incumbent on me to make matters clear.

"You really must never, never, never do this again," I demanded, unsure whether I meant it or not.

Yet it happened a few times more. I persisted in insisting that it must stop. In the end she wanted to make confession of her sin. I agreed to counsel her so that she could get it off her chest. We met in church after dark. Giving her godly counsel in church would put an end to the precocious girl plaguing me, pleasant plague though it was. It was a solemn occasion in the vestry where I listened to her disencumber herself and I honestly thought that she was repentant. I pronounced over the girl the assurance of God's forgiveness. But within minutes she was back to square one. Her buxom bosoms were out in the open. How can I get out of this one? She was so infatuated that, to my mind, she had made a mockery of the sacred session that had so recently taken place. Needless to say, I should have made a confession too, since I went along with her whenever she held out a carrot. Having started, it was all too easy to keep taking a nibble. I never got around to making my confession, not before another priest anyway. It was not yet, thankfully, the custom to do so. Had it been, I would nonetheless have considered it unwise to give it a go.

She enticed me into bed shortly after, one afternoon in the rectory. We lay naked but, up to now, had done nothing. Unfortunately, or perhaps luckily when I think about it in a calm moment, the housekeeper came through the front door at the perfect moment, perfect, as I say on reflection, having saved me from a defrocking in a different sense. I did not think Marjorie the housekeeper suspected anything. But sometime later I had an angry visit from Susanna's mother, a local shopkeeper. We were found out. She was justifiably furious, though apparently unaware that the fault was all Susanna's, not at all mine. This, thankfully, put a definite conclusion to our seeing each other. I was eternally grateful that Susanna and I did not meet with the same fate as Betsey and Bill. My life turned lucky yet again. This all took place months before my own wedding. I never got around to telling my Mary about Susanna.

Unfortunately Susanna's friend Lucy was in the know about all that had gone on. She knew about the initial crush and all that had taken place since. Hence my embarrassment when, three years later, I learned that Lucy's brother wished me to officiate at his wedding. I do not think Bill or Betsey knew about the indiscretion. But how would I look the bridegroom's sister in the eye as I performed the ceremony?

Lucy would also be a bridesmaid and one of the witnesses to sign the register. Lucy was the second of Philip and Mary's Lucys. The first died, as we know, aged two. The next Lucy was born five years later when Bill was himself just two and always running amuck. Most children outgrow this time of being out of control, ever on the rampage. I think I did, for instance. Bill never did, not, that is, until he became subject to Betsey's strong influence.

Anyway, Lucy had started to work with Betsey in the lace factory. "Luce the lace" she was called by the girls. The job did not last long. She went into service after that. Neither did that last long, for she married another William and went to live in Oakley, the other side of Bedford. He was another William who was continually in trouble with the law. From the age of fourteen he had a criminal record. He was in court charged with larceny. He regularly contravened game laws. His speciality was night poaching.

Lucy did not last long in her marriage either. It was nothing to do with her wayward husband. So recently married, she died of the same disease that her sister Elizabeth was to succumb to four years later. Lucy was then twenty-four. Everyone, not least myself, was devastated. If only people could have read my mind when I learned of her death. I did not officiate at the funeral, since she had moved away. It would have proved a difficult task, knowing that she had known all about my momentary weakness.

Susanna's mother, whom I desperately kept well clear of, had been a pupil of the Royal School of Embroidering Females. Mrs Nancy Pawsey moved her successful embroidery works from London to Dunstable Street in Ampthill. Most women who trained there were mature and experienced. Not so Susanna's mum, who was seventeen when she spent a year in the school (then run by Nancy's daughter Harriet) not long before it closed. The School had had the financial support and commission of Queen Charlotte. Ampthill women had contributed curtains and hangings for George lll at Windsor Castle.

I am informed that professional people, including many clergymen, sent their daughters to the School. It was too late in the day to send mine there, not that they ever had inclinations in the direction of the fine art of embroidery. It was even too late in the day to send my wife there, and she did have a talent for the same. She was twenty years too young to be eligible. Anyway, she had not even heard of the existence of Ampthill. I picked her up in Derbyshire.

Susanna's mother, on the other hand, was a local girl. As a result of her training at the School she gave private instruction in embroidery and later set up a shop that sold her own work. She passed on her skill to her daughter, which is how she became friendly with Lacy Lucy, and so invited to the celebrated wedding.

My young curate, the Reverend Mr Chapman, had not yet officiated at a wedding. I suggested that he come to see how it was done.

The wedding itself, considering not only that my curate would be looking to pick up hints while wearing L-plates on his surplice but also that I would be on edge due to the presence of Lucy, went off well, apart from a few dramatic moments. The first drama was when I asked if anyone knew any just cause or impediment to the marriage. Nobody was expecting a hysterical outburst from Betsey's mother Mary. A just impediment is supposed to be a legal one. It is not sufficient impediment that the bride's mother take exception to the bridegroom. But that is what she did. She refused to be placated, so it became necessary to get a few strong men to eject her from church before I could continue the service. Hers was the only objection.

Not much further into the service we were about to begin the vows. Bill started to sway sideways, straighten up, then sway the other way. Was he pissed, I asked myself? Then he toppled over onto the stone floor and was out stone cold. I walked briskly down the aisle and outside to the nearest alms-house and banged on the door.

Dressed in a white surplice, minus lace trimmings of course, I demanded, "I need a glass of water." The very old man who opened the door to me reacted to this strange apparition by himself fainting.

Both men, young and old, recovered and the service progressed. I asked the best man for the ring. It had happened to me before, and has happened to other clergy, that the wedding ring has been dropped and fallen into the grating in the floor. Well, that did not happen this time. But Bill's little seven-year-old brother boy George had been wiggling his loose tooth and, just as I asked for the ring, the boy caused a commotion because his tooth had fallen out. It landed on the floor, then bounced into the grating, irretrievable. How would the fairy pay him now, with no evidence below the pillow?

No further mishaps occurred until the bridal party recessed into the vestry to sign the registers. This time it was I who collapsed. The curate used some initiative by taking charge of the signing. In fact he was the only one who signed his name without making his mark. I had to rebuke him afterwards because it was quite irregular for him to sign as officiant when he had done damn all to effect the couple's marriage. He came back at me by asking who else could have signed, since I was incapacitated. Then he informed me that everyone had commented how lovely the service was. It seems that he had earned credit for doing not a sausage. I did indeed feel a degree of relief when I had recovered sufficiently to realise that all was over. What the couple got up to afterwards I can only speculate. I know that in my own case I stumbled back to the rectory and took a double brandy.

CHAPTER 10
THE RECTOR IN CLINK

February 1846 *The undertaker called about a funeral. Later I visited the widow, stroking the fat cat while the lady made me tea. By the time she appeared with the teapot the cat was on my lap. She was horrified. "Oh no! He bites. He scratched my husband to death."*

I visited my parishioners faithfully as soon as I arrived in the parish, without favouring any social class. Ordinary agricultural workers were equally if not more deserving of my time as the gentry. So why, I wonder, did I choose as my first afternoon call the home of Lord Wensleydale and his family at Park House? My diary tells me that that is what I did. From the rectory I set out along Holly Walk, a banked footpath and short cut down to Park House. As I approached up to a steep slope to arrive at the foot of a tall flight of broad stone steps leading to the main entrance via the side wing of the most beautiful mansion I had ever visited, a three-storey brick building encased in stucco, I heard a lady's voice (it must have been *the* Lady's voice) exclaim: "Oh, my God! It's the bloody rector!"

This was a comment I might have expected from an estate worker's house, but hardly here. Before mounting the steps, I encountered a hound. Awaiting a fierce bark, which did not materialise, to my relief I realised that the dog was a stone statue mounted on a pedestal.

The anxiety of being eaten up by a huge hound having diminished, I timidly knocked on the large door. It was opened by a young servant girl. She asked me into the hall, seated me and told me that she would see if Lady Wensleydale was at home. Lady W was at home, as I well knew. (Her husband, a High Court judge, perhaps was out, or perhaps hiding. If he were out, who, I wondered, was Lady W talking to when she made her not-intended-to-be-heard remark? Surely not a maid. Or was it the maid who had sworn and, if so, why? Is it usual to swear before a judge? These questions passed through my mind as I waited.) Anyway, Lady W greeted me as if she were truly delighted to see me. "Oh, my dear rector, how lovely to see you. How kind of you to come. Please do come through to the drawing room."

Whereupon she rang the bell and summoned afternoon tea for two.

My next visit was not until the following day. As a curate I had reckoned normally to make six calls each afternoon. Six cups of tea were sufficient for one day. It became essential to learn the whereabouts of suitable places to relieve myself, bushes included. If I were lucky enough to be offered whisky instead (preferably accompanied by a cigar) then I would walk back to the rectory, without completing the quota of six calls, to sleep off the effects before the evening engagements. But an encounter with Lady Wensleydale was more than enough for one day; I had expended a six-fold amount of nervous energy.

The next day came. The first and last of the day's visits did include a generous tumbler of scotch. It was at Ampthill House, close to the church. The house had been built twelve years before my arrival in Ampthill, the home of Joseph Morris who was the wealthy owner of the brewery. But Joseph had died three or four years before I came. His daughter Catherine was left the mansion in his will. She, however, had decided to marry and moved away, letting it out to a tenant. Who the tenant was, until I gained entry, I had no idea.

I meandered up the long sweeping drive alongside colourful central flower-beds, passing the paddock and ponds to the right, to view a fine Georgian Doric portico. Reaching the top of the steps I rang the bell. A maid (one of many, I soon discovered) invited me in and led me through a reception room (one of many rooms), then into a large drawing room, next through double mahogany doors opening into a smaller drawing room where I was told to await my hosts. The tenant turned out to be William Petre, indeed the Honourable William Petre. Both he and his wife entertained me for considerably longer than my usual average twenty minute call. I hope I did not overstay my welcome, because I gather there were nearly twenty guests staying in the house. But, after all, most of them had brought their personal servants in addition to having the services of the Petres' own domestics, so no doubt they were being looked after. My visit took place shortly before William Petre was created a baron.

Were Joseph Morris still alive I should have been disappointed had I not left the premises slightly tipsy from local ale. As it turned out, my head was spinning from the effects of whisky rather than beer. I tried to be careful to avoid falling into the central flowerbeds as I meandered, or, more accurately, staggered back down the drive, conscious that probably I was being observed by twenty guests from their windows, providing them with light entertainment.

I was to be a regular visitor here after seventeen years in the parish, when the Wingfield family bought the house. Sir Anthony Wingfield, who much later was to start Ampthill zoo on his vast estate, was one year old when they moved in. Of the zoo I will say nothing. I was a very old man by then, too old to take up the offer of a ride on an ostrich.

Of course in the process of time I did visit, often on horseback, all types of homes during my incumbency, including more lowly ones like the Low family's. It just happened that two large typical country squire-like houses should constitute my first two pastoral visits.

An elderly lady expressed delight at seeing me when I called. "I've got a bottle of whisky but can't get the top off." I offered her spiritual help in exchange for a tot.

Some of my visits were to the housebound who would have come to church had they been mobile. Often I would take them the sacrament of Holy Communion from my black box. Occasionally my black box confused other visitors, such as the nurse who took me for a doctor.

April 1862 *I took communion to Mrs T. Her care nurse looked at my black box and said, "Good morning, doctor." I let it go. But the next week she was there again. I asked Mrs T about her bruised leg. The nurse addressed me again. "Is this cream I've been putting on the right stuff, doctor?" It was time to tell her that I was the rector and knew nothing about that sort of cream.*

Calling on the elderly took up a considerable proportion of my time. It was a particular challenge if they were deaf. I recall a lady asking me whether she would retrieve her hearing in heaven. I am not sure that she heard my reply.

I frequently visited parishioners in hospital. I talked to a man who I thought was a patient. He turned out to be a hospital doctor.

Another time I picked a lady patient up from the floor. She had fallen. This earned me a stern rebuke from the sister. Perhaps I should have completed the handling and lifting course before helping the patient back to bed.

The same sister I accidentally tripped up as she walked briskly along the corridor. My reactions were quick and I caught her in my safe arms before she could land on the floor. I apologised but there was no reprimand this time. Perhaps she enjoyed it.

Then there was the time when I was in trouble due to being in the wrong place at the wrong time. The curtains were drawn around a patient's bed. A nurse was peering through the curtain, her backside protruding. Another patient, an elderly woman, was passing and gave the nurse's bottom a hefty smack. By the time the nurse had turned, I had approached the scene of the crime too, coming face to face with the assaulted nurse. I protested innocence but do not think that she believed me.

I sometimes looked into the Union workhouse. I had noticed that they were regularly putting out tenders for supplies of meat, groceries, cheeses, oatmeal, potatoes, bread, flour, soap, coal, coke, clothing, drapery, shoes and all sorts. One of the Robinson family, George, was clerk to the Board of Guardians and was responsible for sorting out the tenders, some six monthly, some three monthly. A constant headache it gave him. He also was responsible for advertising for a chaplain. I had noticed that they were offering a salary of £40 per annum. It attracted several clerical enquirers as well as my own application.

As rector I had been invited to be chairman to the Board of Guardians, which invitation I declined. But now I considered taking on the role of chaplain. However, it seemed too arduous a task to fit in with so many other pastoral duties in the parish. That was my excuse when I was not offered the post. When it came to interviews I was beaten to the job by a Strict Baptist minister from Bedford. Perhaps he was more suited to the workhouse's strict regime. The Strict Baptist minister and I engaged in conversation but our interests proved somewhat different. He recommended that I read the Gospel Standard, an excellent magazine, so he said. I told him that I already read the Christian Remembrancer. "I've never heard of it," he said. "What is it?"

"It's a high church periodical," I rejoined. At that he cleared off, calling me an abominable ritualist. Admittedly I was wearing a cassock at the time. It was thought to be so way-out that I never wore it outside the church again. Nevertheless, I have rarely been so rudely insulted. I had not even mentioned the Guardian, for a brief while a Tractarian leading Anglican weekly newspaper. It was short-lived (and so, it turned out, was the Strict Baptist minister). Thank God, I thought, that there is no Strict Baptist minister here in Ampthill - not yet, at least.

Shortly afterwards I found myself appointed chaplain of Bedford gaol, part-time of course. I did two days a week there. Fortunately Ampthill still had Mr Chapman as curate, so he could cure souls in my place. Although time was precious I persevered in the job, not, of course, for the reason that it brought in a little extra to supplement the stipend. My prison responsibilities included visiting inmates of the House of Correction set up for less serious offenders in Bedfordshire like Betsey, though her offence had seemed serious enough to me at the time. The role involved seeing servants and labourers who had misbehaved in their employment, at least according to their masters. Often, it was said, girls were there because of their lewd actions. I put Betsey in this category. The House of Correction was demolished before my first decade as chaplain was out. It became a garden for prisoners in the main gaol. So there was no further lewdness.

I had to deal with more serious cases too in the main prison. With apprehension I would visit those found guilty of murder, of which there were not a few. I counted myself unlucky to have to deal with Sarah Dazley. Sarah was the last woman to be publicly hanged outside the walls of the gaol. In fact she was the only woman to be hanged publicly at Bedford prison. Talk was that she did not deserve it. She had poisoned her husband with arsenic. Probably he did deserve it. But in the end it was clear that she was well deserving of the punishment. It turned out that she had also poisoned her previous husband too, as well as her son.

Sarah, when I visited her, led me up the garden path with her tall stories. Perhaps I wanted to believe her due to her charm and attractiveness. A girl aged only twenty-four, she was tall, her long flowing hair making her appear even taller. She had big brown eyes and used them to convey pity. I did indeed pity her and found her convincing at the time. When all later came to light I could tell in hindsight that nearly every word she had uttered was a lie. I was unable to elicit any sign of remorse. How, I mused, could such beauty and evil exist in one person?

She was executed on a hot August day, with literally thousands of people come to watch the hanging. Having delayed my week's holiday, I accompanied Sarah to the gallows having already said prayers with her in the cell. This was the worst job of my life to date. I wished I had got the job at the workhouse.

I remember my initiation in the gaol a couple of years earlier because it was the year of my marriage to Mary. I went to care for men and women who had lost their freedom. I had now lost my own freedom by being shackled in matrimony. I would stay in the prison overnight once a week, simply because it was impractical and inconvenient to travel the seven miles there and back in a day. Some wicked scandalmongers suggested that it was to have respite from my wonderful wife. The accommodation was basic, marginally less comfortable than the parsonage. There were no bars in my cell windows, and I had a key to get out.

Mary complained about my absence, naturally. I solved the problem by buying her a dog to keep her company and to shoo off unwanted callers. The labrador could certainly bark but was friendly towards all comers, especially if she were offered a biscuit. In fact the bitch would do anything for food and thought nothing of thieving. She stole joints of meat, cabbages, cakes, even ropes, whatever she could find. It was worth a clout with the rolling pin. It was worth being violently sick. We had the dog on 29th June, Saint Peter's Day. So we decided to call her Simon. Perhaps that is the reason why she was so neurotic.

Mary took Simon for a walk in the park. My grandmother was with her. The dog began to do her business in full view of everyone around but nothing happened. She strained and strained but nothing fell off from her backside. "You'll have to pull it off," suggested my grandmother. In the end that is what Mary attempted to do. She tugged and pulled and pulled and tugged. The sausage kept coming out, growing longer and longer. An audience had gathered. To Simon's eventual relief the whole stuff came free. It was not excrement but a length of rope. Mary received an embarrassing round of applause.

One of the first cruel actions my darling Mary carried out after our wedding was to confiscate, or rather throw away, my treasured set of cut-throat razors. Perhaps she was nervous that I would use one of them for foul purposes should I become tired of her. But I would not have been so cruel. I suppose at the time she could not be certain of that, especially when I related some horror stories of domestic abuse, the cause of some husbands being locked up.

January 1842 *Mary has been reading the Table of Affinity in the Book of Common Prayer and found out that after my death she is forbidden to marry my father. Good. It means that after her death I cannot marry my mother-in-law.*

Off the Maulden road there was a quiet track called Cut Throat Lane. Perhaps Mary's imagination led her to think that one day I would take her for a walk along the lonely lane and do the dastardly deed. Anyway, a new gas works was built there three years after our wedding and the track was renamed Gas Works Lane. The town's five lamp inspectors were familiar with oil lamps but now needed to get accustomed to the new gas lights.

Our first daughter Jane's birth was a few years before the coming of gas to the town. Mary was not yet used to giving birth. She did not realise what was happening, assuming that all she had was an extreme attack of wind, especially when in the middle of the night I told her to get back to sleep. So she thought that she was full of gas, and desperately wanted to let it out. We thought that gas had already arrived in Ampthill. It had not. Nor had it arrived in our bedroom. The outcome of Mary's attack was neither gas nor wind but the first baby. The gas, when it eventually did arrive, would turn out to be the means of a tragic suicide for one of the family in the distant future. But for the immediate future gas was to become a welcome asset, not least at evensong.

So was our second child a welcome asset. Well before we were to be elated by the coming of gas, we were now equally elated by the coming of Pamela too, and finally by the arrival of Elizabeth. The doctor told Mary, shortly after Elizabeth's birth, that she was too old to have more children. She was twenty-five. Bill's mother Mary had eleven. Betsey had six. Betsey's daughter Eliza had ten. My poor Mary had only three, yet was past it.

Was it due to the new gas works that the character of Ampthill had changed, at least as far as its residents were concerned? The same month that the works opened, the Gentleman's Magazine reported: "Thirty years ago Ampthill was perhaps reckoned to be the most genteel town in the country ... but it has not now that distinctive character; many respected and popular inhabitants are no more."

I liked to think that I was popular and respected. That was not the case whenever I suggested any change. Both my congregation (I sometimes had more than two) and the townspeople did not approve of my suggestions for keeping up with the times. Perhaps it was my eccentric views that did not capture their imagination, if indeed they had any. Or perhaps it was my disreputable appearance that turned them against my good ideas.

Unable to shave, Mary having discarded my razors, I grew a beard. It was black, bushy and curly. Other men wore whiskers in a variety of wild and weird ways, so why should I not do so too? When wearing a black cassock people might have mistaken me for Father Rasputin - had he lived forty years earlier, and had he been nine inches shorter. The white cravat that I often wore, when I remembered to put it on, was nowhere to be seen beneath the long beard. The only disadvantage of the beard was that babies would grasp hold of it when I attempted to dunk them in the font for baptism. It was not only painful but awkward to disentangle their little fingers. Did Rasputin have the same problem? I would need to await retirement before I could ask him.

Mary and I were married nearly a year when Jane was born, as aforementioned. Pamela arrived two years later at five in the morning while I was actually in prison. I was soundly asleep at the time of birth. Not so Mary. Later in the day I was scolded for not being at home for the birth. How was I to know?

September 1845 *Mary was well and truly injected neither by the doctor nor by me but by an angry swarm of wasps.*

Elizabeth, our third and final daughter, was born a further two years later, five years before the House of Correction would be no more. At least our Elizabeth would not be going there, unlike the other Elizabeth who had done me harm. That is not to say that our own Elizabeth was not without need of correction too.

Thankfully our heroine Elizabeth was known as Betsey. So she cannot now be mistaken for Elizabeths of my own family. There was my mother Elizabeth, my sister Elizabeth and now my daughter Elizabeth. It might be easier to refer to them by their second Christian names, namely Irene, Janet and Emily. But we will stick to their first names and call my sister Elizabeth the second and my daughter Elizabeth the third.

I wrote in an earlier chapter that I had officiated at Elizabeth the second's wedding. Contrary to popular opinion it was not the archbishop of Canterbury who was to perform the ceremony at all. It was the curate of Bury St Edmunds.

CHAPTER 11
FOREIGN AND HOME AFFAIRS

The Low family, with their dark complexion, black hair and dark brown eyes, have been said to resemble Latins. Perhaps a Mediterranean character came over to Wootton or Ampthill many years ago and struck up a relationship with a maternal forebear. Anyway, some have mistaken the family for Italians and been taken aback when they spoke with a broad mid-Bedfordshire accent. They would not have understood a word if an Italian had actually confronted them, though such a confrontation would be highly unlikely. Italians were not yet flooding into Bedford. The highly unlikely happened though. There was one Italian who had settled locally and had taken to the Established Church. Salvatore worshipped in my congregation.

Although they were quite unfamiliar with any foreign language, the Low family, with whom I now had regular contact, were impressed when they heard me come out with the occasional Italian phrase. How were they to know that I had spent some months in Italy? How were they to know that I was swearing at them, especially when I had shouted "vaffanculo" to Betsey?

Years earlier I had had the good fortune to study in Italy. It was hardly a grand tour. I was not wealthy enough for that and had to slum it on a limited budget. Simon, my companion and architect friend, accompanied me. It took us three days to get to Dover, cross the Channel on the steamship and arrive somewhere north of Paris. It was a stormy crossing on the first day of January. Many passengers were seasick. In fact one lady whom I had been chatting up in the breakfast queue bought a cooked breakfast and then found that she was unable to face it. It had proved well worth speaking soft nothings because she offered me her fry-up. I gladly accepted, of course, and so devoured two meals. By the time we had crossed the Alps into Italy I had been hungry on several occasions. But from Turin onwards I suffered no lack of pasta or wine.

Although Milano, Venezia, Firenze, Roma and Napoli were enjoyable (perhaps educational is the right word), there were drawbacks. One was the presence of highway robbers. I thought that they were an English hazard to travelling but not so. They were in abundance, especially in Milan and Rome. My pockets were picked not once, not twice, but thrice.

In Rome we stayed at a convent in Rocca di Papa, where the [3]Papa had his summer residence overlooking the volcanic Lake Albano. Sister Amadeus greeted us at the huge entrance door in an Irish accent: "You're a day late, so you are." I did not care, as long as we were not late for dinner. We entered the refectory in perfect time for the meal, as if they had been waiting for us to arrive. We sang a hymn to Mary (not my wife) before going to bed.

The next day there was a visit by a score of young people. I was asked if I would be prepared to talk to them in the chapel about the Church of England, Sister Amadeus acting as my interpreter. Following my short oration I invited questions. A boy asked whether my church at home had a confessional box. I answered that it did not but that I sometimes would be asked to hear a confession, in which case I would find a private corner of the church to carry out what they, the Roman Catholic Church, would call the sacrament of penance. The next question was a straight forward one from a girl who asked what the board was with five rows of numbers. Sister Amadeus was expecting me to tell the truth that this was the board to inform the assembly of the hymn numbers. Instead I brought light relief by saying that the figures referred to the number of confessions that I had heard over the last five weeks. Nobody, I think, believed me.

It was a hot, sunny and peaceful morning when I sat on the Spanish Steps daydreaming. My bag containing little of value except a packed lunch was at my side. All of a sudden I was rudely woken from the reverie by a lanky lad running past, at the same time snatching the bag. Immediately I sprang into action and gave chase. There was no way I could have caught up. But I bellowed and boomed (I think I shouted "bastardo"), which caused the thief to turn his head. Luckily for me he

---

[3] *Papa* is Italian for Pope.

tripped and stumbled. I retrieved the bag and let him go, feeling rather pleased with myself.

Our horse and cart had a rocky ride on the way to the catacombs along Appia Antica, where Saint Paul had once been led prisoner into Rome and where now prostitutes occupy the sides of the road waiting for men who do not have their wives with them. Simon and I, of course, did not stop.

My brief account of various kinds of pilfering attempts does not include the French robbers. They seemed to be interested not in money but other items. They stole my research notes. How were they to know that my briefcase contained material for a major academic work? Perhaps they thought that it was hiding priceless jewels. The fact is that I had prepared a paper on church architecture and planned to write a book on the subject, with Simon providing the sketches. Little good did the study notes do to the filthy thieves but it succeeded in turning my book into a tiny insignificant booklet, most of it comprising Simon's wonderful drawings. Simon made many sketches of cathedrals and churches and, to rub salt into my wounds, of highwaymen.

In Orvieto we were not robbed but, for a change, our carriage collapsed. While the horses and I awaited help Simon took the opportunity to sketch the carriage, one wheel lying on the ground. So I entitled our booklet "Nervous Breakdown in Italy".

Because the study that I managed to do was minimal we focused on other, more interesting, things to occupy our time, like drinking and eating as well as the early evening passeggiata. I did, however, return home with a get-by knowledge of the language.

Moreover, we both returned home with ideas of altering the church interior. Simon was now not only my friend but also churchwarden. I said to him while still in Italy, "Simon, the rector has always been responsible for the sanctuary. I've always thought it's in need of restoring. You as warden are responsible for the nave. Why don't you use your talents as an architect to design a better space for our worship?"

Simon replied, "Charles, you took the words from my mouth. I was about to utter the same proposition. Brilliant minds ... and all that."

And so our plans for change began to develop. They turned out not to be universally appreciated. Some of the parishioners were always objecting to change of any description. But in the end we won almost everyone over.

February 1831 *Simon and I went into a bar in Rome for an espresso. On returning to the street it was now pouring with rain. This reminded me that I had gone into the bar with a hat and left it behind. It was nowhere to be seen. So I went to ask the waitress, in my best Italian, " I have left my hat (cappello) behind." She looked at my head in puzzlement. What I had actually said was "I have left my hair (capelli) behind."*

At that stage of life I had not lost my hair, so the poor girl was as confused as I was.

Simon, of less years than myself, never lost either his hat or his hair. The bishop had advised me, as he did all his clergy, not to make close friends within the parish. This advice of course I ignored. We were great mates. Mary and I had meals at theirs and they a few at ours. Mary was quite envious of Lesley's kitchen and up-to-date equipment. She invariably came away after an evening with Lesley and Simon quite pissed. It was late after one evening of revelry when Mary and I, having made fond farewells, tottered down their drive onto the cobbled road. I realised that I had left the rectory keys behind. I propped Mary beside a cart while I returned to collect the keys. She clung on for dear life, praying that the horse would not bolt forward. She was too inebriated to realise that there was no horse attached to the cart.

We arrived home safely. But our youngest daughter Elizabeth was already home sitting downstairs with a new boyfriend. I will not forget the look of astonishment on his face. Nevertheless we tried to step towards the staircase without attracting further attention. But profuse giggling did not permit us to be imperceptible. We crawled upstairs. By the time I had enjoyed a lengthy pee in the toilet I went into the bedroom to find Mary spread-eagled naked on the bed. I undressed too. Then Mary said that she too needed to go to the toilet but was incapable of moving. Being strong I lifted her from the bed. I managed a few short steps but, mainly due to an uncontrollable chuckling, collapsed beneath her weight. We fell to the floor, Mary's body crushing mine below. Elizabeth came up to investigate the commotion and found two nude parents on the floor, at which point she joined in the giggling.

I related some Italian travel adventures to my new friend Salvatore. Apart from the robberies we had been caught up in floods en route. Moreover our lodging house in France had burnt down. Yet we survived. It was difficult communicating all this to Salvatore in his own tongue, partly because I was quite inadequate at expressing myself (Mary tells me that I can hardly express myself in English let alone in a foreign language) and partly because he wanted to improve his English, which was a thousand times better than my Italian. He made an offer to teach Italian to me and anyone else who might be interested. I took up his offer by organising a small group to meet twice a month to learn Italian. It seemed a good thing to do since there was a ready-made teacher in Salvatore, even though I was unlikely to venture abroad ever again. Salvatore lived on Woburn Street. Though few in number we met in Hannah's house on Slutts Row. We will come to Hannah shortly. But for now let us change the subject.

While I was in Italy an outbreak of cholera occurred in Bedford. By the time I was settled in Ampthill the disease had broken out again, not only locally. It was widespread all over the country, lasting as long as eighteen years. People were well aware of the scourge, but now it was too close to home for comfort.

If Betsey's brother-in-law Joe had actually had cholera, as the doctor had surmised, though he was fortunate enough to recover, Betsey's sister Ruth was not so lucky. She did succumb to the disease. Little did the Robinsons suspect that it would hit their home, especially since they had heard that it happened only in homes destitute and poor, where sanitation was bad. There was always clean water to drink in this home. Also it was a decade since the outbreak had first occurred locally.

Betsey's sister Ruth had been to visit a friend who was very poorly. Four days later Ruth went down sick. She craved for drink, yet could hardly do so without great effort. She was vomiting painfully. Suddenly her eyes became sunken. Her hands and feet became wrinkled. Her skin was cold. She got cramp in the muscles. This went on for several days. She died as quickly as the illness came. The family made all arrangements for the funeral, which concentrated their minds, but they could not help fearing that the infection would spread to others in the family. It did not.

Lydia was another of Betsey's sisters. She had been a lace maker too, working at Carlton Hall in Harrold, north-west of Bedford. She died on the job. In fact she died on my eighth wedding anniversary. Lydia was at the factory working on a lace tablecloth, together with her friend and work-mate, Ann Harris, when she held her head in her hands in pain and suddenly fell unconscious. Soon afterwards Lydia became paralysed. The doctor said that she had ruptured a blood vessel in the brain, causing her immediate death. Lydia was twenty.

Betsey had another sister, Mary, who had moved away to St Albans to be in service. Mary's mother Frances had been friendly with a doctor's wife and when the doctor moved to a practice in St Albans Frances kept up correspondence. This was three years after Queen Victoria, King William's niece, came to the throne. She paid for the correspondence by buying the new penny black. This had the Queen's head engraved on the stamp. It was a novelty for Frances to go to the Post Office, buy a stamp and actually lick the sticky gum to put it onto the envelope. When she received a reply she was intrigued to see that the stamp had been cancelled out by a mark. There was no chance that she would be able to use the stamp again. The PO were not stupid. If her letter ran to lots of pages, as they sometimes did, she would need to buy a two-penny blue.

From Maulden the family moved two miles up the road to Ampthill, to aptly named Rascals' Row on Dunstable Street. The area had once been called Trollops' Terrace but residents had fought successfully to get the name altered. Not so lucky were the residents of Slutts' End on Woburn Street, who had to wait several more years for their address to slide into history.

The following is an example of the goings-on in Slutts' End, though by no means all residents lived up to the name. That it was spelt with a double "t" did not help their reputation when the address was mentioned verbally; not that most of them were spelling bees in any case. Many occupiers were ordinary, some a trifle dirty, some slatternly, some slovenly, some sloppy, but not necessarily downright immoral.

There was at least one lady, though, who did tend towards the immoral, one Hannah. We briefly met her earlier in the chapter. She provided a few of us with a daytime venue to meet and attempt to converse in Italian. Unfortunately she also provided a night time venue for a few who definitely did not call to learn Italian.

The lady lived next door to Enoch Knightly. Hannah was not averse to an occasional side dish. Enoch, one of Hannah's admirers, would do all he could to win her favour. But in him she was never interested. Enoch was not one of the many men to whom she had an attraction. Nevertheless, he pursued and pestered, sometimes calling her "my sugar", sometimes "my sweet". Living next door, he had an inkling when Hannah's husband was on nights. These nights were not infrequent since he was a night watchman at the rope factory. On a few occasions, Enoch would call in by the back door for a friendly chat. One evening he had had too many glasses of ale. It was not long before he suggested they go up to bed. "Please, sugar. sweet." He must have pleaded with her a dozen times. But she was having none of it.

She tried to distract his attentions and intentions by suggesting a cup of tea. Onto the stove she placed the kettle of water. When steam came ejecting from the spout, she poured two cups of tea, having taken as much time as she could to warm the teapot and allow the tea to brew. She handed him a spoon and sugar bowl. Enoch sugared his tea and went to put a spoonful in Hannah's cup. "No, no. No sugar for me. You keep telling me I'm sweet enough, Enoch."

They finished their tea, he quickly, she slowly. Enoch had not forgotten what he had called for and persisted with his plan to get Hannah upstairs.

"No," said Hannah. "I told you, I'm not having you put your dirty spoon into my clean cu…"

The word 'cup' was cut short. He stood, took her hand and almost dragged her into the hallway. She succumbed. At least she agreed to go part way and led him upstairs.

"Take your trousers down." Then, "Take your pants off."

She took nothing off. She just stirred his spoon, thinking that all the beer that he had drunk would affect his potency.

"This will get no bigger than a little coc…" She was trying to remember the Italian word for teaspoon, that she had heard during the class earlier in the day. "This will get no bigger than a *cucchiaino* after all his drinking." Hannah had learned this by experience, since her husband was next to useless in bed after a night at the pub.

However, she soon found that she was stirring a dessertspoon. Indeed, it became a tablespoon. In the end it was a ladle. Hannah was amazed by his ability. She chucked him a towel to wipe his now shrivelled cucchiaino.

"That was one heck of a shot," Hannah ejaculated. At least, though, her own cup remained dry, unsoiled, unspoilt and empty.

As a result of his partial success that night Enoch's visits became more frequent. Enoch would even dare to knock on her front door. Hannah opened it only slightly ajar.

"Who's there?" she would demand.

"Enoch."

"Enoch who?"

" 'e knock 'nightly."

He had cracked the first ever "Who's there?" joke.

We must shortly progress our story from (door) knockers to knickers, or rather drawers as they were called. However, before this we will go on another long journey, not to Italy this time but to Germany. It was after I had been twenty years in the diocese that I had built up a reputation as a reliable horseman and coach driver. The dean of the cathedral asked me if I could take some of their choir on an Easter pilgrimage. Wishing to prove my prowess I instantaneously agreed. But where would I be asked to take them? I was invited to make a suggestion.

"Well, Mr Dean. I have already driven a successful pilgrimage to Norwich cathedral. I've also taken youngsters all the way to Sizewell."

"I was wondering," said the dean, "about somewhere further - like Kevelaer."

"Kevelaer?" I repeated. "Where's that? Near London?"

"No. It's a town on the Rhine in Germany, not far from the Dutch border. They have a basilica, where thousands of pilgrims go from all over the world. I'm surprised you've not heard of it."

"I have now," I muttered. "But it's impossible. I couldn't possibly drive that distance. There are too many problems. Anyway, I'm too old for that sort of adventure."

There we left the matter. But the more I slept on it the more I relished the challenge. Of course I was not too old. In the end I acquiesced and a date was fixed. We were to depart on Easter Monday. A concert tour for the small section of choirmen and choirboys was organised and it was arranged for an exchange of Easter candles between the cathedral and the basilica. We duly set off. I will not recount the hazards of the journey except to tell that as we were travelling along at good speed, the horses performing wonderfully, the right wheel fell off and rolled down into a ditch. I recall receiving a round of applause for reining in the horses to a gradual halt and avoiding us all following the wheel and missing a bridge by inches. I was commended by the dean for my skill and presence of mind. It was he who organised a replacement carriage.

Towards the end of vespers, at which I had been invited by Monsignor Richard to preach (in English) and bless the paschal candle that was to be taken back to the cathedral, I was asked to give the choir an "A" on my flute. Impressed by my single note the monsignor said, "Father Low, would you like to give us a whistle?" I had neither sheet music nor the ability to play a flute by ear. In any case, I misheard what he said. I thought he had asked me to give not a whistle but a dismissal. I stood up and pronounced the blessing. The service, I thought, had gone on long enough anyway.

On the last night of our visit, following a speech in which he extolled my proficiency, I was presented by the dean on behalf of the choristers with a bottle of wine, a fat cigar, an icon and a picture of horses and carriage with one wheel missing. We were then shown the library containing Martin Luther's books in the first edition. We retired to Father Richard's room for a goodly number of drinks, after which I retired to my own room to smoke the cigar. Sadly there was nothing with which to light it. So I retired to sleep.

The Bedfordshire Times later reported, CARRIAGE DRIVING RECTOR SAVES CATHEDRAL CHOIR.

We now go back at last to Betsey's drawers. Betsey, unlike Hannah, did not live on Slutts' End but on Rascals' Row. Unsurprisingly, since they were now next door to each other, Betsey had soon met Bill. Following the events described in chapter 2 Bill took Betsey to bed a few times and enjoyed better comfort than their first frolic on the farm. She gave birth having become pregnant after the very first tentative adventure, as we heard.

They named the girl Eliza. Then they married, their wedding also already having been described.

Philip, after originally counselling caution, had insisted that they marry. In truth he saw the chance to be finally shot of his son and to pass the responsibility to another. Bill claimed he was marrying not because his father said so but because he definitely wanted to wed her, baby or not.

She was a plaiter by the time she married, having given up her previous work in lace. She now worked, somewhat less salubriously, in straw. So the marriage register had her down as a straw plaiter. Betsey made her mark "X" in the register, the entry that my curate had signed although he was no more than an onlooker at the service. It was rather strange that she made a mark. She had told me in captivity that she could read and write. This hardly appears to have been quite truthful. Everyone in prison seemed to tell me one lie after another. Perhaps that is why she threw away my Pilgrim's Progress, because she could not even read it, let alone comprehend it.

Betsey had an affair in the early years of her married life. Alfred was as burly a chap as her husband. She saw a lot of Alfred in every sense. Bill knew that they had regular contact, yet never suspected any cheating, not in all the four years that they were misbehaving. All that Bill was aware of was that Betsey became moody and touchy with him. But he put that down to the ways of married life and the idiosyncrasies of women. Betsey resented Bill's taking her for granted, not least his thoughtlessness in being out at the Sun most nights. On the remaining nights he would be at other pubs, often arriving home well after closing time, by which hour Betsey had already been asleep some considerable time.

Little did Betsey know that while she slept Bill stayed behind at the pub after closing time, when the landlord had locked the doors. A dozen or so stayed on drinking in the tiny intimate tap room, where the landlord had arranged for a stripteaser to perform for an hour. It was not always the same girl. One night Sarah danced. Being in the taproom the entertainment became known among customers as tap dancing. Sarah and Bill caught each other's eye, so that after the dancing ended, instead of Sarah disappearing into the lounge to get dressed, she came and sat on Bill's knee. Somewhat embarrassed, not least because Bill was getting some jibbing from his mates, he nevertheless held on to Sarah's waist and asked softly, not thinking what other question he might pose, where she lived. Sarah gave her address and said that he would be welcome to call any time, but that it would cost him. At that, she jumped up and scuttled away.

Bill was unaware that Sarah had more than once been arrested for soliciting and taken to the police house. She got away without charges so never had to appear in court.

Before Ampthill had its purpose-built court house some cases were heard in one of the locals. If only the magistrates had known about the after-hours goings-on not only would the licensee have had no licence but he would have been behind iron bars rather than the wooden bars of his inn.

A proper court house was eventually built on Church Street. The county court sat there once on alternate months. Before this, inn quests, or rather inquests, were held at the Sun. One inquest, for instance, touched on the death of an illegitimate child aged four months. She had been found dead by the side of her mother. The verdict recorded was that she "died by the visitation of God". I was appalled by the theology implied by the wording and was moved to write to the Bedford Mercury to say so.

All the family's females worked on the top of people's heads. That is to say, they were plaiters, like Betsey herself; or they provided cover for their heads, as bonnet sewers, again like Betsey. The men, on the other hand, like her father John and her brother James and, of course, Betsey's husband Bill, worked on the land. The exception was her brother John. He worked to provide cover for the bottom end of the body - the very bottom, that is. He made shoes and boots.

One day when the working week was over Betsey wanted to take the children to Bedford to see the very first regatta on the Ouse. They had a big argument. Bill was set against it. He did not remember the dreadful day thirty years earlier when James was drowned in the floods. But it was engrained in his subconscious. Betsey had not experienced the horror of that day. His children were never to go near the river, not as long as he was alive to forbid them. Contrary to what was said about Bill not winning any further arguments, this time he had his way. They went to the Firs instead, and continued into the park with a picnic.

Betsey's younger sister, Lydia, had an affair too. She was unmarried, so perhaps we should call it a fling. The liaison was with a family friend called Rob, who visited Ampthill only now and again. He came by horse and dilapidated trap on business. Lydia and Rob would philander in the cart, not altogether comfortable, but they made do. Lydia began to look plumper than usual. It was not because she was expecting. It was because she found it convenient to leave her corsets at home. Her waist, therefore, did not look its normal slim self. It was simpler to lift her shift at the last minute, rather than mess with lots of unhitching and disentangling when time was at a premium.

Betsey's sister, Ruth, had no affair during her brief married life, but the youngest sister, Ann, did. She bravely owned up and admitted that she had been seeing Peter rather too often during the course of several months. Looking back, it made sense to her husband, Fred, because he recalled the party at which he and Ann had shared a table with Peter and his wife. Ann looked ravishing that night. Her dress was low-cut. In fact, her succulent breasts were nearly on full display. There was even the slightest ripple of a nipple on view. Who would not be tempted to lust after her? It came back to Fred how Peter had taken hold of Ann's bust and hauled her up from the floor, where for some unknown reason she had slipped down under the table. He could hardly resist looking in admiration of the cleavage. When Ann told Fred of this business, he asked why she should want to do this. She said simply, "It was nothing." No doubt she was alluding to Shakespeare's *Much Ado About Nothing*.

Betsey, her husband, her sisters and her brothers-in-law all gradually learned to overcome the clouds of storm because through them shone the rays of love.

CHAPTER 12
ENTER ANN

May 1875   *Today has been a scorcher. Some of the young ladies from the church arranged to go out for dinner. They thoughtfully invited the rector. I sat between beautiful Beula and jovial Joy but opposite obnoxious Adele and amorous Ann Farmer, whom I'd not previously properly met. My Mary was further down the table. Adele did give me her dessert, so perhaps she was not all bad. But Joy offered me her cherry, which of course I readily accepted. As for Ann she was amiable enough but ate everything in front of her.*

Ann Farmer was not an unusual girl in that she too came from a working-class family, one of eight children. It was a working class family with aspirations. Her father George worked not as might be expected with a name such as his as a farmer but as a clockmaker. In practice he did more cleaning of clocks than making them. Although George considered himself to be an ordinary man in the street he had higher connections for a time. He had been summoned to fix a clock at Park House and, having successfully got the clock ticking, was enticed to stay on as personal gentleman's servant to Lord Wensleydale.

Ann had an older sister, Mary, who, like Ann, was unmarried. Unlike Ann she had not one child but four. The five grandchildren, who together with their aunts and uncles all lived with their harassed grandparents, liked to call their granddad "Grandfather Clock".

She had many dislikes. For instance Ann disliked cats intensely. She even kicked one feline off a wall and down a steep embankment. It survived of course. Moreover Ann disliked most people too, though I am not aware of any attempted assassinations of other humans, however catty they may have been. In other words Ann was bigoted, opinionated and unfeeling. Any sympathy that she had she saved up for Bill. In her favour, though, Ann had a firm faith and was a good Christian!

Ann herself was another straw plaiter. She was unmarried until she reached thirty-six but had a daughter, Ellen, when she was twenty-five. Ellen too did not marry but she in turn had a child, Florence. Both daughter and granddaughter lived with Ann until she died aged seventy-seven. The exception was while Ann was nursing and caring for a family on Bedford Street, during which time Ellen stayed with her grandparents. It was during this period that Ann first met Bill, who occasionally called to visit the same family. He and Ann became friendly, though never intimate in their relationship.

Their friendship began like this. While they were both at the home on Bedford Street Bill was a little embarrassed because a button came off his waistcoat. This was not altogether surprising because he had a habit of fiddling with his buttons. Betsey would have removed his waistcoat and sew the buttons back on. Ann did not offer to do this. Instead she produced a safety pin, with which she proceeded to do up his top button. This caused Bill's heart to go thump-thumpety-thump. He could well have struck up a love-match had opportunity favoured him, and, unlike his bonding with Sarah, the sex would have been without financial cost. But it did not happen. Not yet.

But it did happen after Betsey's death. Betsey saw her final sunset before suddenly suffering a huge haemorrhage of the brain when she was forty-two. She died while she was giving birth. The baby saw neither sunrise nor sunset. Bill was shattered. It was the last straw in a sheaf of sadnesses. Bill was altogether unable to cope. He had lost so many children. Now his beloved Betsey was gone after twenty-two years of marriage, with all its ups and downs, its bright periods and the overcast moments of black clouds, not least the latest eclipse. He was numbed. He gradually began to feel the pain, the loneliness, the devastation, the anger. Eventually he began to cry his heart out, which had not happened immediately after the loss.

After some time Ann came around to see him, to offer comfort. It was then that the relationship grew deeper and her comforting became intimate. Ann entered the scene and Bill entered Ann. But now it was not illicit, as it might have been some months earlier.

It was the following year that Bill married Ann. The sex was, of course, free of charge (which had not always been the case with Bill), but the marriage was a costly one. Ann had expensive tastes. She wanted good clothes. She insisted on the best food. She was not so content with making do as Betsey had been. She did not sew. She just replaced things with new. It meant that Bill had to cut down on drink, which is not what he was inclined to do, as he continued to sorrow. Bill never got over his loss, although he survived to celebrate eight anniversaries with Ann. In fact they had a child, Emma, the year following their marriage.

Such a long time ago Bill had been banned from the Old Sun. Now Bill saw the very very old sun go down for the last time at the age of fifty-four when he suffered a stroke. He was taken quickly into the Bedford infirmary. But nothing could be done. He did not see the old sun rise again. Now Ann lived in Bill's house with her two half-sister daughters and her granddaughter. She soon sold up and the four women moved to a more up-market house on Austins Lane.

My Auntie May had died only a few months earlier. She had lost my Uncle John four years previously. Unlike Ann, May loved cats. She died with her cat sat on her lap. It would, therefore, have been appropriate had she died of a stroke, but it was not the case. I had seen more of my aunt and uncle in recent years since they had moved to Ampthill from Westoning. Family life, however, never stood still. Around the period of Bill's death my three daughters married in quick succession. I officiated at all their weddings. Then the grandchildren started to appear, first Marie, then Derek, next Frances, followed by Jonathan. Mary and I had to wait until the next decade for the births of Wilfred and David.

Ann's new home was along from the Alameda. The Alameda was a successful imitation of the Almeida in Madrid. There were no bull-fights but I do remember as a little boy running like Jehu along the Alameda and jumping hard onto a big boy's back and grasping his neck with all the might I could muster. I was fed-up (or had had it up to the neck) with his bullying. He survived the onslaught but it taught him a lesson not to mess with me.

The Ampthill estate was sold to the Duke of Bedford after Lord Holland died. There was resentment when the gates were removed. It was claimed by the Duke of Bedford, so his workmen said, that they had been worn away by boys playing Duck. That, surely, was a tall story. Though I must admit that as a boy I did indeed play the game, using the gates for climbing. But I cannot believe that we did all that much damage. I never regarded myself as a young vandal.

In my boyhood I hardly appreciated the beauty of the Alameda, the Slipe as we called the walk, and the plantation. But Ann did and, like so many others who came to visit, she loved going for walks and picnics so close to her home, not least in the Firs.

Although, as I say, there were no bull-fights (albeit a little bullying) the Alameda was the venue for a cattle fair that took place between the start of May and the close of November.

My father had gone to the fair once a week and eyed up the cattle, speculating how many succulent joints of beef they could provide for his butchery. But now my father had gone altogether. He died in Bedford infirmary the same year as Betsey. He went to heaven at four o'clock in the morning as the birds began to sing.

INTERLUDE
A THICK BLACK CLOUD

...and the light grows dark with clouds.
Isaiah 5.30

Poem

by Anthony Thwaite

Clouds now and then
Giving men relief
From moon-viewing

LUCY LOW IS DONE FOR MURDER

Lucy was the only one of Betsey and Bill's six children to marry. Apart from Lucy and Eliza, and we will come to them shortly, the others all died in childhood. Lucy was born the same year as my Pamela. Nineteen years later I officiated at Lucy's wedding at St Andrew's. She married Charles. They moved away to Leicester, where he laid plates on the railway before working at an iron works.

But before we go into Lucy's sister we will consider the tragic case of another Lucy Low. I knew Lucy at Bedford prison and had to perform the distressing duty of ministering to her after she was condemned to be hanged.

Lucy was born eight years before Lucy Low, Eliza's sister. Aged nineteen she married Sam Ellis. Sam had been in trouble with the law since he was fourteen. He was done for larceny and breaking all sorts of game laws. In short, he was a poacher, an activity he usually practised by night. Lucy was already expecting a baby when they married. Her husband Sam died only five months after their wedding. Lucy was left to bring up her son Henry alone. Four years passed and Lucy met Ellis Low, a labourer from Wootton. No doubt he was related somehow to Eliza and Lucy Low, whose granddad Philip, we recall, came from Wootton. Ellis married Lucy. It seems that Lucy had a habit of falling for people called Ellis. They had four children in addition to Ellis' stepson. But Henry now lived with his grandparents.

Ellis left home after nine years of marriage. He never came home again. He disappeared from the face of the earth. There is no evidence whatsoever that Lucy took him for a walk along Cut Throat Lane. But he vanished. Lucy could not afford to keep her children and they had to go to the workhouse.

Lucy went to find work and tried her luck in London. She found a position as domestic servant in Hampstead, where she worked in the vicarage for the Reverend Theodore Kirkman and his wife. After three years she left the vicarage because she was pregnant, though that was not the reason she gave to Mr and Mrs Kirkman. There was no suggestion that it was the vicar who caused Lucy's pregnancy.

Lucy lodged in Bedford, where she had her baby, a girl. Mrs Hull, Lucy's landlady, was helpful and kind to her.

"How is the baby?" asked Mrs Hull, after Lucy had returned from a visit to her sister in Derby.

"She is well", replied Lucy. "But she had a fit when she was a week old. I've left her with my sister."

Lucy may or may not have had a sister in Derby. She probably did not go to Derby. If she did, she did not leave the baby there. The baby was left in a black parcel hidden in undergrowth in a village not far from Bedford. The bag was found by the gamekeeper of Colonel Higgins. His gamekeeper prodded the parcel with his foot and was shocked to discover that the bag contained the body of a baby. He called the local policeman. The baby was twenty-one days old. She had been suffocated.

Investigations led, of course, to Lucy. She was found guilty in court by the jury. "We find the accused guilty, M'lud. But we ask for clemency."

M'lud ignored this appeal and sentenced Lucy. "You will be "hanged by the neck until you are dead." " Perhaps the learned judge wondered whether Lucy had also murdered one or both of her two husbands.

Being the chaplain in Bedford prison I was as helpful to her as I could be. Just before the appointed hanging the Home Secretary wrote giving Lucy a respite. Her sentence was commuted to life in prison. I saw a great deal of Lucy during my visits. I had written to the Home Secretary myself, asking that her sentence be shortened. I claimed that she was ill and mentally disturbed, which she certainly was. I was pleased that Lucy was finally released after serving ten years in prison, by which time I was no longer there myself.

PART 2
Eliza and Pop

Our ancestors were all under the cloud.
I Corinthians 10.1

Stanza XVIII (final) of Verses written on the Alameda

by Jeremiah Holmes Wiffen

Farewell! in childhood's careless prime
It soothed to list the hum of bees,
To pluck wild flowers, and lisp wild rhyme
Beneath thine immemorial trees,
Sweet Ampthill! and for joys like these
'Tis fit I strike an idle chord,
To sing these rising Groves of thine,
And in thy grateful service twine
One laurel for thy Lord!

CHAPTER 13
DELIVERY OF POP

Eliza's brother William died when he was two. Her brother George died when he was one. Her brother John died before he was one. Another brother died at birth. He was not even given a name. He it was who caused Betsey's death. Eliza's half-sister Emma died, unmarried, when she was twenty-six.

The only ones to survive into old age were the first and second born, the two sisters, Lucy, who lived to three score years and ten, and Eliza herself, who lived to four score years and five, before she finally slept with her ancestors.

As I have already said, I married Lucy. On the other hand I did not marry Eliza for the simple reason that she did not get married, despite her ten children.

At their marriage preparation I offered Lucy's fiancé Charles a glass of grappa. This was a mistake. He obviously had not tasted the delightful drink before. He spat it out and clearly took a dislike to both my drinks cabinet and to me ever after. Ever after did not last long because the couple moved away following their wedding. Whenever I asked Lucy a question during our interviews she would first rub the side of her cheek. Her eyebrows lifted; her eyes would almost pop out as if in amazement; her chin thrust forward and her lips pursed. These actions were a preliminary to her verbal response to each and every question. I wondered what sort of conversations Lucy and Charles had in private.

By the time Eliza moved from Dunstable Street to Saunders Piece her sons and a few daughters had left home. But this still left a household full of females, granddaughter included. (Her first three children were boys. The remaining seven were girls.)

Eliza was faithful. She never knew another man except Pop. Pop popped around to visit her often. Eliza lived on Saunders Piece, a row of houses that Pop actually owned. This is how she came to live there:

Pop made his first call on Eliza when she still lived with her parents on Dunstable Street.

Eliza was an upright young lady, prim and proper and even prudish. Her few boyfriends never got far with her. They were shooed off if they made unwelcome advances. Unlike her sometimes under-drawers-less mother, Eliza was always well protected. It was unlikely that any man would penetrate her armour.

However, the unexpected eventually happened. It nearly happened one morning when she answered a knock at the door. Her parents were out at work. Her sister was out at school. Eliza's first thought was that it was the milkman on the drag. She was wrong. It was the pop man. Pop and Eliza were immediately attracted to each other. And she had not yet got around to putting on her body armour in any case. Enjoying a lie-in, since she was working a late shift at the bonnet factory, Eliza was wearing her milk-white dressing gown.

Pop fled. It was unlike him to feel embarrassment but for some reason that was what he felt. The feeling though was not powerful enough to stop him wanting to call again. And again. Sometimes - damn it - her parents were at home. He would curse his luck when her father Bill answered the door. Usually, thank God, they were out. He often called just late enough for Bill, Betsey and Lucy to have already left the house, but early enough to catch Eliza still in a dressing gown. Eliza was drinking more mineral water than she had ever drunk in her life.

Sooner rather than later, early one morning, Pop knocked on the door with his usual delivery. Like the brewery, which used horses to pull the wagon loaded with barrels of beer, so did Pop use a horse to deliver his softer drinks. It was not difficult, then, for Eliza to hear his approach and see the horse rein to a halt from the window.

"Come in," invited Eliza.

She was still without body armour. She had not yet put her skirt on let alone the wire crinolines underneath. But she was not without enamour. Uncharacteristically, following the usual initial polite verbal exchanges, Eliza stood in front of Josiah, for that was his name. He was startled when her loose gown from her body slipped and fell. She caught him in her arms. She kissed him softly. She whispered gently (for it was all she could think of), "My darling, how do you like this?"

He liked it very much.

CHAPTER 14
THE RECTOR'S MATCH

April 1861 *A party of 20 or so turned up at church for a wedding rehearsal, some eating chips and drinking from a bottle of wine. The bride's father can't stop talking. The mother arrives late on crutches. She has had a stroke and can't talk much. Her father died this morning. All ask lots of questions but nobody listens to my answers. The bride, six feet tall, is nearly nine months pregnant so I have difficulty not touching her with my own stomach. The groom is little. They suggest he stand on a kneeler. The bridesmaids are also lean and lanky and will need to stand on one side if the guests are to have any chance of seeing the bridegroom.*

May 1861 *A fat rector marries a fat bride.*

June 1861 *The landlord of one of the inns called on behalf of his sister-in-law who is to be married in another town. For the sake of his customers (and no doubt for the sake of trade) they are following the wedding with a mock ceremony before serving refreshments. He wants me to perform the pretend wedding. I advised him to find an actor.*

There was no pretence when a girl called to swear at me. She came to swear an affidavit for a marriage licence. She was scared stiff. But she did it. Then I told her to do it all over again - this time holding a Bible.

July 1861 *A couple came to arrange their wedding. The girl's parents came too. I tolerated their presence this once but suggested that next time I would want to see just the couple to be married. Damn me if the parents didn't turn up yet again. I told them to scarper.*

December 1861 *The bride appeared at the church door and announced that she had a problem. Her garter had slipped. I wanted to help but decided it was really a job for one of the bridesmaids.*

Before writing of my marriage to Mary (who was not the fat bride, by the way), why should we not have a forward view of three more matches, those of our three daughters? Although they enjoyed, as we will hear later, sundry Ampthill admirers they each came to marry boys from Suffolk. I married them. Of course, I married my wife some years previously. But I married our girls to their respective husbands, all of them in St Margaret's Leiston, a new church less than twenty years old at the time. Each of them had come to my study, in turn, to ask if I were willing to let my daughters go, and naturally I was delighted to agree to part with them.

Having spent my second curacy in West Suffolk I had been attracted by an appeal for a locum priest to relieve the new vicar of St Margaret's so that he could go on holiday. I took advantage of my Ampthill curates and absented myself to spend some time by the Sizewell seaside. It was during these busman's holidays that our daughters fell for their fellows. The vicar, the Reverend Mr Blathwayt, who had been at the church since its dedication, kindly allowed me to return to officiate at their weddings. He did for the first two, anyway, and would have done so for the third had he not inconveniently died the year before.

The last shall be first. The last daughter Elizabeth was married first - first in every sense. She was married on the first day of the first month of the first year of the new (seventies) decade and at the first minute past 1 o'clock. But, not to be outdone, the first daughter Jane announced her engagement on the eve of the last's wedding day. Elizabeth had not yet begun to wear the trousers. Neither did her husband at the wedding. Having drunk Scotch almost nonstop since his stag night two days earlier, "Beefburger" Ben Lomond turned out in a kilt. During the vows, when she ought to have been concentrating on her sister's solemn promise, a bridesmaid's eyes fell upon a memorial plaque to Richard Garrett. Her mind wandered to the Agricultural Engineering works that were so famous. The chancel floor was uneven and wedding guests thought that that was the reason why Ben was swaying to and fro. It was nothing to do with the floor. But it provided an excuse. The chancel was floored later the same year. (So was Ben.) The vicar had told the couple that other work to be done later that year was the re-roofing, which was expected to cost £700. He therefore begged the guests to be generous in their giving after the service.

The couple had an extended break following the wedding. It happened to be the country's first Bank Holiday.

The first daughter Jane married Derek the following year in midsummer. Guests, many of them who had walked from the railway station, completed their trek up the long path, through the recently enlarged churchyard. So tall was Derek that I needed to stand on a pile of hassocks to see over his head. I had relegated the church organist and brought in my own ivory player, Andrew Ivory. The organist, the service, the reception, were so good that the evening was followed by not a few orgasms.

August 1872 *I performed another wedding when the rector of Saint Margaret's was away. It was for a big and determined girl called Annabelle Battle. Her husband-to-be was Peter Ship. I can only imagine the fighting that went on during their married life. As far as I am aware she did not insist on using a double-barrelled name.*

There was a congenial family of gypsies in the parish. I did not manage to baptise many babies during my locums. But one was from these fairground people, and to get the baby's name correct was a testing task. She was named Zoah Ebony Rachel Hedges. And those were just the Christian names.

We have missed out the middle one. Lastly and thirdly, three years later, our second daughter Pamela married. Happily the new vicar was also in agreement with my request to officiate. The Reverend Berney Wodehouse Raven not only consented to my stepping in but was supportive in every way. He came to build up the church in the catholic tradition over the thirty-five years of his incumbency at Leiston, and he suggested I make a start by wearing a white stole and cope for my daughter Pamela's wedding. Of course, I needed no asking twice. It was a Christmas wedding. Indeed it was a white Christmas wedding, not only because of the colour of the stole. Some of the stuck carriages had to be pulled out of the snow by horsepower.

Pamela and Nicholas were both schoolmasters. Or more correctly Pamela was a schoolmistress. Many of their guests, therefore, were teachers. They seemed to have a preference at the reception for whisky. I suggested that they should be drinking Teacher's, which little joke went down well. The whisky went down even better.

During my visits to Felixstowe Mary and I had got to know a generous and talented gentleman named Hugh Miller. He invited us to stay at his home at the Coastguard House in Shingle Street. We took up the offer immediately following Pamela's wedding, so that we could have a shorter journey to gallop the horses after a bellyful of whisky. Hugh was not at home. He was gallivanting around Switzerland. He left us even more whisky in his cabinet. The house was brimming with curiosities. It also had (unless I am mistaken due to being slightly tipsy) magnificent views of the sea from the bedroom, and of the countryside from the toilet.

All three daughters were now wedded. It will soon be time to tell of getting married myself. But a further wedding was still to happen before we come to that.

Fifteen years after her first wedding Elizabeth had another go. By then I had ceased to look after the parish of Leiston for holiday duty. Instead I had been invited to help in the parish of Walton-cum-Felixstowe. The vicar, the Reverend Mr Charles Hardwick Marriott never asked or allowed me to conduct services in the parish church of Saint Mary. He did ask me to do so in a small upper room in the Victoria Hall on Hamilton Road. A new enormous parish church to be dedicated to Saint John the Baptist was not yet even a pipe dream for another few years. So the next wedding would have to take place at the foot of South Hill on the seafront where a hut church had just been built. It was not ideal but better than the upper room. It was known as the Iron Church. It was here that our youngest daughter wished to marry again. Of course, her wish was thwarted. Everyone wondered why on earth she desired to have her nuptials in an iron hut. Surely the parish church was by far the better option. But the Iron Church was where I took services on holiday and for that reason alone Elizabeth considered the ugly option to be the romantic one.

When she eventually told me of her wish I rejoined, "But Elizabeth, my love, do you not know it's not even a possibility. It isn't licensed for marriages." I was prepared to marry her. But I was not prepared to marry her on the quiet and then find that she and William were not legally married at all. In fact I was not keen to end up in prison for doing so. Therefore I pleaded with Mr Marriott that he allow me, just for once, to officiate in his church. He finally agreed but with the proviso that he be there to keep an eye on me and he would give the sermon.

In the event I preached briefly before he could do anything about it. Then he had the last word because he followed my humorous sermon by climbing up to the pulpit and thundering out a lengthy evangelical diatribe of his own. What a lucky couple to have not one but two sermons!

Some time ago I had married a girl to a soldier who had been married before and was now divorced. His former wife was inconveniently still alive. Now that my daughter was in the same situation I did not see a convincing reason why I should not do the same for her. That is what I did. She too married a soldier. He was a sergeant major. William did not sway during the service. Nor did he wear a kilt at their wedding. He continued to wear the trousers at home ever after.

Let us at last go back some forty-six years. I returned to Derbyshire for the funeral of my training priest, George. Four years earlier I had lived with him in the rectory. People had wondered suspiciously about our relationship. Two bachelors living together was thought by some to be scandalous. It was not considered quite the thing at that time. But our relationship was innocent, beyond reproach - except that it was often a fraught relationship. George, apart from being generous and patient (he needed to be) was also virtuous and respectable. He was moreover a perfect socialiser. I was perfectly shy and sheltered in his shadow. George was especially charming in the company of old biddies - his pussies as he called them. Day in, day out, one or other of them would invite him to lunch, probably another to dinner. I would tag along. It was not a bad lifestyle since Phyllis the housekeeper would always have provided us with a cooked breakfast on our return from matins.

My antics were a challenge to his genteel life-style and good taste. He was proud of his home and the valuable collections of best china. I was thrilled one day when he entrusted me with the organisation of a parish pilgrimage to Norwich cathedral. Transport arrangements were up to me, and I had not yet worked out how we would get there, apart from making part of the journey on foot.

One Friday evening a lady called at the rectory door wanting me to add her name to my list of pilgrims. I was undressed when she called, having just stepped into a tin bath in front of the living room fire. Normally I would bath in the back kitchen but George was out. So I took advantage of a luxury scrub in front of the coal fire. Having forgotten to draw the curtains I saw the lady look through the window as she passed. She saw me too. In a panic I stepped out of the bath vigorously catching my foot on the side of the tub. The bath tipped over, spilling gallons of water onto the new floor that George had had laid only the previous week. I was unpopular with the disgruntled George. But that was nothing compared to the remonstrations of Phyllis, his angry housekeeper. The lady, after all that, decided she would not join my pilgrimage.

One of George's old pussies was Mrs Bates. She was so old that she was at the time unable to care for herself, so was living with her daughter Dorothy and son-in-law Frederic. Fred had two assets. One was his brilliant scientific brain. (My brain was neither brilliant nor scientific but he considerately came down to my level.) The second asset was his luscious teenage daughter. We lunched with the family on Saturdays. Most summer Saturdays recorded in my memory were scorchers. We would walk through the back gate and find the daughter, also a scorcher, basking in the sunshine with minimal covering. Of course, we would linger for a friendly chat in the garden. In admiration of the voluptuous flesh lying before us we would stand upright. We probably stood upright even when we were sat down on the garden bench. Fred would appear and spoil the fun, calling us inside for a drink. The daughter sooner or later followed us in. She joined us for lunch, but now (like the salad) was fully dressed.

That was all four years ago. Now I stayed for two nights not at the rectory but at the home of Leslie, the parish clerk. He too had a teenage daughter, Mary. I sat with Mary and her mother Frances at George's funeral. It was a requiem Communion presided over by the diocesan bishop. The bishop looked black in both dress and expression. That is all I recall of the service except that, sat next to nineteen-year-old Mary, I experienced a tingling feeling in the pit of the stomach.

The same evening Mary's dad, Leslie, invited me for a drink at his local, the Crispin. After a couple of pints he confided in me a family secret. I thought that he was about to tell me some unpalatable information about his daughter, perhaps to warn me off courting her. Not so. He told me that he was parish clerk in name only. He helped the rector during services and accompanied him at all sorts of parish functions. But it was his wife Frances who did the administrative work at home. It was she who wrote correspondence, completed registers, kept records, and all the rest. She was considerably more efficient clerically. All he did was add his signature and take the credit. Nobody else knew this other than Mary and, now, myself. Relieved that his secret was not as serious as I had expected I enjoyed the rest of the evening but notwithstanding found myself wishing that I were back at my lodgings in the company of his adorable daughter. Time was at a premium. There was one day and one night to go before returning to Ampthill. Next day I went with Mary into Chesterfield and we found ourselves in the parish church, the Crooked Spire. It was rumoured, Mary informed me, that when a virgin walks down the aisle to be married, the spire would straighten forthwith. I had heard that said before at my ordination. Mary told me she preferred not to marry in Chesterfield.

I plucked up courage to do two things later in the day. First I asked Mary if she could lend me some money to buy cigars for my journey home. "Yes," she replied. Secondly, I asked if she would like to visit me so I could show her around Bedfordshire. "Yes," she replied. (I had so far only invited her to Beds, not to bed.)

Before there was chance to swing a cat (not that I ever had one), she had made the journey. I arranged for her to stay with Marjorie, my housekeeper, who lived on Church Street. It was not a good idea to invite her to the rectory. Not yet. This housekeeper also used to come in to do me cooked breakfasts after matins. This was a reciprocated visit by Mary after my Derbyshire visit and she too stayed two nights. I took her to

Houghton House, to the great park, to my church and to my father's butcher shop.

I summoned up courage to do two things before she returned to Derbyshire. First I asked Mary whether she could cook. "Yes," she replied. Secondly, I asked her if she would marry me. "Yes," she replied.

It was funny, all these yesses. After our wedding it was always "No".

Later in the day Mary and I returned to the butcher's. The shop was by now closed. Arthur let us in. He was doing orders for customers. "Dad," I ventured, "Mary and I are going to get married."

Without looking up at us, he continued, "That's a pound of sausages for Mrs Albion, some suet for Mrs Bunyan, some stewing steak for Mrs Crompton, and ..." Then at last he looked up from the order book and peered into Mary's eyes. "Do you love him?"

"Y......es," she replied.

His eyes dropped back to the order book. "And tripe for Mrs Downton."

Next I took Mary to my grandmother Maud's on Saunders Piece. She took an instant dislike to poor Mary. Perhaps it did not help that I jokingly introduced her as my new girlfriend "Matilda". The trouble was that my grandmother was taken with my previous girl (the one I took behind a bush in Oxford) and expected us to be married. So my Matilda Mary was a disappointment. Her prejudice against Mary continued a long time - until we visited one Christmas with a tin of mince-pies which Mary the magnificent mince-pie maker had made herself. It proved the way to Maud's heart.

But my grandmother's coldness towards Mary was undoubtedly hurtful to Mary's feelings. A rift in the clouds came only after we had left the house and talked and walked to the other end of town. Mary's tenseness was alleviated somewhat by my romantic overtures. Then I suggested that she see my old school on Bedford Street. We did not quite make it. Instead of passing the Prince of Wales inn we stepped inside and ordered a drink. She was by now back to her effervescent self. It was here that we began to make tentative plans for our wedding.

Laughing later at my father's reaction to our news, I asked Mary, "Do you *really* love me?"

"Y......es," she replied. "I do love you. But I hate your beard."

Wishing to satisfy her I shaved it off. This was something she had in common with my opinionated grandmother, for she hated it too. I delighted two women with one razor.

Mary had by now celebrated her twentieth birthday. We continued to make preparations for the wedding. Normally a couple who wanted to be married in church had to go through marriage preparation with the parish priest. Because in this case the parish priest was myself it was expected that our preparation would be done by the bishop. It did not happen. He made it known that he needed to meet Mary before we marry. Mary made it known to the bishop that she was quite happy for the bishop to interview her. But she added:

"He knows where I live."

To this retort the bishop replied, "She'll do."

Two weeks before the wedding Mary moved her bags into Marjorie's house. The first week I said that she needed to pack her bags again because I wanted her to join me at a youth camp. I was due to take twenty of the parish's youngsters to Sizewell-by-the-sea. We were allocated the upstairs floor, girls on one side of the corridor, boys on the other. Mary had a bedroom at one end and I at the other.

Tired from the long journey we retired to our rooms soon after supper. About to doze asleep I was surprised by a knock on the door. In walked Mary in her nightdress. "This is going to be a wonderful night," I thought. I was no longer feeling tired.

Mary panicked, "I'm not sleeping down there. My room's full of spiders. We're changing rooms. Get up! This is now my bed."

We moved, of course. I eventually fell asleep. I had not slept with Mary. Next morning the young ones caught me coming out of her room. When at breakfast we tried to explain the reason none of them believed a word of the story about spiders. I suppose the week away with the parish youth was a sort of pre-nuptial honeymoon without the sex.

The second week before our marriage Mary did spend at Marjorie's. My pastoral visits that week were, first, to Marjorie, secondly, to Marjorie, thirdly, to Marjorie, and so it went on. Marjorie kept having me on, "Sorry, she's out." But I did not believe her.

At last the fourth of September arrived. I was nearly late for the service. In fact I arrived after the bride, because I had gone to the tobacconist's to stock up with cigars. (Mary, by the way, never saw her money again that she had lent me to buy cigars the previous year. But she was well compensated in other ways.)

St Andrew's was packed. Eight clergy robed, some local, others from Suffolk, and hordes of people came from Derbyshire. I myself did not robe but I did wear a white cravat, so I claimed. It was not visible for I had by now re-grown my beard, much to my grandmother's displeasure. She blamed Mary for this, of course, for allowing me to appear so dishevelled. Clearly Mary secretly did fancy me in a beard after all. Anyway, as well as the nine clergy, not forgetting myself, there were eight hymns during the nuptial Communion.

Inquisitive parishioners came to see our wedding, many content to stay outside and watch the bride arrive. Others came into the church for the long service, presided over by my second training priest, Kenneth. George, by now himself married, preached the sermon. Those inside the church included Betsey and Bill, not themselves quite yet married, and many of the Low family.

On our wedding night I pondered the question: If I had married Mary in Chesterfield parish church would its spire have straightened? I will never know. Nevertheless, we spent a happy night in the rectory.

Then we travelled to my great aunt Em's for the honeymoon on the Isle of Wight. Thankfully my telegraph had arrived and she was expecting us. It was not as exciting a stay as it might have been because Mary suffered from asthma attacks and spent nearly as much time with the doctor as she did with me.

In due course we returned home. As ever, I went to church in the morning. I rang the bell in church and said matins, walked back home through the rectory door and sat down at the dining table. I waited and waited for my customary cooked breakfast to appear. It did not. Married life is different, I discovered, from living with a housekeeper.

The week after we arrived back home a young lady called Mary knocked on the rectory door. She wanted me to marry her. Of course I would. But I wondered how I could cope with two Marys. Just one is as much as I could manage.

Mary learned how to be a rector's wife. In fact that is wishful thinking. She never did. And when I look back I am thankful that she did not. She was outspoken, was Mary. She was her own woman. She gained a reputation for being the only rector's wife to swear at the bishop, not only once but every time they met. She was, however, in reality an excellent rector's wife. I have to say that. She is still alive. And I say it even though she does not do cooked breakfasts!

Another benefit of married life was that I was no longer plagued by Susanna, or, for that matter, any other young girl with a crush on bachelor clergymen.

CHAPTER 15
JOSIAH'S HATCH

June 1888 *The National School processed to St Andrew's. This time I gave the children a lesson on baptism. I shook the doll to dry her long tresses and inadvertently soaked the headmaster.*

Unlike the National School, the British School never processed to the parish church. But they had heard about my colourful teaching on christening. Instead of inviting a Nonconformist minister for a change they asked me to go into the school and demonstrate a Church of England baptism. I took up the offer.

July 1888 *This time I used a teddy bear. The headmaster stayed away.*

August 1888 *I baptised a real baby. Both headmasters and children of both schools stayed away. The mother, unlike most parents, did not call me "rector". She called me "Luvvy".*

September 1888 *It was a riotous baptism. The child grabbed hold of his father's wallet and dropped it into the font. Perhaps he didn't understand how we do the collection.*

Josiah's father, Edward, and mother, Susanna

Edward met Susanna (not the Susanna who met me in the vestry) at the constable's house in Luton. Susanna was there to report a robbery. Ted was there to provide intelligence about a different robbery. Father Ted was something of an amateur detective. He could see that the constable, even had he been capable, even had he the time and resources, did not have any real intention of following up the crime of which Susanna was the victim. Ted told her that he himself would do what he could to solve the crime, even if he was unable to recover the lost goods. In the event poor Ted did neither. What he did manage was to strike up a relationship with Susanna.

We do not need to go into the details of how the relationship led to their marriage. What we do need to know is that Susanna was a Methodist and Ted a Baptist. This was no problem until, after the wedding, Susanna found herself embroiled with a whole family of ardent Baptists. Ted suggested that Susanna be baptised.

"But I'm already baptised", she insisted.

"No, darling. Unless you were baptised as an adult it doesn't count. You must be born again."

"But my minister told me you can only be baptised once."

"I'm sure he was quite right. But you haven't actually been baptised at all, darling. You didn't know anything about it. You didn't agree to it. You didn't ..."

Ted won the argument, mainly because he had his strong-minded and insistent relations on his side.

Susanna agreed to be baptised again, against her better judgement. What harm could it do?

The baptism was duly arranged. The minister had only recently been called to this congregation. It was to be his first baptism here in Luton. The chapel had a large pool. The floor boards were lifted up to reveal an impressive bath.

My own three children were to be baptised many years later in a much tinier tub of water. It was considerably older than the chapel's as well as substantially smaller. But it was sufficiently large to immerse them. This is what I did, for I administered my children's baptisms myself. And I persuaded Mary that they be done naked. As Anglicans they were babies and could be immersed easily into the (warm) water in the font. And even if the baby daughters did not know anything about it, did not agree to it, did not remember it, yet it was, I firmly believe, entirely valid.

August 1846 *The next baptism after our daughter Elizabeth's was different. The father had knocked on the rectory door and enquired, "How much do you charge for a baptism?"*

"Nothing," I replied.

"I want five," he said. Then he introduced me to his wife. I had married her only last year - but not to the man who wanted the baptisms.

At the rehearsal the children's father asked if it was all right for the godparents to wait outside the church until the actual baptism bit - because, he said, they didn't like going to church. I suggested that perhaps they could make a special effort just this once. Probably they should have stayed outside after all, because it was the new curate's first sermon, a thunderous one. Not only that - the roof collapsed.

The Rector of Millbrook was suffering from stress. He asked me to help by leading a service for the patronal festival on Sunday 29th September in the afternoon. Yes, I could manage that. It would mean missing my afternoon sleep but I told him that I was happy to help. I love the feast of Saint Michael and All Angels. Then came the sting in the tail. "Oh, by the way, there are also four baptisms. Is that okay?" Having already agreed I could hardly now say that it was not okay. It simply added to my own stress.

The four to be baptised were children in the same home. The visit to the family to prepare them for baptism was precarious if not perilous. They lived down in the vale, thought to be John Bunyan's Slough of Despond. I was indeed full of despondency when I called at the house. None of the children was at home when I knocked on the door. The mother Lauretta answered. Had my visit been a hundred years later she was the sort of woman who I could imagine with tattoos all over her big body. Her first words before inviting me inside were, "Are you afraid of birds?"

"Only my own," I replied, not quite sure what I meant.

"Then come in."

There were three big birds in the room, out of their cages and looking ominously as if they were ready to pounce on a nervous stranger. There were six more birds in the garden, she told me, but they were too dangerous to keep in the house. Lauretta was a formidable bird herself. As if she did not already have sufficient protection from a strange man of the cloth, her equally large husband suddenly appeared from upstairs. She told me that he had been on night shift and that I had woken him by banging on the front door.

Sunday, I thought, should be fun. And so it was. The font was small but I successfully got the children soaked. I had the protection of Michael and the flight of angels, but not a bird was in sight.

Rather differently in the prominent pool inside the Baptist chapel, a candidate for baptism would step down to where the minister was standing, dressed in his white robe, in the (warm) water. He would push them under, taking them by the neck and round the waist, and gave them a thorough ducking. "In the name of the Father ..."

He would dip them again. "... And of the Son".

Then he plunged them a third time. "... And of the Holy Spirit."

The newly baptised would splutter, "Amen." The newly baptised would be taken by an elder into the vestry to dry off and dress. If they were lucky they might be allowed a little of the minister's brandy. They were, in fact, never lucky. If the minister drank brandy he was certainly not going to let others know it.

This was not a dissimilar pool, except for its age, to the baptistery I had seen at Milan cathedral where Saint Augustine had been baptised by Saint Ambrose, probably without brandy.

The new minister's new way of doing things would involve the candidate to strip first. A screen would be set up so that the congregation could not see the baptism. It would be administered in private, except for any inquisitive child who might peep through the screen. The only witnesses would be a female elder (if the candidate were a woman) or a male elder (if a man), and, of course, the male minister. The nearly baptised nude would step into the pool and the newly baptised nude, the neophyte, would rise up and be covered by the elder with a white robe. They would go to the vestry, as previously, and, after using the towel, dress, preferably into a pure white dress. (The men were not expected to wear white, and definitely not a dress.) Then might follow a small tot (of water, that is, not brandy - nor an inquisitive child either).

This was the theory. But every elder without exception objected to the minister's crazy idea. It would perhaps be fine for male candidates. But a female minister ought to baptise ladies. Of course, this was out of the question. Women ministers did not exist. Neither could they. How could a woman be a leader in the church? Their job is to be submissive and silent.

Anyway, the minister got away with baptising Susanna naked. But she was the first and last. After that baptism war broke out between the minister and the elders.

When they went to bed that night (Susanna and Ted, not the minister and his elders), the bride put on her nightdress. It was pink, not white. She slid into bed with Ted. Ted pulled up her nightie and said, "I would like to baptise you again."

"No," insisted Susanna. "The Methodist minister told me you can be baptised only once, not three times."

But baptise her he did. And in due course Elizabeth was born.

Ted was adamant that someone could be baptised once only. He was not so resolute about having more than one woman. Sadly, Ted left his wife when he told another young lady that he was able to help her solve a crime. Again he was unsuccessful. But he enticed the other woman into a relationship. At first the grass was greener. It remained so for ten years.

It took that time for him to realise that he had made an enormous mistake. One thing led to another (to cut the story short) and Susanna, to everyone's dismay, took him back. It was after this considerable time that their second child, Hannah, was born. She was followed by Rachel. She was followed by William. And he was followed by Josiah.

CHAPTER 16
POP DELIVERS

We will skip Josiah's early days, since he grew up in Luton, where his first job was a groom. He was not yet, however, a bridegroom. Josiah arrived in Ampthill in his early twenties. He started a business as a soda water manufacturer. He lived in Oliver Street next door to the Flowers family, Joe and Fanny and their children. It was several years yet before he would pass the top of the street and see the sign with a finger pointing down the road directing passers-by "to the Foundry". When the foundry was built he decided that he would canvass them for business. Indeed he established good relationships. But before all this he established an even better relationship with a young lady round the corner from the sign that was eventually to mount the brick wall. For Josiah a finger was pointing towards the home of Betsey and Bill Low. The reason that he followed the invisible finger was that Bill and Betsey had a daughter. To get past Bill to chat up his daughter was itself like mounting a brick wall.

Eliza was seventeen, living in Dunstable Street, when she met Josiah. This was the beginning of what became a prolonged affair. We have already noted the story of how it all started. The fruitful consequences of the affair were nigh-on multitudinous. That is a hyperbole for saying that they reached double figures. Their son William was born when Eliza was still seventeen. Josiah was ten years her senior, so perhaps he should have known better.

Three men and two boys worked for Pop not too long after his mineral water business had taken off. His wife Sarah's brother Len did the bottling. Len lived next door on the other side from the Flowers. That is not to say that Len did not also have an array of lovely flowers. Years later Josiah enticed Joe, Joe's son, to leave his job with his dad, a master bricklayer, and work for him manufacturing ginger beer. Pop had a nephew James and two great-nephews, James and William, who were mineral water workers. It was very much a family business.

Not everyone drank mineral water. Katherine, one of my flower ladies, tripped over a hole at the bottom of the church path. Fat Kat, as I called her, told me that she would make a claim against the church. I told her that she would never get away with it, since she was carrying a bunch of flowers in one hand and five empty wine bottles in the other.

James lived at Russell Villa on Arthur Street. When Pop took a back seat in the business, otherwise known as retirement, Josiah and James swapped addresses because Pop's home in Oliver Street had all the equipment. James had now taken over as manager of the aerated water firm. James the younger was a bottler and William was responsible for sales. Josiah relaxed at Russell Villa with Annie and their twenty-two-year-old Emily. His business manufacturing mineral water and pop was successful. Pop was well able to afford looking after his many illegitimate children financially. And he did so.

Clergy and pop-men (but not, I have it on good authority from my younger brother, milkmen, because they operate much too early in the day) have something in common. They visit homes and are liable to catch people at awkward moments. During hot weather I would sometimes purposely make calls via the back-garden gate rather than knock at the front door, and so have been known to find a housewife sunbathing wearing next to nothing.

Pop's nearest customer was Fanny Flowers. Pop, his motive more innocent than mine, had no response at the front door and so called round at the back. By a bush in the garden sunbathing and lying on her back was Fanny. She was wearing a top but nothing else. At the sight of Pop she scrambled up, ran into the house and put on some bottoms, but not before Pop had seen her bush. Pop was to have so many encounters with her Fanny in years to come. Or, to make matters clear, Pop was to have so many encounters with Fanny's niece Fanny in years to come. Fanny Flowers the younger was to marry Pop and Eliza's son Albert. Fanny the elder felt embarrassed whenever she saw Pop after the scare in the back garden, unable to erase from her mind that first meeting. Neither could Josiah erase it, not that he wished to.

Josiah led an interesting private life, not that his private life was private. The two women in his life were public knowledge and the subject of common gossip, not least because he was outwardly an upright churchman. Yet he was held in respect as a figure of the community.

Josiah, still only twenty-six, was among the great and good of Ampthill to be invited to the opening of Bedford Midland Railway Station.

He often needed to travel to Bedford. Pop owned another mineral water business in Bedford. He could catch one of the many stage coaches passing through the town. But once Ampthill station was built he would catch the train. It was not ideal, being a good mile from his home. No sooner had he begun to read the paper than the train entered the long tunnel.

A schoolboy told me that he (the boy, not Josiah) used to take the opportunity on his journey to school to kiss the head girl, with nobody (except the head girl) any the wiser. He enjoyed a nice lengthy kiss, for the length of the tunnel made it worthwhile.

Three years later Josiah stayed a night at the recently opened Midland Hotel. He had sat down to a sumptuous supper in Bedford with twenty-five other tradesmen. He enjoyed regular dinners with other businessmen in both Bedford and Ampthill. It was not unlike a gathering of a Rotary Club, had one existed.

Josiah much relished the few occasions when he was summoned for jury service. Whether this was due to his community spirit or because he enjoyed seeing prisoners put away is uncertain.

He continued to be a pillar of the community throughout his business life. Josiah's prominence was confirmed when he became elected to the new Local Board in Ampthill, established when he was a young lad of sixty.

The rector, my successor Mr Nichol, was one of the unsuccessful candidates at the election onto the Local Board, with only one hundred and forty-one votes. Josiah was not at all sorry about this, being an ardent worker for the Union Church. In any case, Josiah was himself elected onto the Local Board, almost topping the poll with two hundred and seventy-two votes, and immediately became caught up in the sewerage controversy. An outbreak of gastric fever was blamed on the drains. There was not yet a brain drain. But there was certainly a drain blame. Josiah tried to persuade his fellow councillors to sort out the problem rather than continue their negative attitude always with the excuse that the work was too expensive.

Josiah's wives, Sarah and Annie

Eliza never married. Pop, however, had two wives (one at a time) in addition to his mistress.

Sarah was Josiah's age when they married. They were nineteen. Contrary to gossip, they did not have to marry, because Sarah, like her biblical forerunner, was barren. Abraham's Sarah did eventually and incredibly have a child in her old age. Not so with Josiah's Sarah, who did not live into old age. It was after eight years of marriage that Josiah met Eliza, and before Sarah's death Josiah gave his beloved mistress ten children. They were known as Pop's deliveries. Sarah had been married to Josiah thirty-one years.

If she gave him little satisfaction in bed (or if there was some satisfaction there were no results to show for it) she did nevertheless provide much help in his business, making mineral water and soft drinks. As we have already seen, it was Sarah's brother who was Josiah's right-hand man. And her nephews were involved in the business too. Sarah was the backbone in the background of an amazingly successful business - the prop behind the pop.

The smaller bottles had a marble in the neck that needed to be pushed downwards in order to release the drink. This was a clever ploy, because boys badgered parents to buy as many bottles as possible so that they would be provided with more marbles for their collections and games.

Annie married Josiah shortly after Sarah's death. To add to Josiah's ten children, Annie also presented him with just one child, Emily. Josiah was now fifty-five and decided enough was enough. Annie was more daring in her dress than Sarah had ever been. She wore garters and her drawers were attractively trimmed with lace. Sarah would not have been seen dead in such alluring underwear. Now she was indeed dead.

Why did Pop not now marry Eliza? He liked Eliza as a mistress but preferred to keep her at a distance. He would have found her overbearing to live with and the package would have had to include living with her daughters, so many little Elizas. In any case he had rather fallen in love with Annie. The real truth of the matter, though, is that Eliza would have nothing to do with matrimony, and certainly not after all those years of spinsterhood combined with childbearing. She was content as she was, thank you.

Pop, like Eliza, was faithful to both his mistress and wife, apart, that is to say, from the other woman. After all, he was a good Baptist.

But his relationship with Eliza had caused Sarah untold distress. She was lonely both physically and mentally. She saw little of her husband, especially in the evenings. He said that he was out at meetings or business dinners. Often he was. But she never really knew whether he was out with trading partners or with his bedroom partner. So Sarah was resentful if not jealous. She felt inadequate that she could not provide Josiah with offspring. She felt inadequate that her husband was attracted to another woman. She felt sore that her husband's money was going outside her home. Probably all this is why Sarah immersed herself, not literally, in soda water. She led a sod of a life.

Annie, on the other hand, would not tolerate Josiah's affair. He had no more children by Eliza since Sarah's death. Annie insisted that he break off any intimacy with the other woman forthwith. Annie made him swear that he would have nothing more to do with Eliza. He agreed that she would no longer be his piece but insisted that he would keep up calls to her home on Saunders Piece. He would not be denied visiting his children. And after all, he still had to deliver Eliza's pop.

And what did Eliza think of Josiah's wives? As for Sarah, she just did not care. Josiah gave her what she needed. He kept all the children fed and clothed. It was an expensive business but he could afford to provide for them. And he kept her content upstairs.

Emily tried as she grew up to avoid her older half-brothers and sisters. In particular, she had no desire to be acquainted with old Eliza. But she gradually got to know some of her half-siblings and discovered that they were not all that bad. Some of the females of the family she met at work. She was not really a born hater. Neither was Emily a hatter. She was a needlewoman. The work overlapped since her sewing services were required in the hat industry as well as her making and stitching other clothing.

As for Eliza, Emily might have discovered that she was not quite the witch she imagined, had she tried to make contact. But she did not.

CHAPTER 17
FATHER CHRISTMAS

Mary walked into my study. "Good morning, Mister Low. May I come in?"

I was a trifle annoyed. "May I?" She had already entered. She addresses me as Mr Low when she is either in a frivolous or sarcastic mood. Which was it? Sat at the desk I was trying to concentrate on choosing next Sunday's hymns. We were in Advent and I was considering "Lo, he comes with clouds descending." This beautiful hymn was written by Charles Wesley and John Cennick in the last century.

Mary was holding an envelope in each hand. Two Christmas cards had been delivered, she told me. One was to herself from flower lady Katherine (Fat Kat). Kat had asked that she convey Christmas greetings to Mr Low. Now I was more than a trifle annoyed. Why did Mary need to interrupt me to tell me this?

Then she apologised for opening the other envelope by mistake. My annoyance abounded. "It's from the bishop. He wishes you a good Christmas. He included a personal message hoping that you are getting on all right with your difficult parishioners, and ends, 'Sock it to 'em'."

Yes, Mary was in her frivolous mood. The card was actually also to herself from her friend Ann Bishop. (It was from the Bishop after all.) Two cards for her. None for me.

I knew all along that the bishop, especially the Right Reverend Thomas Turton, would not be sending Christmas greetings to me. He had many clergy spread throughout Cambridgeshire, Huntingdonshire, Bedfordshire and West Suffolk. And he would certainly not have told me 'to sock it to 'em'. A bishop would not be saying that sort of thing until Richard came to the throne 130 years later.

December 1850 *Mary and I were invited to a Christmas (or pre-Christmas as I would prefer to say) fancy dress party. Mary and I went* *as Father and Mrs Christmas. We sat opposite a rather attractive nun. The serving wench had healthily plump wobblers which I prayed would completely fall out whenever she bent over in front of me. My prayer was not answered. I recall that I ordered breast of chicken.*

Mary, as I will shortly relate in a later chapter, bought me small Christmas gifts, like a notebook, but with loving affection. My presents to her were not always so small. For instance, because I was often away from home I bought her a brand new lightweight cart with two wheels that could be pulled by a single horse. She would be able to pack a picnic, put it in the back with the children, severely forbidding them (I could picture the scene) to eat anything on the journey until they reached their destination. It was a problem hiding the present, but with the complicity of a neighbour it remained a surprise until Christmas morning. I had wrapped up a set of reins, which I gave her first. This caused some puzzlement until I revealed the bigger item. From that moment she had aspirations of driving a mail coach.

It was later on the same wet Christmas Day when I took a stroll into the town and, to avoid a downpour, was about to shelter in the King's Arms Yard. But I did not evade getting wet because before I could step away from the edge of the road a carriage pulled by four horses hurtled by at some speed, straight through a puddle, drenching me and spoiling my best clothes. The water was cold. The carriage was travelling not quite fast enough for passengers not to hear my loud cry, "You bloody bastards!" Heads turned. Perhaps they did not know (so I hoped) that it was the rector who was yelling. I felt justified because a stagecoach should never have been travelling at speed, if at all on Christmas Day, and especially not splashing the rector.

We had a different kind of disturbance at the end of one Christmas service. An elderly lady was attacked by a young man waiting for her to come out of church. He was a neighbour with a grudge. I held him by the throat with my left hand while shaking the congregation's hands with my right. Mary had run off to find a constable, who was easier to locate than a churchwarden. He took the young man away, while warmly shaking my hand, saying, "The peace of the Lord be with you."

Another Christmas George, the bitch, was afraid to venture outside for her late night pee. It took a while to realise that she was terrified of the snowman that the children had created.

Snow could be a problem in the churchyard. Apart from anything else the funeral director could not find soil to accompany my words of committal, "earth to earth". I suggested that I could substitute "snow to snow" but immediately had second thoughts.

If Josiah was known by a large number of people as Pop, I was never known as father not by our children and certainly not by parishioners. My children called my father-in-law "Pop-Pop" but me they called Dad to my face, and various other names behind my back. They refused to call me "father" because they felt that I was severe enough already, without needing to draw attention to it when they addressed me. They craftily thought that they could get round me if they tried to soften me up by informality. Also the children were aware that I would have liked people of the parish to address me by this more staid title, even if it was unheard of for anyone actually to do so. Perhaps they thought that I was secretly envious of the Roman Catholic clergy. So the children were resolute that they were not going to comply either.

Jane, Pamela and Elizabeth were good friends to each other as they grew up. We gave our middle daughter an unusual name. She loathed the name, particularly as Pamela got a little older. Perhaps she was ridiculed by other children. Perhaps it was due to her being thought unusual, even odd, for she knew no other girl of that name. But she had to live with it, just as she had to live with being the middle child. The eldest always received the best of everything. The youngest received all the attention. She, however, was the one left out, the Pammy in the middle. Or so she complained.

Elizabeth, on the other hand, complained that she was treated as inferior because she was the one, in her opinion, always left out. She was the unnoticed one. She was the one left behind. So she lamented.

They all grumbled that their father was never at home, had no time for them, was always busy with parish affairs, was always away on army duty, spent all his time in prison. When he was at home their father was too strict, too cross, too severe, too demanding. Of course, it was all far from the truth.

It did not count that I had spent time teaching them in turn to ride a horse expertly. They became able riders, if recklessly not always heeding what I had taught them.

Neither did it count, I suppose, that I spent one hour quality time with them once every week when I was preparing them for confirmation. One of the reasons that it did not count was that twenty-five others were in the class too. Among them were the curate's three daughters.

January 1858 *I'm not sure that one of the boys is ready yet for confirmation. I asked him, "Where did Jesus die?" He buried his head in his hands and murmured, "Oh, Christ!"*

On their confirmation day, still in the Christmas season, the girls were clothed in white dresses and veils, with white cardigans to provide a little warmth. So we had three children fathered by the curate, three fathered by the rector, their Father in God (the bishop), their godfathers, a stepfather stepping in for a godmother, and too many godmothers to mention. The bishop complained that there was so much chatter in the front pew coming from clergy daughters that he could hardly get a word in edgeways.

The curate was one of the best the bishop sent me. He followed the short-stay curate, the one who dumped his wife and two daughters on the parish and bunked off with another woman. The bishop made amends by sending me this one, the Reverend Walter Clifton and his wife Catherine. They had four children, three of them girls who were confirmed with ours.

Our girls grew up to be beauties, Jane blue-eyed, Pamela and Elizabeth brown-eyed. They were eyed up by many of the town's boys. They all loved to party and it caused me untold anxiety when they arrived home later than the deadline that Mary and I had set them – much, much later. It was usually on a Saturday night when they were not home until the next day, which caused me distress because the next day was my working day. One Saturday the youngest daughter was not home by the midnight curfew hour, so I sat up by the front door of the rectory and waited angrily. When she finally appeared and faced my wrath, perhaps slightly cooled due to relief, she rejoined, "But what's the problem, Dad?" I was silenced and retired to bed.

I always thought that Jane was the talkative one. But as the years went by I realised that not any of the three had the upper hand in that department. But then they were typical of the Low brood. They either had nothing to say or else everything. They certainly differed in other respects. One was good in the kitchen. Two were not. (Their husbands made up for their lack.) One was good upstairs (in the brain department, that is). Two were not. One had common sense. Two did not. One was good at raising girls. Two were good at bringing up boys. Similarities included the ability to make friends and get on with everyone (almost), due to a most pleasant personality. So their father was proud and thankful, especially after they had left home.

The children were beautiful in looks but equally beautiful in personality. And their husbands were pretty resplendent too. Of course they differed in character as did the girls. But they were all full of vitality, manly, sporty and athletic, often excitable, hardworking, indeed hard in every sense. But they were good fathers even if they stood for little nonsense. And they were good husbands, even if they stood for little nonsense. At least they liked to think that it were so. They could all compete with their wives when it came to chatter, which is saying a great deal. They enjoyed food, which kept them in my good books. One would eat so quickly, though, that his plate would be empty before the rest of the family had had a few bites. He would hope that his children would not finish their dinner at all so that he could pounce, setting into theirs too.

Back to the parish, I had tried time and time again to persuade the church to either purchase or use our embroidery ladies' talents to make vestments for the church. In the end they gave way, but not until I had handed over to my successor. For him they purchased a full set of gothic vestments.

Although I was sometimes referred to as a man of the cloth, I was at last known as "Father" at Christmas. The festival was an exception. One Christmas I was out and about in heavy snow. My white necktie was indiscernible. The black beard became iced and white. Not only did I suddenly feel an old man but children nick-named me Father Nick after Saint Nicholas. The name stuck. They all knew well enough that Father Nick was aka Santa Claus, even when the snow had melted.

That same Christmas I was invited to sit in the grotto dressed up as Santa Claus. Getting dressed was itself a problem. I put the red jacket on back to front. A mother told me that I had forgotten to put the wig on my head. Everyone seemed to be aware that I was only pretending and that I was really the rector. Everyone, that is, except my little daughter Jane. She did not recognise me. I had totally fooled her.

It was so hot in the grotto, dressed all in red and white, on top of my normal warm clothing. I even had to put on a false white beard to cover up the black one. I had chocolate in a pocket, which I attempted to eat between child clients coming into the grotto, but it had melted, so I managed to get brown stains all over the white gloves and beard.

A little girl came to sit on my knee, not my daughter this time. "What would you like Santa to bring you for Christmas?"

"I would like a doll, please... And my mummy said she would like a baby for Christmas."

I said that it would be difficult to comply this year but if she was patient I would call to see her on Lady Day and see what I could manage in time for next year. (No, I did not really say that. How dare I?)

Out of Santa uniform I appeared so respectable in my rigid starched collar. I had begun to wear the so-called Roman collar. People passed pleasant comments about the new type of band around my throat, but they would not have been so favourably disposed had they known what it was called.

Every Christmas we were visited by Mary's parents, Frances and Leslie. Since they came all the way from Chesterfield they decided to make the most of their visits and stay on for Mary's birthday, which was not until mid-January. Nobody who stayed a night in the rectory ever went to bed before the next day. Frances was no exception. She sat and sat while I willed her to go to bed. My willpower must have been weak because she never complied. By the second half of January I was exhausted.

Mary was bereaved of her father and mother and brother Rex in the space of four years. Rex died first when he was forty-one, then her father Leslie, followed by Mary's mother Frances. It involved a lot of speedy galloping from Ampthill to Chesterfield.

Christmas was the only time of year that Mary and I played cards. Playing each other at whist one night I dropped several cards onto the floor. We both bent down together to pick them up and our heads collided. My head-butt sent Mary unconscious for a while, so I put her to bed and declared myself the victor. Ever since, the game has been known as knockout whist.

Later during each year Mary and I would find time to visit her parents in Derbyshire. Not long after our marriage we left my parents-in-law at home and went for a long walk up to Pudding Pie Hill. I was ahead of Mary and heard her voice behind me, "What do you think of the view?" Aware that she was proud of her home county I shouted back, "It's exhilarating." I turned around and saw that she was holding her dress in the air. She had no drawers on. Yes, the view was indeed exhilarating.

Frances and Leslie had been with us only two or three days one Christmas. It was Boxing Day. It was also Sunday. What with late nights and Christmas services I had prepared a sermon for the feast of Saint Stephen very hastily. I said to the curate before the service: "Make sure you pray for the bishop today in the intercession prayers." Last week he had forgotten to mention him.

My curate replied, "He's here."

"Don't be daft," I said. "Of course he isn't here."

But he was. The bishop's name was Nash. He was sat in the back row. I suppose that he was either taking a Christmas break or he was checking up on me. I was aware that one of my strait-laced congregation had put in a complaint, something to do with my being immoral - which, naturally, was both unfounded and untrue. Anyway, there he was. And there was no time, even, to nip home and search out a better sermon.

Late January we were usually visited by mother Frances' cousin Williamson and his wife Barbara. Of course, they never went to bed early either. But Williamson liked to go for a drink every night. He never drank beer from a pint glass. It was always a half pint. But he had very many half pints during the course of the evening. Williamson would need to get up several times during the night to let out the ale. The toilet was adjacent to the spare bedroom. All he needed to do was take a turn to the left and he was there. One night we were woken at three o'clock by hysterical yells from Barbara. Williamson had turned right instead of left. Instead of finding the toilet he had found the top of the stairs, which he proceeded to tumble down to the bottom. We found him in a crumpled bloody heap, naked and helpless.

Barbara was flapping. Mary was embarrassed for him and tore off my dressing gown to cover him up. Now I was standing naked and embarrassed. Once back in their bedroom I watched Barbara trying to encourage Williamson to dress himself into her slip, lest he should leak blood all over the clean sheets. Williamson refused to wear the slip, at which point I left them to it, doubled up in laughter. By the end of January I was doubly exhausted.

Returning to the theme of being addressed as Father, some of the old soldiers who had fought at Crimea called me Father. But they used the Latin, Padre. Oddly my Roman Catholic reservist colleagues in the army would not contemplate the title Padre. They stuck to Father. One of them actually had Christmas as a surname. He was the only Roman Catholic I know who blankly refused to be known as Father.

Mary and I invited the Roman Catholic curate to supper. He harangued us about the sins of married clergy. Mary had had enough. She retorted, "Who's cooking your bloody supper?" and forthwith took away his plate.

Then we invited the Roman Catholic parish priest, Father Benjamin, a lovely man but deaf and aged. It was as well that Mary had prepared a fish pie. It was Friday. But he did not eat anything other than fish, he told us, for fear of nightmares. While we were still eating dessert at the table he abruptly stood up and announced that he had to go home to bed. This was unlike most of our guests, who stay for ever. We hoped that he would not go home to nightmares.

CHAPTER 18
MISTRESS ELIZA

I had been in Ampthill two years when Eliza was born. I remember the year because of a fatal accident. Dr Edward Drax Free was hit by a cart when crossing the road. The accident hit the news in a big way. Edward Free, a Fellow of Saint John's College, Oxford (well before I was at Oxford) had until 1830 been rector of Sutton, just thirteen miles up the road from Ampthill. During his twenty-two years tenure the Doctor of Divinity had caused a scandal not only in the vicinity but up and down the country. Not only did he keep pigs in the churchyard; not only did he profit by selling lead from his own church roof; not only was he offensive to parishioners when drunk; not only was he offensive to parishioners when not drunk; not only did he keep pornographic writings and drawings; not only did he seduce a series of housekeepers; not only did he father five illegitimate children; he also charged excessive fees for baptising and burying. After barricading himself in the rectory to avoid being charged he was eventually deprived of the living. The defrocking occurred while I was innocently enjoying myself in Italy. But now, about to celebrate his eightieth birthday, his collision with a horse and cart brought the affair back into everyone's topic of conversation.

Eliza's birth was thus overshadowed.

Eliza was a handful for Betsey while she was going through the early teen years. To others outside the immediate family she came across as such a charming, pleasant, vigorous little girl, indeed a young lady. To those who lived with her day by day she was immature, impetuous and stubborn. She was bothersome and burdensome. She took pleasure, it seemed, in provoking her mother. Betsey referred to her as "my vexatious and cantankerous girl". She was prickly, sharp-tongued and, often, downright rude.

However, before her teens she was lovely. She helped Betsey in the home and was always prepared to help with housework - other than tidy her own bedroom. So it was difficult for Betsey to refuse her when she wanted to do something special. After spending hours cleaning out cupboards and sweeping and polishing and dusting she thus perfectly timed a request to her mother to see the summer boating spectacular that she had recently heard about.

Eliza was ten years old when she had her first excursion to Bedford. Eliza desperately wanted to join the crowds to watch the much-publicised Bedford Amateur Regatta on the Ouse. Rowing events and races had taken place over the past few years, but this was seen as the very first official regatta. Since the railways had taken off, navigation on the river as a major industry was in decline. The picturesque river began to be used for leisure. So the scene was set for a great fun event. This was certainly more Eliza's idea of fun than staying at home for a musical jaunt around the piano, which is what her best friend's family did every Sunday. A piano was her friend's parents' latest acquisition. Eliza was pleased that there was no piano in her home. Instead she was desperate to persuade her parents to take her to the Ouse.

Bill, however, was set against the idea. He remembered nothing of the incident, but he was well aware of the tragedy of losing his elder brother in the floods some thirty years earlier. Against his better judgement Betsey persuaded him, as only she knew how, to take her and their three children to see the spectacle. Another flood is not going to happen, she assured him. Eliza would help look after five-year-old Lucy and little William.

As it turned out, the weather, despite it being August, was horrid. This did not prevent them having a marvellous day out. There were no tragedies either. An awful tragedy was still to come at the regatta some sixteen years later.

The poor weather did not deter competitors in the eight races. It did not deter good crowds along the embankment. It did not deter the umpire doing his job from the back of his horse. It did not deter the said umpire spotting the winner of the sculling event catch hold of another boat and getting himself disqualified. It did not deter ladies sitting down by the wharf to drink their tea. It did not deter people watching the Bedford Brass Band along the High Street and, later, playing from a large barge. It did not deter fiddlers accompanying dancers by the riverside. It did not deter the bells of St Paul's ringing out all afternoon. Why should it? The ringers had the driest place of all inside the tower. It did not deter the winners putting a smile on their faces. After all, they came in for welcome cash prizes.

Eliza's first regatta was a hazy memory when she next went. But for the rest of her long life she would vividly remember her next one when she was twenty-six. She witnessed a tragic and fatal accident. She was there early and was in front of the crowds at the start point. A sergeant of the 82nd Regiment, stationed in Bedford, had the responsibility of firing the gun to signal the start of the races. A little girl, a local landlord's daughter, ran in front of the canon as it was being fired. She was shot through the neck and died before she arrived at the hospital. The sergeant was traumatised. He was also arrested. The coroner's verdict, however, was indeed accidental death. Eliza never went to the regatta again.

After spending her working week in the hat factory Eliza would often take the children on Sundays for a walk in the park, admiring some of the largest oak trees in the country. Pop hardly ever went with them. If he walked in the park on Sundays it would be with his wife Sarah. Pop was not aware until he moved from Luton what a gem Ampthill Park was. King Henry VIII had clearly thought so too. He had come regularly, when the park surrounded the Castle. Henry had stayed at the Castle when he came to hunt deer. The king's stalking and hawking among the oaks took him as far as Houghton Conquest, where in years to come my descendants were to keep a different Royal Oak.

Katherine of Aragon was also fond of Ampthill. She too stayed at the Castle. She was there during her divorce proceedings. On the site of the Castle is now a cross (Katherine's Cross). Some say that a lucky person one day in the far future would find a treasure buried nearby.[4]

Much more recently than King Henry and his first wife, only a hundred years before Eliza and Pop were separately enjoying their walks, the park had been landscaped for the second Earl of Upper Ossory (who later was to have a public house named after him). The work was carried out by Lancelot "Capability" Brown (who did not have a pub named after

---

[4] Ken Thomas and his dog found the golden hare of Masquerade by Kit Williams in 1982 in Ampthill Park.

him). He built the reservoir, or "rezzie", the banks of which I used to roll down as a boy, and pull up without tumbling into the water.

Soldiers who camped in the park told stories about the park being haunted by a ghost. It appeared as a knight in armour riding on a white horse. Perhaps they had had too much to drink. In any case, unlike the spirits in the two pubs, I was not invited to get rid of the knight, or the white horse for that matter.

Everyone made the most of their Sundays off. Skilled workers were beginning to have Saturday afternoons free. But the family in question were hardly in that class. It was on one of her Sunday jaunts in the park that Eliza, with her one-year-old daughter Elizabeth Eliza, bumped into their friends Charles and Martha Shotbolt with Walter their son. Walter was also in a pushchair. They did not know then that before the century was out their babies would be marrying each other in the parish church. Lizzie and Walter were fond of each other as they grew up. But it was not until they found themselves working together in the tailor shop that they felt completely suited. They got to know each other's bodies intimately by using a tape measure, he to check her vital statistics, she to examine his vitals.

The same August that the early pushchair collision took place between Elizabeth and Walter, the foundation stone was laid for a new Primitive Methodist chapel across the road from Eliza's home. It was too late for Elizabeth Eliza, but Eliza wondered whether it might be far easier to have her future children baptised almost on the doorstep. But she never did. She did not give way to the temptation to take the easier way. Eliza continued to lug the family all the way to the parish church.

Pop, of course, went to the Baptist chapel, though not usually in Ampthill. He was an elder at Westoning. He did, however, go to the opening of the enlargement of the Union chapel. It was extended a little while before the much smaller Primitive chapel opened.

Pop told Eliza that not only his Church but most Dissenters were strongly supporting the separation of the Church of England from the state. Although Nonconformist Churches differed among themselves, they all seemed to unite in opposition to the Established Church. Neither was this a one-way phenomenon. Many of my fellow clergy, for instance, were sore that the government allowed licences for weddings to take place in Nonconformist chapels.

Building work was also going on where Pop lived with Sarah on Sand Road. This was not another chapel but a foundry, clearly such due to its tall chimney. The works made agricultural equipment and ironwork for ordinary homes, as well as parts for steam engines. Josiah was one of the first domestic customers. He took down his garden fencing and had a fine set of railings made to surround his house. He thought it would look classy in comparison with his neighbours' houses. It was, until they started copying his idea. The iron works was on the corner of what became Foundry Lane. The works also made the splendid gates to the Alameda, set into a red brick wall. There was an outcry (but no rioting) when the Duke of Bedford's workmen demolished the wall and took the gates away.

The same year Eliza's daughter-in-law's brother-in-law (that is to say, Eliza's son Albert's wife Fanny's sister Harriet's husband George) died the year after their marriage at St Andrew's. He died of smallpox. A severe epidemic hit the town. It was brought by a tramp who had been looking for refreshment and shelter. No less than a hundred and fifty people went down with the disease and were taken to the workhouse.

Then they had to close their gates to everyone. Bulletins were posted on the gates. People in homes affected by the disease were isolated and had provisions left at their doors by friendly neighbours. There were nineteen deaths, of whom twenty-year-old George was one. This was a harrowing time for everyone, not least for me, who bore the brunt of the funerals. Their burials took place at night to reduce the risk of infection. Regulations were laid down that dead bodies had to be laid down (buried) within three days if the deaths were caused by infectious diseases. Otherwise five days were permitted.

The same year it was necessary to extend the churchyard. A referendum was held to ask people if a public cemetery should be provided. The answer was "no" because it would increase the rates. So it was left to the parish church to extend the churchyard at their own expense but for the benefit of the community.

Eliza worshipped at St Andrew's every Sunday. She also did her bit at church socials, not only baking cakes but taking charge of the cake stall, dressed of course in her most fashionable hat. She came into her own at the annual parochial tea. Volunteering her many daughters, there was hardly a limit to the involvement of, or more correctly monopolising by, the Low family.

Eliza's big problem was punctuality. She was, apart from always turning up at the factory on time, a serial late arriver. Never did she turn up for an appointment, a family event, a meeting, whatever the occasion, on time. Perhaps that is why Pop rarely took her with him to a function, even when his wife was safely at home. If Eliza was required to be somewhere at a given time it was necessary to lie through the nose and tell her that an appointment was at least an hour before it really was. But she soon twigged the trick. Perhaps the failing explains why Betsey had to wait so long for Eliza before she decided to leave the womb. What on earth she did while everyone else was waiting is a mystery.

But it was Eliza who drew my attention to a hundred missing prayer books. The church had re-stocked supplies. Had I taken them away to use at an outdoor service? Had I lent them to a neighbouring parish? Had I not ordered them after all? Had they been pilfered? Had someone used them for a bonfire? Eliza and I searched in the most unlikely places (behind gravestones, in the rectory loft, under the altar, on top of the tower) before telling anyone else of the disappearance. It remained a mystery for months. Then I was contacted by the police. There was a man who had been apprehended for stealing from a bookshop in Keswick. He lived in Houghton Conquest and the police found every room of his house to be crammed full of religious books. He had a fetish for them. The police asked us to collect a hundred copies of the Book of Common Prayer from their storeroom. We did. But they were not ours. They were older. Another church must have taken the new ones!

Perhaps we have painted a more attractive picture of Eliza when she was grown up than when she was making her way through puberty. It must be said, however, that Eliza never lost her ability to amass untold jumble in the home. She was unimaginably unorganised, untidy in the extreme. She was good and skilful at work. She was caring and went out of her way to look after others. She was extravagantly generous. But we cannot escape the fact that her home was a mess. It was not unclean - far from it. But it was crammed full of accumulated stuff that she would never need. In other words she was a compulsive hoarder.

Apart from this and her terrible timekeeping Eliza was a truly remarkable and likeable lady.

Eliza's sister, Lucy, and Charles
I had baptised Eliza but it was my colleague, the Reverend Mr Maule, who baptised Lucy.

Lucy (not, of course, the Lucy of the Interlude) could not have been more different from her elder sister Eliza. Growing up they never saw eye to eye. But then we need to take account of the six years' difference between them. Lucy rather resented that she had grown up in her big sister's shadow. She sought independence from her and finally found it when she found Charles.

Charles Read could have been an honorary Low insofar as he was soft-hearted and easy-going yet was perfectly capable of flaring up when riled. His exhibitions of anger were real if rare. He was usually tolerant, accepting, accommodating. He was an honest and principled man. And he was sociable (even if he did turn down my best grappa), a good mixer in company, which he always relished.

Charles was a hard-working railway worker from Leicester. His job was to lay plates, a job that took him all over. His previous job had been in Nottinghamshire. Then he was sent to Bedfordshire, which is where he laid plates immediately before he met and laid Lucy. He proposed to Lucy but told her that they would be moving away from her family. Lucy was not unhappy about the prospect. I married them in church and that was the last Lucy saw of Ampthill or Ampthill of Lucy. They went to Mansfield, on to Broughton, from there to Wellingborough and finally they settled in Leicester, where Charles left the railway and got a job in an iron works. He set up Eliza's eldest son Albert with a job at the works. Albert was fourteen and this was his first employment. He stayed at his aunt and uncle's until he had had enough of smelting.

Eliza missed her little sister but she was too occupied being unmarried to let it prey on her mind. While Lucy was bearing lots of legitimate children, Eliza was bearing them rather less virtuously.

CHAPTER 19
AT WAR

May 1855 *Half way round the fitness test course the sergeant major yelled at his soldiers: "Come on, boys. Don't let the Padre beat you - for GOD'S sake."*

Eliza's brother, William

Everyone remembered William's birth. There was some panic, not only to do with the premature birth but also due to many Ampthill men at the time joining the 3rd (Reserve) Battalion of the Bedfordshire Regiment. They were to reinforce other regiments being mobilised for the Crimean War. Our country was at war with Russia.

Soldiers were being recruited. Chaplains were needed to minister to them. Numbers of regular army chaplains were inadequate. But the Society for the Propagation of the Gospel had opened a fund to send twelve chaplains to assist with the spiritual ministry to troops. I was fortunate to have two curates at the time. One of them was as yet only in deacon's orders. He applied for a posting. I urged him to withdraw his application because he was abysmally inexperienced. I think he hardly knew a couple of swearwords even. But he persisted. On his application form he listed as his motives for applying:

I am unmarried, young and healthy.

I am not trying to escape any creditors.

I have a love for the souls of others.

It was in his favour that he was unmarried and healthy. As for being young, I considered he was too young. Would he cope in a hospital dealing with the vast number of soldiers dying from infectious diseases? Or what if he found himself in the front line? I dreaded to think. As for creditors, I happened to know that he was badly in debt, just as I had been as a curate, and still was for that matter. As for his love for souls, I wondered how he would manage to love the stinking bodies in the terrible conditions of rampant disease.

My fears were allayed. He was given the thumbs down.

Most Ampthill residents had little understanding of why the war was being fought, especially after it had gone on for two years with little progress. Losses were far higher than expected. Soldiers from my parish suffered terribly and misery was brought to their families. A few young men never returned and some did return but broken.

"What a dreadful fiasco," the unhappy public were saying. "The war is a disaster and unnecessary."

They were doing more than complaining. They were protesting through demonstrations. These took place in Trafalgar Square and Ampthill Market Place. How did they protest? Heavy snowfalls gave the clue. They held snowball riots. They showed disfavour against the war by pelting horse-drawn omnibuses, cabs, pedestrians, whatever was in the way, with snowballs. The police intervened. So they got pelted too. The snowball fights were replicated in Ampthill. But no one took a lot of notice.. They had had enough of more serious rioting twenty years earlier over the poor law.

The Market Place was a gathering place for people, not only on market day. They came to meet at the town pump and obelisk, erected by the Earl of Upper Ossory, where, below the clock tower with its two bells, they could tell when it was time to go home for tea.

It was at the Thursday market that Pop caught sight of a recent customer, William Spriggs, recently moved down from Darley Dale in Derbyshire. Their son, also William, was not yet born. He was destined to marry Minnie, Pop and Eliza's fifth of seven daughters. If Charles Darwin was right about evolution, Minnie would be the best evidence I could summon to second him. She resembles an ape more than anyone else I know. We will return to Darwin in the next chapter.

The sixth girl, Florence, many years later, in the late 90s, went out with Frank Inskip and they spent hour upon hour sitting in the market square courting. Flo was a straw hat sewer. Frank took off people's straw hats and cut their hair. Frank left home. He left his wife. He left Ivy their daughter before she was a year old. Florence and her daughter moved back in with Eliza. The household now comprised mother, daughters and granddaughter. Frank was now cutting hair in Brighton, where my mother was born a hundred years previously. As well as a gents' hairdresser Frank was now keeping a tobacconist shop. He had certainly quickly got Flo out of his hair.

But we must return to the time of the Crimean War. It came to an end after two years. So did William Low's life. He lived through the short duration of war but, with a greatly swollen head, he died of water on the brain, and then bronchitis.

Two things happened at the end of the war. First, I was asked to be chaplain to the 3rd (Reserve) Regiment. My curate, who had been turned down as a regular chaplain during the war, was utterly disgruntled by my appointment. He wanted the position. He considered himself more suited. In other words he thought that I was too old at forty-two. I urged him to dwell on what the military required in a padre, youth or experience? I still had plenty of energy. I was fit. I was willing. I related easily to men. (I related well to women but that is another story.) I was capable of conducting a good drumhead service in the field. The commanding officer complimented me on my accomplished talent as a flautist, for I played the flute to accompany hymns. By no means was I a good flautist but I could play marginally better than I could sing. If my voice could not inspire the soldiers to sing, the sergeant major did. He was encouraging from the back, "Come on, sing, you bastards, sing."

My colleague was not convinced that I was the man for the job but that did not worry me; he left shortly after for another parish and we lost contact.

There was, as ever, paper work to complete. There was a form that I was asked to check, sign and return. It showed correct details except that under the heading "Religion" it had "unknown". That seemed a fair description for a Church of England chaplain.

I had services to conduct for the regiment. Sadly, the first two were memorial services for a private and a lance corporal who had died in the war.

The third service was two days before Christmas. The regiment formed up together with wives and families who wished to join in for a carol service. I asked the regimental sergeant major's wife to read a lesson. Laughter broke out when she read, "But how can this be, since I am a virgin?" I sternly rebuked the soldiers for their hilarity, telling them how difficult it had been to find a virgin.

A benefit of the appointment was that I could escape the problems of the parish for a while. Unfortunately it meant leaving problems with Mary (again, my wife, not the blessed virgin). But she coped better with many of them than I could have done. For instance, we were asked to put up a sixteen-year-old girl who had been thrown out by her parents after having a miscarriage. She came in and I went out - to camp.

The regimental medical officer and I, together with the medical orderly Private Albone (otherwise known as Private Bones) arrived at the park in an army ambulance and were met by an explosion. It was nothing to worry about - just an exercise using simulated civilian casualties. The scenario had been planned to test the battalion's medical resources and response. We were not meant to be part of the exercise but out of the blue the ambulance turned up complete with doctor and padre. I gave excellent spiritual care to a casualty but forgot to do anything about his bleeding. He is now dead. Perhaps the curate was right after all. The next curate was worse, as I will explain shortly.

Before that I will recount another adventure with the doctor. We slept in the ambulance on a stretcher, or more correctly on two stretchers. This is not a comfortable way to spend a night, made worse by the RMO being a prolific snorer. We had just turned into sleeping bags (the doctor in pyjamas, I without) about midnight. Within half an hour he was called out to attend to a captain with chronic gut ache. I recall his muttering as he re-dressed: "Chronic. Chronic. Chronos. Time. Why this bloody time?"

He came back to his stretcher bed at 5.30, the captain by now being in hospital. I visited him the next day at a more sensible hour.

The medical officer and I, like good buddies, would put camouflage cream on each other's faces. The brigadier came to visit. He asked me why I had my forehead marked with camouflage cream in the form of a cross. I had no idea what he was talking about until the RMO chuckled.

He was the same doctor who had given me a medical on joining. It was thorough, including pants down and cough. But when he completed the form listing every possible ailment he should have ticked the column that indicated "no". Instead he inadvertently ticked the "yes" column. The army now had a totally physically and mentally deficient chaplain. Probably nobody even noticed.

Anyway, the following day we drove to another area in the park to visit "B" Company. Unbeknown to us the Company had been briefed, as part of the exercise, that infiltrators were expected to penetrate the area in the guise of a medical team. Our ambulance, therefore, was regarded with extreme suspicion. We were surrounded by soldiers, guns, police, police dogs, the lot.

As I was packing for another summer camp I received bad news. The paymaster, I learnt, had been murdered, while packing his own kit. The following day I wrote to his wife with my and the battalion's condolences. The day after I heard that condolences were not an appropriate emotion. She and her handyman lover had been arrested for the murder. I was introduced to the new paymaster.

This was the camp when I had forgotten to pack shoes. I had boots, which fitted most occasions. But they were inappropriate for a dinner night. A fellow officer had some to spare. This solved the problem except that they were size eleven, three sizes too large. But that was preferable to three sizes too small. I wore them with mess kit and all was well until after dinner, having ordered a brandy at the bar, the officer came to demand his shoes back. He needed to return home in a hurry. I spent the remainder of the evening trying to avoid the general. But the attempt was unsuccessful, to my embarrassment.

I was asked if I would marry one of the officers. This I declined until I realised that he meant me to marry him and his fiancée. I then accepted and the wedding took place in Houghton Conquest where he lived. In the sermon I caused eyebrows to be raised when I confessed to the bride that I had slept several times with her husband-to-be. Some were slow in realising that I was referring to sleeping on exercise in ditches or barns or under the stars.

During a camp in the park I was visited by some brigade padres. We celebrated a Communion service together. It was open to everyone but nobody else came except us three chaplains. One was Frank, a young man. He felt a spider crawling under his shirt during the confession, which he tried to squash behind his back. I thought at the time that it was a new expression of mea culpa. But he showed me the dead spider afterwards. The other chaplain, Jim, suggested that we had a chaplains' briefing. However, I explained that I had a late breakfast booked in the mess, so, leaving them to it, I went off for a fry-up.

It was not only the spider that died. Not long after our service Frank killed himself, leaving behind a young wife and children. I had no idea that he had big problems.

September 1855 *A young soldier bought me a beer. He insisted he didn't want me to pay. But he did want me to pray. The drink was in exchange for a prayer to keep him safe when he goes live firing tomorrow.*

Returning to the next curate, he had turned up in the parish with his wife and two young daughters as I was about to go away (all of half a mile) to summer camp in the park with the regiment, a few incidents of which I have just been describing. I had suggested that he use his time, while I was away roughing it in a tent (or on a stretcher), to settle in his new home. I would show him the parish ropes on my return. When I arrived back he had disappeared, leaving his three females in the house. It appears that he had eloped with another woman. Luckily neither the News of the World nor the Church of England Newspaper got to hear of the scandal so it was unreported as far as the public were concerned. It seemed to me to be a set-up job, so that he could provide some short term security for his deserted wife.

The army chaplaincy, then, was my first appointment. Secondly, a year later the bishop told me he wanted me to accept the post of rural dean of Ampthill. This involved oversight of surrounding parishes; keeping an eye on their errant clergy; acting as go-between them and the archdeacon; keeping the bishop up to date with what was happening on the ground; looking after parishes when the vicar had moved off to another post, or run away with the organist or the postman; organising chapter meetings of the parish priests. (Why are they referred to as "local" vicars or rectors, I often wonder? Are rectors and vicars not all local?) I was also expected to keep an eye on their wives. I called on a neighbouring parish's vicar Francis, and his wife Elsie, to whom I gave a cuddle. Unfortunately I held her too tightly just where she had broken her collar bone.

To start our regular chapter meeting I had asked the clergy to arrive half an hour earlier so that we could begin with a celebration of Holy Communion. They all turned up as I had bid. I presided, reciting several parts of the service by heart. I knew the Comfortable Words from the prayer book, so when we got to them I did not even bother to find the page. Somehow I panicked and forgot my words completely. I desperately turned pages but the right page would not appear. My answer was to make up my own version, which was no more than a breathless gibberish. Although I was unaware of it for a long time I was known behind my back as "Comfy Low".

The clergy meetings ended with prayer, or so the minutes recorded. When I read the minutes of one previous meeting I was taken aback to see that, instead of stating the usual "The meeting closed with prayer", it read, "The rural dean closed the meeting saying that he was hungry."

I also tried to create good ecumenical relationships in the deanery. I got on well with the Methodist minister. He called at the rectory to ask if I needed some spare hymn books, which he had brought in a big bag. No, they were hardly the hymns we sang at the parish church. The point, however, is that I greeted him naked, having come straight out of the bath. I returned the books at a later date to his wife, explaining that they were of no use to us. She said that she was only sorry that she had not brought them round to me herself.

The bishop was crafty. He suggested that we went for a meal together with other rural deans and the archdeacon. To make an impression I offered to drive the group to an inn. It was not difficult to persuade the White Hart to loan me their horse-drawn omnibus, especially when I explained that it was to take out the diocesan dignitaries, one of whom was no less than the bishop. I did not explain, of course, that we were to go out to dine at another inn. The venue chosen was a lovely public house in Pulloxhill. Almost at the end of the journey things began to go wrong. Both horses developed hoof problems and were unable to pull a carriage overloaded with corpulent clergy up the final hill into the village, which was not called Pull-ox-up-the-hill for nothing. I bade the bishop remain inside and asked the other clerics to jump out and do some pushing. With a big heave and a little assistance from the lame horses we made it to the inn.

The journey home was better. The horses had been shod. It was downhill. The only problem was that I had left one of the rural deans behind. He had stayed to talk to someone. Why should I count my passengers? They were supposed to be adults. At least it was not the bishop who was left behind. Had it been, I would not any longer have been rector let alone offered the job as the diocese's newest rural dean.

The offer arrived two days later. The bishop wrote to ask me to take on the extra work. He went on to pay tribute to "the intrepid driver, who has no misgivings about asking his passengers to get out and push the coach up the hill, or even leaving half his passengers behind - but he calmly drives on to live another day."

The bishop was unaware of how much responsibility I already had in my two chaplaincies, not to mention that I was supposed to be rector of a vibrant parish and that its vibrancy was due largely to me. However, I could hardly tell the bishop to sod off. I decided I had to relinquish the post of prison chaplain. At the time I knew there were interregna to deal with. I simply could not cope with the workload. Mary, though, said it would be a mistake to give up the prison. I could hardly tell my wife to sod off. She persuaded me to stay on, which I did until after Lucy Low's reprieve twenty-two years later. Somehow I coped.

It concerned me that my priorities might be compromised. But I was determined to find time first for prayer, mindful of the saying "Vicars do it on their knees." (There were pathetic jokes going around at the time, like "Farmers do it in on the haystack" and so on…)

It turned out to be a relief when I eventually gave up the prison. I was no longer rural dean by then. But my time was immediately taken up by new tasks. More time was available to go walking and swimming. It is not only bishops who "do it in the see".

CHAPTER 20
ORIGINS

Eliza's brother, George

I baptised George in February and officiated at his burial service the following year, on Hallowe'en. He too succumbed to bronchitis.

Six weeks later I visited Betsey and Bill again, to follow up the comfort I had tried to offer on the death of yet another baby son. They were doing their best to prepare for Christmas but knew it was going to be another sad one. I returned home to Mary feeling depressed and upset and, indeed, somewhat guilty, because I knew that for Mary and me Christmas was likely to be a happy time. We were blessed with three healthy and spirited daughters, albeit naughty ones. But we could not forget, especially at Christmas, the sorrow of other families like Betsey and Bill who had lost children.

We almost did lose our three children in one go when they were little. I might have lost my own life during my stay in Italy when our lodging house burnt down had I been asleep in bed at the time. The fire at the rectory on a hot Whit Sunday evening could have been worse. I was all right because I was officiating at evensong. Mary was at home looking after the girls, the youngest being eleven months old and sound asleep in the cot. Clouds of smoke rapidly descended from the ceiling. Mary somehow grabbed into her arms and carried outside all three children. It was a superhuman feat of strength that would hardly be possible other than in a desperate emergency. God has a mysterious sense of humour. At precisely ten to seven the incident happened, the very time that I was in the pulpit preaching on the text, "Come Holy Spirit - in fire." He surely did.

The Fire Office in the Market Square took on more significance for me whenever I passed by in future. And in years to come Eliza's son Albert was to work there. He started work as a fireman as a boy and slowly earned promotion as the town's chief fire officer.

The rectory fire was some unlucky thirteen years before George died. When he died Mary and I had been married eighteen years. I remember the year because my grandmother Maud died the same month. She had had a hard life, not made easier by the bad luck of losing two husbands who both died not long after marriage. Her husband George had survived just long enough to have two daughters, the elder being my mother. She married a market gardener, a rich Jew named Samuel when I was nine. They were married three years before he too died. My grandmother did not inherit any of his money. Samuel's sons contested the will, claiming that Maud had married only for his money. They stopped short of accusing her of killing him. Although she lived a hard life it was nonetheless a long one. "With long life will I satisfy him", says the Psalm, and so she did.

That year I recall also because Mary gave me an odd Christmas present. It was a notebook. I must add, it was a lovely and beautifully-bound notebook. But it was only a notebook. There was nothing in it. Was there any thought put into the present, I pondered?

In fact there was. Mary had intended to buy me a copy of Charles Darwin's "the Origin of the Species". It had been published the year before and I had expressed an interest in the book. But there was not a hope in hell of Mary procuring a copy for me. They sold out immediately. She tried to get one for my Christmas present when the second edition was published. They cost fifteen shillings (rather more than the notebook, I imagine). But again the book was out of print and she was out of luck. Or, rather, I was out of luck, except that I was nearly fifteen shillings better off, since I always had to pay for my own presents.

"Why did you buy me a book with nothing in it, darling?" I dared to ask.

"I'm glad I couldn't get hold of Darwin's book, dear Dave. You wouldn't have understood it anyway."

Then she added, "I thought a book with nothing in it would suit you. After all, your head is usually empty."

I am sure she was right that I would have found it hard going to grapple with the idea of natural selection. But I needed to be up with what people were saying about evolution. Thinking people, even in Ampthill, were asking questions about how life began. The new ideas were controversial. Science was still tied up with the church, especially with the Established Church. Science was no more or less than natural theology.

Yet here was a reputable scientist saying that species were not separately created but that natural selection is the main agent of change and that selection in nature is caused by the struggle for existence.

The Church, on the other hand, was saying that humans are unique. We are not related to other animals because we, unlike them, have a spiritual nature.

Unlike some, I never took the Genesis stories of creation as historical, and certainly not literal. I still felt that Darwin's theory (though I confess I have never read any of his books) of evolution was not any threat to religious belief. If Charles Darwin saw life as something complex that adapted over much time and after struggle for survival, then why should God not have designed it so? God creates life through the laws of nature. God, in other words, created evolution. He created natural selection.

If animals are not spiritual how come we can be descended from them? Well, perhaps God intervened when it came to creating human beings. Perhaps it was his Christmas present to us.

Anyway, this book is supposed to be about the Lows' human ancestors, not their animal ancestors.

Sadly though, young George was among the weakest, and did not survive.

Seven years later I subscribed to the new Theological Review. It had an article on the Origin of the Species. Mary was quite right. I did not even understand the article, never mind the book.

Eliza's brother, John

Neither did John survive. He lived an even shorter length of time than his slightly elder brother. He was born the year after George died and John died within a week or two of his birth. He was one of many victims to be hit by tuberculosis.

Betsey hoped she would not only not have to suffer the loss of another child but indeed that she would not be put through the trials and tribulations of having to bear another child at all, even if the baby were to live long. Her wish was not to be granted. She would have to face one more traumatic pregnancy. It would be the final labour. She had to wait another six years for it to happen.

The gap of six years before Betsey had her next and final child felt like a well-deserved respite from child-bearing. The nine months since conception was as hard as any of the previous ones. Giving birth too was worse than any previous. The baby boy was not to fare any better than her other three sons who died before reaching the age of two. This one died at birth and was not even given a Christian name. Unlike all their other children the "infant" was the only child not to be baptised. This was Betsey's last baby because she herself drew her last breath as she gave birth, not surviving an almighty haemorrhage.

Eliza's sister, Emma

The year after Betsey died Arthur, my father, had died surrounded by his family around the hospital bed. It might have been an elephant in bed, so enormous was his frame, mainly belly, quivering like a jelly at each difficult breath. During his hearty life he had eaten his fill, grown fat, bloated and gorged. But until his heart attack he was happy and carefree. Looking back it seemed ironic. I had returned from a six-mile walk when I heard the news that my father was in hospital. Had he come with me and kept fit (and eaten less chocolate) perhaps he would not have had the heart attack. On the other hand, although I kept myself in good trim, I confess that I abuse my stomach almost as much as he did. I resemble merely a baby elephant in bed.

Arthur's younger and only brother John went hysterical. Slightly behind the post, John relied on Arthur. Now he would be bereft. He looked up to his elder brother. Now all he could look up to was an elephantine mountain beneath the hospital bed linen. I and the rest of the family left the brothers to spend a while alone.

I took some air and wandered the streets. But it was impossible to escape the hospital. I found an old man doing the same as me, wandering the streets. He, however, was dressed in pyjamas. This was a give-away. He must be a patient, I assumed. I gently led him back to the hospital. It seemed that my assumption was correct, for I was treated by staff as a hero. If the old man did not belong to the hospital, well, he did now.

My father eventually died, as we heard at the close of part 1, at four o'clock. The staff nurse kindly brought us some tea and biscuits. John asked her if she would bring him two slices of toast with marmalade. She complied.

At the funeral the flowers were arranged in the shape of "heavenly gates". I was unsure whether the gates would be wide enough to let through such a large coffin. At the wake a fellow butcher shared some memories. He referred to Arthur's work at the brick company; his goalkeeping; his drinking; and his betting. The same butcher had made for the wake a monumental pork pie, of which I am sure that my father would regret not now being capable of partaking.

We have already heard that after Betsey's death Bill married without delay. To Bill and Ann there was born Emma. Emma was never a well girl. As a teenager she was handy with a needle. I do not mean that she nursed and stuck needles in patients' arms to take bloody samples. I mean that she stuck needles in pieces of cloth and skilfully embroidered tablecloths and the like. But she was not fit, really, to carry out even this physically undemanding task. Emma had the same consumptive disease as John, but she suffered with it for much longer than he did. After ten long years she was utterly exhausted and her body finally gave way when she was twenty-six.

I had dropped Emma into the baptismal water when she was a little baby. Twenty-six years later Ann asked me to officiate at her funeral. I had to say no. Otherwise it would not have been fair on the new rector, Mr Nichol. He had already been rector for four years when Emma died but people still were calling him the *new* rector.

It was a disadvantage for me to be still living in the town after my retirement, because having been almost fifty years in the parish everyone wanted me to officiate at their funeral. Well, not quite everyone. But in particular I was in demand if I had previously baptised or married the deceased. Emma was not married but I had christened her by dropping her into the font. Of course, it had been a controlled drop, for I quickly lifted her out again. Perhaps it was a good thing I did because Ann had prepared some hot water to be added to the freezing water already in the font. The problem was that I forgot to add it. Hence the screaming and howling. Ann must have forgotten the incident, for she now asked me if I would do the burial. Although I turned her down at least I attended the service.

CHAPTER 21
UP THE HATTERS

Luton Town would one day have its famous Girls' Choir. It also had its less famous girls working in a thriving hat industry, with factories all over the place. Many girls from Ampthill went to work there. They could earn more pounds, shillings and pence than they could manage in the smaller Ampthill hat factories. But the Ampthill factories were also given work provided by the larger Luton concerns. At the top of Station Road was the Wing, Arnold and Wing hat factory making mainly straw hats. Betsey's daughter Eliza worked there. There were other small hat works, such as those on Arthur Street and on Woburn Street. Many women, moreover, manufactured hats in the more comfortable surroundings of their own homes.

I was most interested in these places. Of course, as rector I was not involved in production work, much as I should have liked to make my own Canterbury cap out of straw. (What a challenge!) The reason that I showed an interest was because I had indeed worked in a hat factory too. This was in Luton itself. I joined the Luton girls, though I would not have been allowed anywhere near their girls' choir of course. Earlier I described my failure as a butcher. At university I also made a mess of dons' hair, for I was the college barber. Hairdressing does not lend itself to those who seek to be self-taught. That is what I was. So it could hardly be expected that I would turn out to be a good barber. Neither was I. But I did learn to use a cut-throat razor on some of the students' beards reasonably competently, because I practised on myself. I must have averaged about three cuts a day in the first weeks. Not many scars still show. Despite the degree of competence, no university fellow ever came near me when I wielded a lathered shaving brush. To be honest, not many fellow students did either.

Having tried my hand at cutting meat and cutting hair I stayed up at the top of the head and helped the hat industry. This I did for a year. Theology students were encouraged to acquire some industrial experience. They wanted to send me to Coventry but I ended up in Luton. Naturally I was not allowed to do anything to the hats themselves. This was the domain of the women. I was not allowed to do anything to the women either, not with the boss breathing down my neck. What I was allowed to do was to labour for the maintenance carpenters. I had cut meat poorly. I had cut hair poorly. I was not permitted to cut wood at all. That was left to the chippies. I carried their tools, timber, whatever was required. But it did give me the opportunity to wander all over the factory floor.

Sidney Lockwood, the boss who breathed down my neck, incidentally and coincidentally, retired to my parish in Suffolk. He was by then blind and housebound. So I took him Communion at home. I provided the wine and he provided the bread, for he made his own.

How did I find my way into a Luton factory? After two years at St Michael and All Angels college, before returning there to concentrate on the study of theology, I decided to step into the big wide world, if Luton may be thus described. The idea was to provide students with work experience. For me it became a test of vocation. Being in Luton meant that I could get home occasionally. Not that I wished to, because I had made friends with other male factory workers, who were rather heavy drinkers. So weekends on the piss were not uncommon. My friends included an Irishman who mixed many pints of mild with many pints of Guinness. I, of course, was more moderate. I just drank many pints of mild and no Guinness.

Speaking of testing my vocation, it did indeed put mine to the test, since I was boarding with another labourer, Jim, and his wife Phyllis. They had six daughters of various ages. It was like living in heaven. Or was it like living in a harem? Who would want to return to a few more years of college life after that? But I did.

One evening I held hands with one of the young daughters. She was twelve. She (I cannot remember her name) was experiencing her first period. I did my best to comfort her. Another evening I held hands with an older daughter. Pat (I can remember her name) was eighteen. She was not experiencing her period.

The prosperity of the hat industry contributed towards the formation of the Hatters, otherwise known as Luton Town Football Club, some five years before my retirement. Although Ampthill Town Football Club had been going four years before Luton's, I took hardly any notice, since I had precious little time to spare for spectating. I had played at college when the game was a free-for-all. I not only played for but was instrumental in the foundation of the WASPS as a curate. This, as almost everyone will know, stands for Wingerworth Amateur Soccer Players. Our games were friendlies. They were anything but friendly. This was many years before there were rules against kicking opponents on the shins.

There were no rules, for instance, about the colour of goalposts. I decided to paint our goalposts in red and white stripes in an attempt to startle and put off the away teams. The clever idea did not work.

The game was getting popular in Ampthill as elsewhere in the seventies. But by that time I was well past it physically, even to stand on the goal line. In any case there was no time to watch football on Saturday afternoons when there were sermons to prepare.

However, I always took a great interest in the ups and downs of the Luton Hatters, and this interest grew into an obsession once I retired from parish life (not that I no longer had homilies to prepare).

It was in Luton that I took a liking to all sorts of hats, whether considered fashionable or not. They were usually black. I sometimes wore a Canterbury cap. Occasionally a billycock hat was seen on my head, which usually caused a smirk if not an outright laugh. I found that my broad-brimmed felt hat did not appear too conspicuous. Having worked in Luton and later being rector of Ampthill I thought that a straw hat, to go with my short jacket, would be appropriate, even though it made me look like a Broad-Churchman. But rarely could I keep a hat for long. I was constantly leaving them behind. The hat left in the Roman bar all those years ago was no lone incident. In years to come women often called at the rectory and handed a hat to my long-suffering wife, saying, "The rector left his hat at mine."

That leads us back to Ampthill. It is enough of Luton. Let us return to Eliza fourteen miles up the road.

CHAPTER 22
ELIZA DELIVERS

I tried to hold healing services once every month. They did not last long. People said that they were unable to be there because they were not well enough.

July 1898 *I offered to lay hands on the sick during the morning service last Sunday. Gladys on the way out of church today told me that after she got home her eyes became badly inflamed. She would never ask for healing again. (Then one of the young people had a fit under the lych gate.)*

Gladys did, in fact, ask for healing again. But it was at the Methodist Church instead. They held more fervent services than I did. She loved the modern hymns: "They're much nicer", she said, "than your tunes at matins and evensong." I responded by saying that nothing was better than Hymns Ancient and Modern. But she was not slow to tell me how she came away with a glowing feeling. And her eyes, she told me, were now better, entirely due to the enthusiasm of the lovely minister.

Occasionally I was in need of a healing service myself. One morning I went back to bed with the shivers. Mary sympathised because she assumed that I had 'flu. The second day I continued shaking, shivering, aching, burning, sweating with fever. The fever had gone by day three. But the left leg below the knee was inflamed and swollen. It was also painful, especially when I tried to stand or hobble. It was not 'flu. The doctor told me that I had cellulitis, probably caused by pricking myself on a thorn in the garden. I had a different theory. I believe that Mary had scratched me during the night with a big toenail.

June 1889 *In Sunday School the children were asked, "What does the vicar do?" Because I lay hands on their heads and bless them, little Ada answered, "He mends heads."*

This chapter, first, is about Eliza blessing her children, without necessarily laying hands on them. They were all born at her little house on Saunders Piece. Eliza's benediction on her children starts with the youngest, then she blessed (or cursed) backwards.

O lovely rotund **Rosa**, how rosy your cheeks and your cheek; how chic the outfits you machined for the butchers; how gratifying to have you as next door neighbour; how you ogled Bert the choirboy; but how he became a thorn that pricked you as your husband; how Bert died young in battle; and how your next husband Harry pricked his rose too, but lost his life at the brickworks. O sad Rosa!

O sweet flatulent yet favourite **Florence**, how you sewed straw hats so skilfully; how you flirted until your final fling with Frank; how you watched him dress men's hair; how you helped him sell tobacco; but how upsetting he left you when he fled to cut men's tops in Brighton and then deal tobacco in Tunbridge Wells; how you clung to your climbing Ivy, your only darling evergreen. O poor poisoned Flo!

O my mysterious **Minnie**, how white you laundered your linen; how neatly you trimmed your beads; how much you loved your darling Darley Dale from Derbyshire, from whence came your bridegroom Bill. O magnanimous Min!

O adorable **Ada**, how far you pushed the boat out; how skilfully you fitted the boater; how well you worked the spindle; how you lived to great age a spinster, no child to nurse. O lonely Ada!

O elegant **Elizabeth Eliza**, how likable my Lizzie who bore my name; how you loved dressing up; how you became a tailor; how you shot your bolt; how you married another tailor, your Walter Shotbolt; how frequent your enlargements. O smart Elizabeth the second!

O elegaic **Elizabeth,** how you were the apple of my eye; how you brought laughter as a babe; how little was your coffin which you entered not yet four months young; how you brought tears to my eye. O tragic Elizabeth the first!

O unjammy **James**, how you saw your first birthday and then were no more. O afflicted James!

O ungorgeous **George,** how you deserted us as a lad; how you sweated in the iron works; how your rebellious Rebecca followed you thinking you could do better in Kettering; how you missed us and returned home; how you were such a grumpy old bugger. O grisly George!

O alarmist **Albert,** how with alacrity you sped to put out fires; how rhythmically you conducted the town band; how you fell for Fanny the percussionist; how you wanted to tinkle her triangle with your baton; how you wed her and played on her isosceles. O melodious Albert!

O jovial **Josiah,** how you blessed me with all these offspring but suddenly were not allowed to issue me more fruit for the womb; how your new wife wanted you only for herself. O Pop, how you made her heavy with just one more child, but blessing Annie (not me) with your seed: **Emily**, your last-born!

The chapter, secondly, is about Mary and me blessing our grandchildren (all of whom call me "Granddad No Hair". All their other grandfathers were still well-endowed).

Marie drew breath the same year as Ada.

September 1875 *Marie came to us for a sleep-over. She entered the bathroom as I stood in my underpants. "Granddad, can I see your willy?"*

Derek came into existence the year after.

November 1876 *Derek came to us for a sleep-over when Mary and I were celebrating our thirty-fifth wedding anniversary. He was astounded. "Blimey, that's a lot of years"! Mary was cleaning the house. He decided to help by brushing in the toilet. Derek locked the door from inside. I calmly talked him through how to open it, which he eventually managed but not before his mother arrived. Jane will never entrust us with him again, not at least until we reach our fiftieth..*

Frances entered the world the same year as Eliza's Minnie.

March 1880 *Frances came to us, with Marie, for a sleep-over. I took them to play in the park. Frances climbed a fence and got her leg stuck between iron railings. I tried to extract her leg. The more I tugged the more pain and crying resulted. Workmen rushed to the scene and hacksawed through the railings. The leg was released but I got the blame.*

Jonathan first saw light the year Eliza's Florence was born.

January 1880 *Jonathan came to us, with Derek, for a sleep-over. I took them for a walk and pointed out to Jonathan the names of items we passed. For example, "That's a litter bin." "No," he insisted. "It's a big bin, not a little bin."*

After he's gone home things are invariably found to be missing, sometimes hidden under the pillow, sometimes in the laundry basket, sometimes their whereabouts forever a mystery.

Wilfred popped out of the womb when Eliza's William married Rebecca.

May 1884 *Wilfred came to us for a sleep-over. Next morning he put his clothes on - all back to front - and got me into trouble.*

He doesn't hide things. He just fiddles with them and messes everything up.

And **David**'s nativity was the year when Eliza's Rosa was incarnated.

July 1886 *When David was barely a year old I collected him in a pushchair. It was pelting down with rain so I had come prepared with a cover. Not knowing me too well at that stage he had not yet come to put trust in me. (For that matter, he never did.) So he fought vehemently against being shielded from the weather. I therefore let him get soaked to the skin. When I arrived home Mary, naturally, scolded me. I claimed, though, that the fault was entirely David's.*

This is how David came to us for a sleep-over. He's an incessant snorer asleep. Awake he's incessantly accident-prone. This time he returned home with no more than a black eye. Pamela pointed out that before we look after her children again we should complete a risk assessment.

What did our grandchildren think of us and did they come to see us under sufferance? They gave a few clues in what they said to us. No doubt there were other things that they did not say and would not wish us to know. But they liked to hear stories, especially wicked ones, about their parents when their mothers and fathers were growing up, things their parents would prefer them not to know.

Perhaps we gave them too much advice, whether they needed it or not. Probably they thought that we fussed too much. "Put a coat on or you'll catch a cold."

They saw Noo-noos sat in her chair always looking out of the window watching people walk past, perhaps assuming that they might sometimes long for them to call to visit.

When they, the grandchildren, called, the first thing we would say was, "How tall you're getting". As far as they were concerned we, the oldies, no longer grew upwards but outwards.

I certainly had a reputation for being forgetful. Whenever I went to their houses I never came away without leaving something, usually a hat, behind. When we left our own home I would lock the door and when we got to the garden gate I would need to return to make sure that I had done so.

When their mothers complained about their behaviour Mary would say, "Remember when you were little and I caught you dipping your finger in the pie?" (No doubt our daughters picked up the habit from me.)

They thought we dressed as if we were old-fashioned, especially when they saw Mary's drawers on the washing line. "Wow! Just look at those bloomers!"

In retirement I would easily fall asleep in the armchair. But I would immediately wake up when food, my favourite word, was served. I would also wake up when one of the girls tickled me or one of the boys shouted into my ear. After the meal I would go back to sleep - until they played the next trick. In earlier days I might rough and tumble with the boys. But later in life they definitely considered me past it.

But I was stricter than their parents in one respect. I expected them to eat up all their food, even things they did not like. Then the rejoinder would be, "But granddad, *you* don't like sultanas", to which I could not find an adequate answer.

CHAPTER 23
DISPATCH BOX

Several politically-minded characters required a special box to hold their important and official documents. Some, like George Claridge, kept them at home. George's father William had founded a prosperous grocery business (Claridge and Berwick) on the corner of Woburn Street and Dunstable Street, the very spot where my father had his own butchery shop. My socialist father, Arthur but known as Sidney, was forever arguing about political issues. His house was known as "Steak and Sidney's". George, who took over his grocery business from his own father, had a large house on the border of Ampthill and Maulden known as "Lard and Treacle Villa". This would have got one over on my father, had he not already been committed to the earth. George was a Liberal. He became the first County Councillor for Ampthill. So, of course, he had to have a dispatch box well before he required one as a coffin.

The secretary of the Town Council had a dispatch box in which he kept the lively minutes and correspondence concerning the controversy over Ampthill's sewerage. After one stormy meeting of the council, and as a direct result of it, the secretary had a stroke from which he died. The dispatch box was no longer any use to him. But he was dispatched in a much bigger box.

The brewers, Morris and Company, also kept a dispatch box in a strong room in their offices on Market Square. On one famous occasion the keys were accidentally locked inside the strong room. Nobody could gain access to the box for three days. It took that long to make a hole in the wall to get in. They had a hole in the wall before any bank thought of the idea.

Next to the brewers' office was a small bakery. The baker on one occasion had the misfortune to fall through the cellar floor and straight into a passage which led into Dunstable Street. It was bad news that he broke his leg. The good news was that he had discovered a new exit.

I had my own sort of dispatch box at the rectory in which I kept confidential files. The bishop had received anonymous letters of complaint (not, surprisingly, about me, but about my curate). The bishop actually sent me the letters which the unsigned had dispatched marked "confidential"; he sent them by mistake. So now I knew who had made complaints behind my back and behind my colleague's back. The bishop quickly became aware of his error and insisted that I burn the letters. I could not find a match, so the letters are in my box (dispatch box not matchbox) to this day.

Life in the rectory was a cultural change after living in a different part of the town as a boy. Although we were not as poor as many we lived among people who lived in conditions of overcrowding and squalor. My parents (some would call them humble but that was never a description that I would apply to my parents) were working class, living down the bottom end of town, and now I had risen in the world to the top of the hill where the rectory was located, rather inaccessibly, but reckoned by some to be up with the gentry. And Mary and I had several servants and even a stable boy.

Even the bats were superior. The church itself had bats but they were merely the common pipistrelle. The rectory ones were the long-eared bats. Moreover the rectory loft was the maternity hospital for them in the locality.

The rectory was even less accessible when, after I had been ten years in the parish, the diocese built me a new rectory on Holly Walk. My home at the top end of town did not mean that I rose in class, except that my professional calling with a mansion to go with it gave me a pedestal to stand on. But I was not given the money that often accompanies the status. The pedestal had been provided by none less than the lovely flower ladies.

In addition to a pedestal to stand on we were provided with a new path to walk on. It came about following the archdeacon's visitation to inspect the church silver. It was a soggy day and, following tea, during which George wagged her tail and knocked over the archdeacon's wife's sherry glass, spoiling her pretty dress, he got not only his shiny shoes but his gaiters muddy when I took him across the garden to the track leading down to the church. (My churchwardens, I discovered later, had been hiding behind the hedge, making an appearance only after he had left.) But the muddied archdeacon subsequently arranged for a new path to be laid so that I could always have clean black shoes. We named the path "Archdeacon's Walk". It is not relevant to relate that the archdeacon's wife's name was Violet and her nickname Violence.

Quick on the archdeacon's tails to inspect the church inventory was the architect to inspect the church fabric. I led the way but in the wrong direction. He pulled my arm (not my leg) and rebuked me: "Let me tell you something, my boy. Never walk around a church anticlockwise. Or the witches will get you."

A churchman from Bedford became a good friend of the parish. He struck up a partnership with me transporting people who were up for an adventure around local churches. I held the reins on our excursions; the more daring of the congregation sat in the carriage; he sat next to me behind the steeds. We pulled up outside a church, always a church situated next door to an inn, and he, we will call him William the Tricker, would voluminously deliver a lecture on the history and architecture of each church. We started going around the outside, clockwise of course. Then we ventured inside for an interesting talk. We might cover three churches in a day. It would have been more but for the necessity of calling next door for refreshment, a euphemism for ale. William was intelligent, witty, charismatic, eloquent, excitable and many other things besides. His voice was a thunderclap. Some would say he was a crank. If so, he was a lovable one and open-hearted. He thought well of everyone. William called my Mary the Reverend Mother. What he called his own wife, Anne, was seemingly uncomplimentary but always spoken in humour, for reading between the lines his comments were endearing and congenial.

I have written of my half-brother and half-sister, who were born four years before I moved into the rectory. Two decades earlier I had grown up with two younger brothers, Roy, born prematurely in a field when my mother jumped over a fence to evade a bull; John, born undramatically at our Maulden home; and a sister, Elizabeth, born in place of a fish bone at our established Ampthill residence. My mother never described any of the births, even John's, as uneventful.

Roy had a stutter, which he never lost, caused no doubt by the rampaging bull. The stammer was a trifle worse than my own, which I did lose. Roy was less docile than I was and stood up to our father, giving in argument as good as he got (except when they argued over politics). They worked together in the butcher's shop, where the rows persisted. Unlike me, Roy took naturally to the trade. He learnt from the old man, which is more than I can claim. I could dispatch meat orders moderately well and even make uneven sausages. Beyond this I was useless. Roy was also trendy and fashionable, which attributes have never been ascribed to me. Roy, unlike perhaps our brother John who loved all things Spanish, was no bull fighter, but he did own a racehorse, Oryx Minor. The only time that I ventured into the bookie's to place a bet was when it had a run of wins so I gambled a funeral fee on the horse. It came last.

I had been spotted in the bookmaker's. A parishioner had gone home and told his wife, a regular worshipper, that he had seen me there. She told me later that she had rebuked her husband: "Well, the rector's bleedin' human, ain't 'e"!

I got my own back later. I buried the bookmaker. Naturally I preached on the text from Philippians, "I am racing for the finish."

Roy and Lorne had three children and several sons and daughters-in-law. One American girlfriend was immediately out of favour with Mary when she disrespectfully (if accurately) called her roly-poly.

My other brother, John, was named after my grandfather (called John, but for what reason only God knows, for his name was actually Arthur. He was the original Arthur Low.) John left home at an early age like me. He went not to college but to an equally hard life on a training ship to enter the Royal Navy. He travelled the world and hated it. What he hated was not the world but the navy. But after leaving the navy he regretted the decision. He became a milkman - not a pop man. John was a man of few words, fewer even than me.

Brenda, his wife, also said little in company. In the company of one another it may have been a different matter. But even that is doubtful, for all the Lows spoke only when absolutely necessary.

After Brenda died John decided that he would move to Spain once he was retired. Some years later he was ready to pack his bags but realised just in time that he was not as old as he thought. He unpacked and did another year's work before reaching retirement age. At the second attempt he packed his bags. He made the move but before John could settle down he died of a heart attack.

Elizabeth was twelve when our mother died. She was the only one of us siblings who had to live with our father in anything but heaven when the new regime took over. She was like Cinderella but never had the opportunity to go to the ball. The rest of us had fled the nest, Roy moving down the road with his young wife Lorne, embarking on his chosen meat trade, and in the course of time bringing up their three children; John sailing the oceans and calling in at the world's ports; and I moving to academia with a view to sacred ministry in the Church. After some years of domestic teenage toil Elizabeth ran away to marry the boy across the road. It failed, but two lovely children produced by the marriage were a successful outcome. By the time Elizabeth married again I was qualified to perform the rite myself, which is what I did. Frederick, her first husband, had been well and truly dispatched by then, otherwise I would not have dared marry her. (The Church forbade marrying a divorcee. It also forbade marrying one's sister!)

Elizabeth's home would have been welcoming if only visitors (or indeed others of the family) could have found somewhere to sit. Her home reminded me, though far less extreme, of the cottage occupied by Susannah and Richard Bridge at Kidlington, where I used to call when at college. All nooks and crannies, chairs included, stairs, floors, sinks, bath all included too, were piled high with papers, clothes, ornaments and what have you. To navigate the house it was necessary to step over obstacles, including some floorboards not yet laid. Some doors opened with the aid of a nail. The garden might have been attractive but for the junk and scrap between the fruit trees. Furniture could also be found in the garden, simply because there was no room for it inside. But Richard was an enormously patient man and put up with Susannah's hoarding. John was equally patient with Elizabeth, though he did not have quite the same scale of problem to contend with.

However, Elizabeth's second marriage was destined to end in tears too, this time due to her beloved John's early death. They too, though, had a son who grew up to become a wonderful man. He was not so wonderful as a boy. I painfully recall him sticking pins in my backside when my back was turned.

Elizabeth worked for a time for Emily. She was an older lady. Emily was recently widowed and had decided to move to Ampthill. In fact she was destined to become a true lady, namely Lady Ampthill. Lady Emily brought many innovations to the town, among them a nursing association which she formed. She employed a district nurse for herself. My sister Elizabeth spent most of her life caring for others. Now she was about to retire. But Lady Emily put paid to that. She roped Elizabeth in as one of the town's new nurses. Elizabeth was so adept at nursing that she tirelessly continued to look after the elderly and infirm even when she ought to have been cared for herself.

I had moved away from home at a young age to study at Oxford. Circumstances finally led me to return to Ampthill before I had reached thirty years, when I was destined to live in the rectory until I handed over the living with mixed feelings. On one hand there were deep regrets at handing back the pedestal to the flower ladies. On the other there was relief at relinquishing responsibility and no longer doing battle with those powerful women.

One of the onerous responsibilities was the job of rural dean. The bishop had told me that the appointment would be for five years and that would be it. The five long years came to an end, then he asked me to extend this extra work for a further three. Had I done too good a job perhaps? Possibly so, because he held out a carrot. Instead of firing me from the job he made me a canon. I was now hardly ever referred to as rector Charles but as Canon Low. At least people would no longer called me "Rev", a slang title that I hated. Well, no one listened anyway despite my protests and many kept up saying "Rev". It was soon forgotten that I was a canon, except by the army. And they assumed that I was some kind of ecclesiastical big gun cannon.

My daughters bought me a fine Robin Hood chess set as a present. One of the bishops resembled Friar Tuck. Two of the white pawns lost their heads but that was not until one of the grandchildren arrived and pretended that he was the Sheriff of Nottingham.

For my second stint the bishop held out a further carrot. He said that the diocese would pay for some secretarial help. The first secretary was useless at the job but in her favour she made delicious cakes, which she brought to the rectory to make up for her inadequacies.

July 1854 *Last week my secretary would not stop talking, causing both herself and me to make mistakes. Today all is forgiven. She has brought me peace offerings.*

Next I had a younger secretary called Selina. She was delicious too. She knew nothing about the Church and made many mistakes. Her worst howler as far as I recall was a letter to all the deanery clergy to let them know of my learned talk on Saint Paul's teaching to gentiles about circumcision. She wrote, "St Paul, Apostle to the Genitals - his views on circumcision". I did not spot the error until too late but I was happy to put up with anything, so luscious was Selina. I defended her from rebukes from clergy who complained of her spelling mistakes. Sadly Selina married an American and went to live in America leaving me bereft.

It was suggested that my title as new rural dean might become "the Rather Reverend". That would have been preferred to "the Almost Reverend" had I been nominated as archbishop. I was not. But anything would be better than "the Late Reverend".

Shortly after making me rural dean I paid a visit to the bishop, as my diary relates.

April 1855 *I received a message that the bishop wished to see me as soon as I could conveniently make it. I spent a sleepless night wondering what I had done wrong. The bishop was perplexed when I arrived at his door. No, he had no wish to see me. When I related the incident to the curate he simply laughed. It transpired that the curate had written the note himself, not for a moment thinking that I would fall for his April Fool.*

Back to Selina, I called at her house to collect the book of registers that she had written up. The door opened and there appeared before me the shape as of a woman. She invited me in, turned the key and looked at me appealingly. I walked slowly towards her, nonchalantly undid her front and kissed her passionately. It was one of my more pleasant dreams for some time.

I did not in reality, believe me, have an affair with my secretary. But one of my more unpleasant duties as rural dean was to deal with a young married priest who did have an affair. It was not with a parishioner. It was with a police constable's wife. He was living dangerously. In fact his living was taken away. Whereas I had been worried about seeing the bishop, he was called before the bishop and it was no April Fool. He was nevertheless a fool.

There was a saying at this time that things come in twos. The incident was followed by another of my clergy being arrested for indecent assault. He was dispatched too.

As far as funerals were concerned I had dispatched many. People commented favourably on the sensitive manner with which I dispatched the dead. But I was taken aback when I heard a comment that the funeral I had officiated at for a publican's father was "okay, but a bit too religious".

A person I did not dispatch was the Roman Catholic priest. He died himself officiating at a funeral. He fell dead while presiding at a requiem Mass. He was sixty-five. The funeral director told me that he was worried about the next funeral, lest it should happen again. I replied that he could not be as worried as I was, because I was due to bury somebody tomorrow. And I was sixty-five too. However, I survived and went to Father John's requiem Mass, at which there were masses of people.

I did the funeral of ninety-two-year-old Ruth. She had told me years ago that the then rector of Ampthill had married her on Boxing Day wearing muddy boots. I carefully cleaned my shoes for her funeral.

July 1885 I travelled by train to Amersham for Peter the baker's funeral, taking Patsy with me. She read a book during the whole journey there and back. I learnt later that I had expressed some of my dislikes when interviewed by the Bedfordshire Times. They included "women who talk too much".

The funerals included both Bill and Betsey during my regnum. Pop and Eliza were another matter. Both are competing to outlive me. The outcome is as yet unclear.

CHAPTER 24
MY RETIREMENT

February 1890 *The Bedfordshire Times reports that a vicar is nearly bottom of the stress league. He suffers less stress than musicians, journalists, teachers, social workers, drivers, armed forces, hairdressers, postmen. I do a bit of all the above, so I consider my stress level to be high. I will change to the News of the World next week.*

November 1890 *The countdown continues. It's now forty days to go to retirement. But in the Bible forty days is a bloody long time.*

The very day of my retirement there was a knock on the door. The church cleaner had a bundle in her arms. It looked like a present. It was, however, a statue of the Blessed Virgin Mary in thousands of little broken pieces. She had knocked it over and brought it to me for healing.

As soon as I retired my blood pressure suddenly went too high. I decided to buy a bicycle to try to keep active. Flitt Cycle Company was the place to go and I duly went. I came away with a lovely machine. It even had pneumatic tyres. I knew how to cycle, even though I rode slightly wobbly. But as I approached the main Bedford Road my mind had a blockage. In a panic I forgot how to apply the brakes. So the brakes had no blockage and I headed straight for a horse and cart. In fact I collided with the horse and cart. The horse was okay. I knocked out my upper front teeth and buckled the bicycle. I returned it to the cycle shop, where the face of the owner, Albert Grimmer, was a picture. Within seconds of selling me a new polished bicycle I had turned it into a buckled bundle of iron. There was nothing he could do to mend it. I decided to give up cycling. (This was a few years before Albert built Bedfordshire's first steam car. I thought it best not to go to him for a new car. His sister was my day school and Sunday School teacher, and I hoped he never told her of my mishap.)

Then came Christmas Day. Mary said she wanted to buy me two front teeth but the dentist said I would have to go and see him in person. Instead she bought me a toothbrush for my other teeth.

Then came my birthday. Three grown-up daughters had clubbed together to buy me a new bicycle. They went, of course, to Flitt Cycles. "It was not cheap," one of them later informed me. I was not surprised. After all, Albert had designed the bike himself. They wheeled the machine into our new retirement home on the Crescent. I was cross. "Get that bicycle outside. I'm not having you bring your bikes into the house."

"But, Dad," they drawled in unison, "it's for you."

"Oh. In that case, bring it in!"

I decided I would resume cycling. I took more care than Jack Seabrooke, who rode his bike without care and attention and knocked down a little girl in Dunstable Street. The only damage I did was to myself, when I took a bend too wide and crashed into yet another cart. I escaped with a few bruises but (the girls were glad to know) the cycle was okay.

March 1890 *The News of the World reports about a man who took up cycling to avoid a heart attack. He was run over by a horse and cart and died. I think I will go back to the Bedfordshire Times after all.*

Living on the Crescent off Station Road I was right in the firing line for the mid-nineties invasion. It was an invasion of navvies (the six hundred and ninety nineties navvies). The incursion was for the purpose of building a second tunnel near the station and two additional lines. Of the nearly seven hundred workers five hundred were miners from Lancashire. Hoping for a peaceful retirement I was rudely disturbed not only by the workforce, who made considerable noise while working but even more during their leisure hours, particularly on Friday nights when I hardly got to sleep due to commotion, but disturbed also by the excited, noisy and loud crowds come to see the Devonshire. This was the locomotive used for the excavation. So we were attacked from two directions, miners from the north and engines from the south-west. Apart from the northern miners there was also a mechanical digger called the North Star. After the work was completed at least the passengers had a more comfortable journey, since the new huge brick smoke vents were an improvement. Everyone could breathe more easily.

We needed to come to terms living with close neighbours on the Crescent. At the rectory Mary could shout her head off and not be noticed. Here, however, I was open to allegations of domestic abuse. She would scream, "Get off me!" The next-door neighbour would come running, thinking of rescuing Mary from rape. He would discover that it was a false alarm. I was innocent. Mary was simply yelling at a fly.

My early days on constant holiday were taken up with concerts by the town band, joining the lending library, getting involved with the Musical Society. I steered clear of the activities of the flourishing temperance movements. I could and did devote time to chess. It was fun having more control over the bishop. I took the monthly British Chess Magazine. I would have liked to browse the occasional chest magazine but in my innocence did not know whether such existed and, if they did, I never would dare have it delivered. The Church Times I gave up altogether.

More active sports were awaiting, not that I took to the rugby field but I watched from the side-lines. The RUFC had been established nearly ten years before I retired but I rarely found time to go, usually needing, as I have already mentioned, to prepare sermons at the last minute. The Cricket Club started up the very year of my retirement, so at the start of the season I was asked to don the umpire's white smock. I think I umpired rather better than I ever played. Certainly I was no batsman or bowler, though I did pride myself as a fielder. But in my late seventies I could not get my right arm up to throw the ball. It was not the only thing I found difficulty getting up in old age.

Even had I retained some of my former potency (despite Betsey's attempt to neutralise me) Mary was not now robust enough to accommodate my member in any case. She had become more and more unbalanced. Her mental health was not in question. But she would topple over every so often, usually at home but not always. We were out walking with the grandchildren in a darkened forest. As already mentioned they call me Granddad No Hair. Mary they called "Noo-noos". Noo-noos was among the company when suddenly she became invisible. The children turned around but she was no longer with us.

Derek enquired, "Where's Noo-noos gone?" A voice from beneath them helplessly murmured, "I'm down here on the ground."

Mary fell once in the bedroom. It was beyond my strength to hoist her up. To give us thinking time I made coffee, for it was eleven o'clock. We enjoyed a coffee on the bedroom floor before making another attempt to climb up onto the bed.

Retired life allowed us to keep up friendships. We would meet up, albeit infrequently, with Stanley and Marilyn, whom we had known for donkey's years. Such friends we saw rarely but never forgot. Nor did we forget their tireless work for the community in days gone by.

The town had many meeting places for its numerous activities. The Quakers had a good meeting house but this was constantly in use for their own worship meetings. They were a strong community throughout my time as rector and continued to be when I was in retirement. Members included the Morris brewing family, the Mays herbalists and the Allens, their successors. I would go inside to join in when I felt the need for silence, not least to escape Mary's constant chatter. I was sure that I got under her feet being at home much of the time, so I would occasionally take part in community activities which included visiting the Society of Friends. There I was made welcome. I rather envied their hall and wished that the parish church could have such a convenient place to hold its varied activities. Perhaps one day in the future Saint Andrew's would be fortunate enough to acquire the premises.

For all its social activities Ampthill lacked a decent venue for large assemblies. Speaking of assemblies, both schools had ample space. But it was the new court house that hosted public meetings, where the public could assemble for concerts (I went to several Gilbert and Sullivan operas there); lectures were delivered there; balls were held there. Many ladies in particular enjoyed holding balls. And the local board held its deliberations there, when serious matters of drains and sewerage were never off the agenda. Its officials were appointed, including the Inspector of Nuisances. The inspector was kept busy. He reported bad smells from fish being sold at the market. He reported filthy conditions of toilets, no doubt also with their bad smells. He reported complaints about slaughter houses, often the cesspits being filled with blood. It was not so in my father's day. The inspector reported a pigsty being shared by calves and ducks and a heap of manure. Undoubtedly there were bad smells here too. And at my old school he reported the out-offices to be in an insanitary condition. It was always so in my day. He reported complaints that people were throwing their household rubbish into the streets. Some items such as fish tins and glass were not doing the horses' hooves a lot of good. Boys were making slides on icy footpaths. Richard Dalley of Saunders Piece was reported for keeping too many cats. The inspector had an unenviable job trying to cope with the health and safety of both humans and horses, for which he was paid £20 per annum.

The upshot was that, in the early days of retirement, my rubbish started to be collected free of charge by carts every Tuesday and Friday. We had to put our rubbish in a bucket, or other such receptacle, and leave it by the front door. We were even told that we had to take the bucket in again after the bin had been emptied. We were told never to put slops in the bucket. And we must never throw slops, or any other rubbish for that matter, into the streets.

A few weeks previously the parish had given me a wonderful send-off. No doubt parishioners were delighted to see me go, after so many years holding the reins. It was a delight to see Fred Law, the Methodist minister, attend my final service and even come to the bunfight. We might have made a good partnership, perhaps as solicitors: Low and Law.

Jim Kelly from the Baptist chapel wrote to say that he had a previous engagement and I think I believed him. He was certainly preoccupied with the major extension, which was to include a new schoolroom. I did not hear back from the Primitive Methodist minister. The Salvation Army officer was not in place by the time I took my leave, but their barracks opened up shortly afterwards.

I bumped into Jim Kelly in town. Naturally I enquired how things were with him. He said that he envied me living a life of ease. He related to me at some length about the pressures he faced, some of which I knew all too well. One of his problems was a reduction of bums on seats at his large chapel. He bemoaned the opening in other towns of Strict Baptist chapels which were full to the brim twice every Sunday. He had heard rumours that a small Strict Baptist chapel was to open on Oliver Street. But he need not have worried himself. Plans were delayed and it was not to materialise for some years. Nevertheless he attributed his fall in numbers to the popularity of such extra offshoots and could not comprehend why it should be so. I sympathised, of course, but my inward thoughts were that I would not be seen dead in any of them.

A much grander party than my farewell event had taken place three years before my retirement. It was Queen Victoria's golden jubilee. I had already celebrated my own fiftieth anniversary of ordination two years earlier. The twenty-second of June was a general holiday and the occasion was celebrated in Ampthill as grandly as anywhere. The town flew flags and bore banners. Triumphal arches adorned Dunstable Street and Woburn Street. Bells bellowed in the early evening and awoke not a few babies. They woke more than babies earlier the same morning, since celebrations had begun with bells at six in the morning. Bells rang again before and after the thanksgiving service in the parish church. I preached a wonderful sermon (so the congregation said on leaving church). The sermon might have been printed in full in an appendix to this book. But unfortunately I lit a bonfire during the first week of ceasing work and burned fifty years' worth of sermon material. (They included a sermon that I had once preached to a convention of bell-ringers in which I tolled them a story.) Perhaps I should have published the sermons instead of this book. To my readers I can only apologise.

July 1890 *I glanced at an old sermon before burning it. It was about the Devil. Why the devil had I found it such an easy sermon to preach?*

The brass band marched up the Alameda where a twenty-one-gun salute was fired. They knew the national anthem back to front by the end of the day. They had played in church at the thanksgiving service as well as the usual organ being played. They also played during the substantial lunch. My work was not over with the service. I thought I had already done my bit but then I was called upon to say the grace before the meal, at which 901 people (including me) sat down to feast. Some said the figure was 1001, but I reckon that was an exaggeration. Nearly as many young people were entertained to tea, also in the Alameda. It all necessitated a large number of volunteers, many being seconded from the parish church. Unusually, there was little squabbling over who would do what, for there was enough work for every willing lady and little time for cattiness.

The youngsters were all given a handkerchief, a medal and an orange. The men were given cigars, which personally I accepted gratefully and chatted up the men I knew who did not smoke, ending up with a nice full box. They would keep me puffing merrily through the first weeks of retirement. What did the ladies get? Certainly not cigars.

Then we all went to the park for sports, including donkey racing. The day ended with dancing and fireworks. What a pleasant day it was, not least for decent weather. I dropped only one clanger at the close of an otherwise successful day. I had brought a few old ladies (the ones who always were game to ride with me, saying that every time I drove them was an adventure) in my horse and cart. Unfortunately I forgot that the horse was terrified of fireworks. He bolted like a rocket, overturning the cart. No one was hurt but the ladies enjoyed another adventure because they had to walk home.

For the record, after the day's activities and eating I returned home still hungry. Appropriately, after hearing so much bell-ringing, for supper we ate one of my all-time favourite meals, a Bedfordshire Clanger, that is to say, beef and onion dumpling with a dollop of jam. This was a clanger I did not drop.

Ampthill House, owned by Sir Anthony Wingfield, had just been extended - not a very pretty job. But Sir Anthony was High Sheriff and organised an art exhibition in his home to raise funds for the town's schools. This was shortly after the bicycle affair. I went to the exhibition, being retired with little else to do. Naturally I rode the short distance on my bike. I went on the first of the two days, Tuesday the first of August, and saw some rare and beautiful objects loaned by important county families. One of the rare and beautiful objects was the High Sheriff's twenty-year-old granddaughter. But I could only admire and stare from a distance. Touching the objects was forbidden, anyway.

A more serious accident involving a horse and cart took place during the building of a new railway tunnel beneath the Great Park. Edward Smith was driving a horse pulling a wagon-load of earth. He slipped and fell. The wheels ran over his legs. One thigh was badly smashed. Edward was taken into Bedford hospital. The leg was amputated. He died the same night.

Some years later an accident happened on Hazelwood Hill Lane. An engine loaded with flour was making its way up the steep hill (John Bunyan had found it so). A wheel came off. The engine ran backwards and overturned. Fortunately on this occasion nobody was hurt. Several passers-by went home whiter than when they set out.

Sadly my retirement was not announced in the parish magazine for the simple reason that it had not been founded until I had been enjoying retirement for two years. The magazine was the idea of my successor, the Reverend John Nichol, whom we met in the Local Board election in chapter three.

The Ampthill News was founded the following year. At least I could now have time both to read a newspaper and to keep in touch with the parish. Reporters were always seeking a quote from my successor. In me they were not in the slightest bit interested.

The new rector was busy from the start, not least with building work. He saw through a thorough restoration and extension of the parish church. He installed new choir stalls. And he earned acclamation for all his efforts, including good write-ups in the Ampthill News. What nobody mentioned was that the ideas and the initiation of all the work was mine. All he did was to bring them to fruition.

The rector kindly invited me to open the annual bazaar.

November 1892 *The rector won a bottle of wine at the bazaar. Having opened the event it would have been justice had I won it. So I cursed the bugger (beneath my breath). Then I won a prize myself - a bottle of vinegar.*

He took the Sunday School to Dunstable Downs. But again, nobody remembered that the suggestion had been mine, and I would have taken them myself had I not retired.

He was busy in other ways too. A higher number than usual of children were dying, which Mr Nichol found most distressing. I offered to assist but he said that he could cope with the help of his curate.

They did not expect to have smallpox to cope with. It was carried to Newport Pagnell and was found to originate at Ampthill's lodging house for tramps at the Prince of Wales inn. The Inspector of Nuisances was called. He closed down a room at the Prince in which were four double beds.

A new curate arrived, the Reverend Mr Rushforth. The very week of his licensing he was called to a fire. A lot of damage was caused. The stables had been destroyed and, although nobody was hurt, four horses were burned to death. The fire brigade brought their engine to the scene but they were helpless because they did not have any water. The incident was witnessed by Eliza's twelve-year-old son Albert, who decided that he would be a fireman and do better than this useless crew. In the course of time Fireman Low was presented with a long service medal. Albert had the old engine replaced by a new motor engine. He went on to be the fire brigade's engineer, then foreman and finally was appointed deputy chief fire officer.

Then there was the outbreak of typhoid. It seemed to start at the home of the Duke of Bedford's gamekeeper, Mr Hillsden. Not many months later people were alarmed when the same disease was discovered in Brewery Lane.

I was not sorry that it was not I who had to deal with the trauma of all this. But writing of the trouble on Brewery Lane reminds me how particularly sad I was to miss out, having now retired, on the brewery's raucous outing to Blackpool. Instead, I remained at home and had the pleasure of listening to the ring of bells. Five had just been re-cast. A sixth was given a little later, in time to ring in the new century. Not everyone considered listening to the bells a pleasure. There were complaints on Sunday mornings from people whose lie-in was disturbed. There were even more protesters on practice nights, because the noise was, they claimed, waking little children. The complaints were not from parents but from miserable sods who did not even have little children. Fortunately I was not bothered by the complaints - this was one of the benefits of retirement.

If I survive into the next century I will write of horrendous black clouds on the horizon. But we have reached the conclusion of the present century with its dark skies but also its many wonderful blessings poured down from above, for which I am deeply thankful.

POSTSCRIPT
END OF A CENTURY

About to celebrate my eightieth birthday my girls, approaching fifty (indeed the eldest already turned fifty), bought me a a present with a difference. It was a ticket to a match at the Oval in Kennington. There was a condition attached. I was not to go unaccompanied. I was to go with all my sons-in-law.

I had heard about the Oval ground since it opened shortly after I went as rector to Ampthill. However, I never had a desire to go until Test cricket was played there some ten years before my retirement. I avidly followed international cricket, especially when we were up against Australia.

There was a problem. The tickets that my daughters and their husbands had secretly contrived for me (and their men) were not for a cricket game at all. They were for the 1892 Football Association Cup Final. I had no connections with the midland finalists, but I loved to watch any game of football, even as much as cricket. So it was that Derek, William, Nicholas and I were four of the thirty-two thousand eight hundred and ten who went to watch West Bromwich Albion beat Aston Villa by three goals to nil.

Exciting as this game turned out to be, the excursion would hardly be worth a mention in my book apart from my meeting with a particular person who was stood next to me in the crowd.

He was dressed in monastic habit, so I took him to be a member of a Roman Catholic religious order. My assumption was wrong. He had recently founded a religious society within the Anglican Church. His name was Herbert Kelly.

HK, by which initials he came to be known, invited me back after the match to see his "cells", as he described the rooms in the large house at Vassall Road. There were, he told me, two priests and eight students all interested in missionary work. I told my sons-in-law that I would not be spending the night with them in the hotel that was booked but staying in a cell. They wondered what crime I was planning on my first night in London. I assured them that I would be free the next morning to return home with them to be reunited with our wives. And so I was.

Vassall Road in the parish of Saint John the Divine Kennington was the humble beginning of the Anglican Society of the Sacred Mission. The Society moved to Mildenhall in Suffolk and from there to Kelham in Nottinghamshire. It was with that monastic Society that I trained for seven years to be a priest.

Football was almost as important as theology. In fact, it could be described as theological football. It is this environment at Kelham that inspires the mishap described in the opening paragraph of this book.

I plan to write a true autobiography, not contrived to fit a period one hundred and thirty years previously, in which my training in a monastery will be described more fully.

The book will be called *LO HE COMES*!

APPENDICES

1. A map of villages close to Ampthill that are mentioned in the text

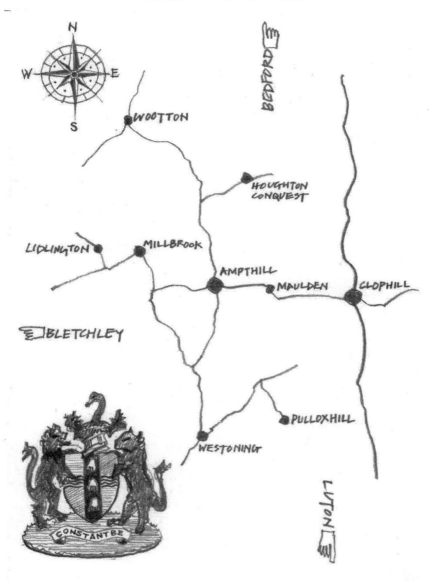

2. The LOW family tree

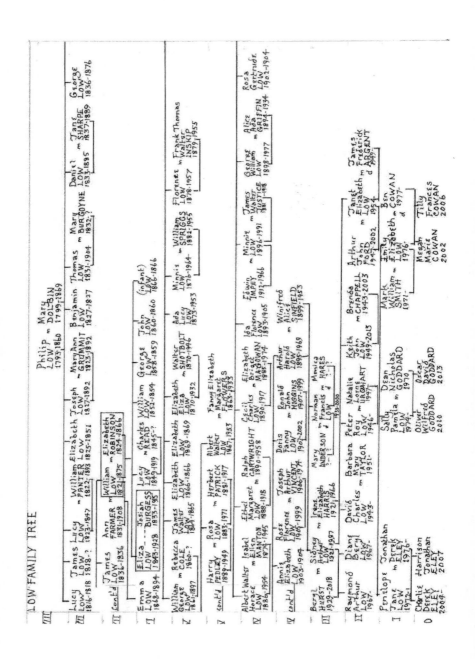

3.The ROBINSON family tree

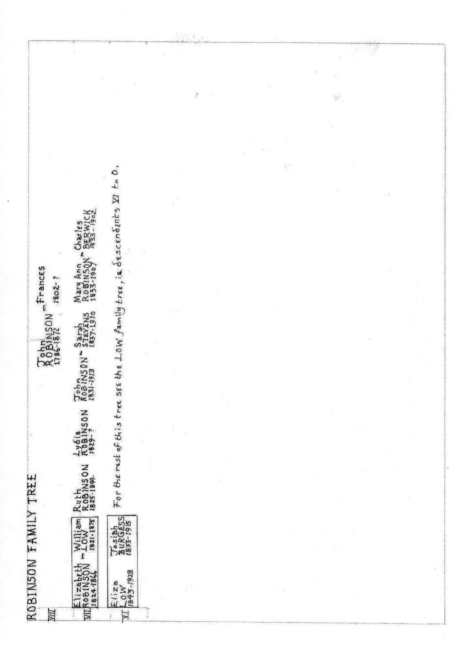

ROBINSON FAMILY TREE

VIII

John
ROBINSON m Frances
1786-1872   1802-?

VII Elizabeth m William   Ruth   Lydia   John   m Sarah   Mary Ann m Charles
     ROBINSON   LOW   ROBINSON   ROBINSON   ROBINSON STEVENS   ROBINSON BERWICK
     1824-1866 1821-1875   1825-1844   1829-?   1831-1913 1837-1910 1833-1907 1833-1902

VI   Eliza   Josiah
     LOW m   BURGESS   For the rest of this tree see the LOW family tree, i.e. descendants VI to O.
     1843-1928 1833-1915

4. The BURGESS family tree

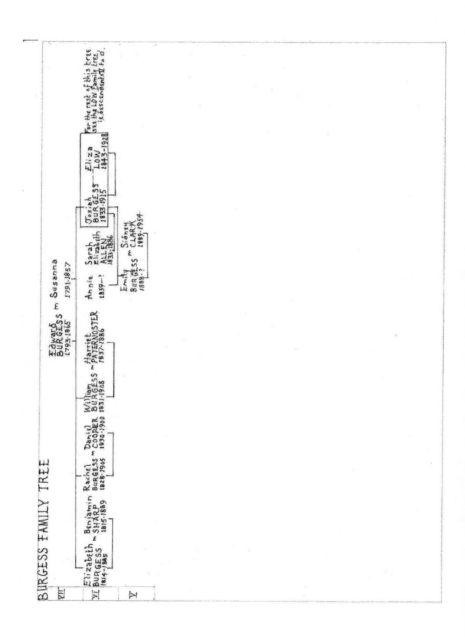

BURGESS FAMILY TREE

VII

Edward BURGESS m Susanna
1793-1865   1791-1857

VI

Elizabeth m Benjamin SHARP
BURGESS 1815-1889
1814-1905

Rachel m Daniel COOPER
BURGESS 1830-1900
1828-1905

William BURGESS m Harriet PATERNOSTER
1831-1908   1837-1886

Annie
1839-?

Sarah Elizabeth ALLEN
1831-1884

Josiah BURGESS m Eliza LOW
1833-1915   1843-1928

For the rest of this tree see the LOW family tree, & descendants t. o.

V

Emily BURGESS m Sidney CLARK
1888-?   1889-1954

5. The BRIDGE family tree

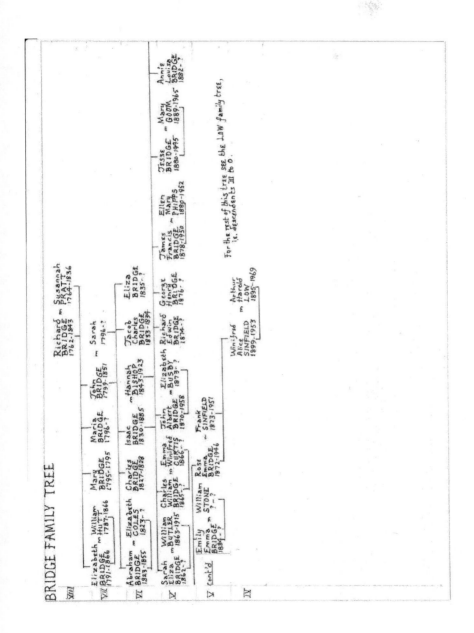

BRIDGE FAMILY TREE

Richard ∞ Susannah
BRIDGE   PRATT
1762-1843 1764-1836

VIII

VII
Elizabeth ∞ William   Mary   Maria   John   ∞ Sarah
BRIDGE   HUTT   BRIDGE   BRIDGE   BRIDGE   1796-?
1791-1866 1787-1866   1795-1795   1796-?   1799-1851

VI
Abraham ∞ Elizabeth   Charles   Isaac   Hannah   ∞ Jacob   Eliza
BRIDGE   COLES   BRIDGE   BRIDGE   BISHOP   Charles   BRIDGE
1823-1855 1823-?   1827-1828   1830-1885 1843-1923 BRIDGE   1835-?
                                                        1833-1894

V
Sarah   ∞ William Charles ∞ Emma   John   ∞ Elizabeth   George   James ∞ Ellen   Jesse   ∞ Mary   Annie
Eliza   BUTLER   William   Winifred Albert   BUSBY   Henry   Francis Mary   BRIDGE   GOOM   Louise
BRIDGE   1863-1915 BRIDGE   CURTIS   BRIDGE   1879-?   Edwin   BISHOP   PHIPPS   1880-1945 1889-1965 BRIDGE
1862-?   1865-?   1865-?   1870-1958   BRIDGE   1878-1950 1889-1962   1882-?
                                                             1876-?

V cont'd
Emily ∞ William Rose   ∞ Frank
Emma   STONE   Emma   SINFIELD
BRIDGE   ?-?   BRIDGE   1873-1951
1884-?   1872-1946

IV
                            Winifred ∞ Arthur
                            Alice   Harold
                            SINFIELD   LOW
                            1899-1953 1895-1969

For the rest of this tree see the LOW family tree,
ie. descendents III to 0.

225

6. The THOROGOOD family tree

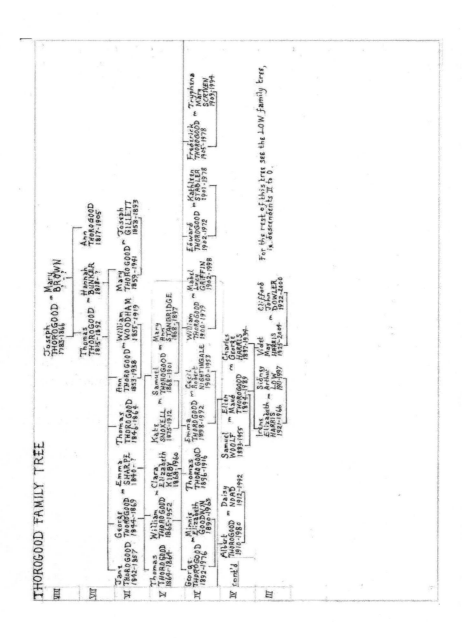

THOROGOOD FAMILY TREE

VIII — Joseph THOROGOOD ∞ Mary BROWN 1783-1866

VII — Thomas THOROGOOD ∞ Hannah BUNKER 1815-1892 / 1818-? — Ann THOROGOOD 1817-1905

VI — Jane THOROGOOD 1842-1857 — George THOROGOOD ∞ Emma SHARPE 1844-1869 / 1840-? — Thomas THOROGOOD 1846-1864 — Ann THOROGOOD 1853-1938 — William WOODHAM 1851-1919 — Mary THOROGOOD 1859-1941 — Joseph GILLETT 1853-1893

V — Thomas THOROGOOD 1864-1864 — William THOROGOOD 1865-1952 ∞ Clara Elizabeth KIRBY 1863-1960 — Kate SNOXELL 1875-1912 — Samuel THOROGOOD 1868-1901 ∞ Mary Ann STANBRIDGE 1868-1897

IV — George THOROGOOD 1892-1976 — Minnie Elizabeth GOODWIN 1890-1963 — Thomas THOROGOOD 1896-1916 — Emma THOROGOOD 1898-1972 — Cecil Robert NIGHTINGALE 1901-1953 — William THOROGOOD 1900-1979 ∞ Mabel Lucy GRIFFIN 1903-1998 — Edward THOROGOOD 1902-1972 ∞ Kathleen STABLER 1901-1978 — Frederick THOROGOOD 1905-1978 ∞ Tryphena Mary SCRIVEN 1909-1994

IV cont'd — Albert THOROGOOD 1910-1980 ∞ Daisy NOAD 1912-1992 — Samuel WOOLF 1883-1955 — Ellen Maud THOROGOOD 1894-1989 — Charles George HARRIS 1897-1934

III — Irene Elizabeth HARRIS 1921-1966 — Sidney Arthur LOW 1921-1997 — Violet May HARRIS 1925-2004 — Clifford John DOWLER 1922-2000

For the rest of this tree see the LOW family tree, ix descendants II to O.

7. Time line of background events

1809 Royal School of Embroidery moves from London to Ampthill

1811 The House of Industry built

1812 Lunatic Asylum opens on Ampthill Road, Bedford

1813 New Wesleyan chapel built on Woburn Street

1820 King George III dies / King George IV on throne / R. School of Embroidery closes

1822 Union Chapel opens

1823 River Ouse floods

1827 Alameda lime trees given by Lord and Lady Holland

1829 Ampthill House built

1830 King George IV dies / King William IV on throne

1831 Cholera epidemic

1835 Riots in Ampthill

1836 Union workhouse built

1837 The Bedford Mercury founded / King William IV dies / Queen Victoria on throne

1840 First modern postage stamp

1843 Sarah Dazely hanged

1844 George Stephenson visits Bedford / The British School opens

1845 The National School opens / The Bedfordshire Times founded

1846 Bedford to Bletchley railway line opens

1849 Ampthill Gas Company supplies the town / Cholera epidemic again

1852 Moot Hall demolished / New Clock House built

1853 First Bedford Amateur Regatta

1854 Crimean War begins

1856 Crimean War ends

1859 Bedford Midland Railway station opens / Charles Darwin's Origin of the Species /
Tuberculosis / Lunatic Asylum incorporated into Three Counties Hospital, Arlesey

1866 Cholera epidemic yet again

1868 Ampthill station opens

1870 Extensions to Union Chapel

1871	Primitive Methodist Chapel built
1879	Continuing sewage problem causes severe illness
1882	Smallpox epidemic /Alameda gates removed
1884	New Wesleyan Chapel opens
1887	Jubilee of Queen Victoria's accession celebrated / Outbreak of gastric fever blamed on drains / Bicycles with pneumatic tyres
1891	St Andrew's parish magazine founded
1892	The Ampthill News founded / Salvation Army established in Ampthill
1893	Further extensions to Union Chapel / Art exhibition at Ampthill House
1895	Accident at tunnel works / Opening of tunnel
1896	Outbreak of typhoid in Woburn Street
1897	World speed record 90 mph on railway line at Ampthill
1898	The great fire of Ampthill / Five bells recast for the parish church
1899	Sewerage system at last / Bedford hospital opens / Boer War begins

8. Time line of Low family events

Events in italics are fictional.

1802   Betsey's mother FRANCES born

1814   Josiah's parents EDWARD and SUSANNA marry

1816   Bill's parents PHILIP and MARY marry / Bill's sister LUCY born

1818   Bill's sister LUCY dies / Bill's brother JAMES born

1821   BILL born

1823   *Bill's brother JAMES dies in the GREAT FLOOD* / Bill's sister LUCY born

1824   Betsey's parents JOHN and FRANCES marry / BETSEY born

1825   Bill's sister ELIZABETH born

1827   Bill's twin brothers JOSEPH and BENJAMIN born / BENJAMIN dies

1831   Bill's brother THOMAS born / Bill's second wife ANN born

1832   BETSEY baptised at Lidlington

1833   JOSIAH born / his first wife SARAH born / Bill's brother DANIEL born

1834   *BILL STARTS WORK on the LAND*

1836   Bill's twin brothers GEORGE and JAMES born / JAMES dies

1838   BILL in gaol

1842   BILL back in gaol

1843   ELIZA born

1844   BILL and BETSEY marry

1845   Bill's sister LUCY and WILLIAM marry

1847   *BILL works with brother GEORGE* / Bill's sister LUCY dies

1848   Bill's brother JOSEPH and MARY marry

1849   Eliza's sister LUCY born

1851   Bill's sister ELIZABETH dies

1852   Bill's brother THOMAS and MARY marry / JOSIAH and SARAH marry

        Eliza's brother WILLIAM born

1854   Eliza's brother WILLIAM dies

1857   Josiah's mother SUSANNA dies

1858	Bill's brother DANIEL and JANE marry / Eliza's brother GEORGE born
1859	GEORGE dies
1860	Eliza's brother JOHN born / JOHN dies / Bill's father PHILIP dies
1861	Eliza's son WILLIAM born
1864	Eliza's son JAMES born
1865	Josiah's father EDWARD dies
1866	BETSEY dies / Eliza's daughter ELIZABETH born / ELIZABETH dies
1867	Eliza's son ALBERT born / BILL and second wife ANN marry
1868	Eliza's sister LUCY and CHARLES marry / Eliza's half-sister EMMA born
1869	Bill's mother MARY dies
	Eliza's daughter ELIZABETH born / ELIZABETH dies
1870	Eliza's daughter ELIZABETH ELIZA born
1872	Betsey's father JOHN dies
1873	*Betsey's mother FRANCES dies* / Eliza's daughter ADA born
1875	BILL dies
1876	Bill's brother GEORGE dies / Eliza's daughter MINNIE born
1878	Eliza's daughter FLORENCE born
1881	Eliza's son WILLIAM and REBECCA marry
1883	Eliza's daughter ROSA born
1885	Bill's brother DANIEL dies / Josiah's mother ELIZABETH dies
1886	Eliza's son ALBERT and FANNY marry / Eliza's grandson ALBERT born
	Josiah's wife SARAH dies
1887	JOSIAH and second wife ANNIE marry / Queen Victoria's jubilee celebrations
1888	Eliza's granddaughter ETHEL born
1890	Eliza's grandson CECIL born
1892	Bill's brother JOSEPH dies
1893	Eliza's daughter ELIZABETH and WALTER marry
1894	Eliza's half-sister EMMA dies
1895	Eliza's grandson ARTHUR born
1896	Eliza's granddaughter MINNIE born

1898   Eliza's daughter FLORENCE and FRANK marry
1915   JOSIAH dies
1928   ELIZA dies

9. Time line of the rector's events

These are events adapted to fit a timescale 130 years earlier than they happened, and adapted to fit different places from those where they happened.

My and others' second Christian names are used if they have more than one.

1812   *Charles' parents Arthur and Elizabeth marry*

1813   *Charles born at the Anchor, Maulden*

1814   *Locks his great-grandmother in pantry*

1816   *His brother Roy born*

1817   *Moves with parents to Ampthill*

1819   *His brother John born*

1820   *Charley's Aunt May and John marry*

1821   *Charles' wife Mary born*

1824   *His sister Elizabeth born*

1826   *Walks home from Luton / Starts working with father in butcher's shop*

1827   *Pours rubbish over his father's head*

1830   *Goes on Grand Tour of Italy with Simon*

1831   *Charles at Oxford University*

1832   *Works in hat factory at Luton*

1835   *Nearly gets expelled*

1836   *Charles' mother Elizabeth dies / Ordained deacon / Curate of Wingerworth*

1837   *Ordained priest*

1839   *Curate in Bury St Edmunds*

1841   *Posted to Ampthill / He and Mary marry*

1842   *Their daughter Jane born / Charles is assaulted / Visits Betsey in gaol*

1844   *Their daughter Pamela born*

1846   *Their daughter Elizabeth born / Marries his sister Elizabeth*

1855   *Moves into new rectory*

1856   *Charles appointed chaplain to the 3rd (Reserve) the Bedfordshire Battalion*

1857	*Appointed rural dean of Ampthill*
1860	*Fire at the rectory*
1860	*Goes on pilgrimage with cathedral choristers to Kevelaer*
1862	*Installed as canon of cathedral*
1867	*Charles' father Arthur dies*
1869	*Starts doing locums at Leiston*
1870	*His uncle John dies*
1871	*Their daughter Elizabeth and Ben marry*
1872	*Their daughter Jane and Derek marry*
1873	*Their granddaughter Marie born*
1874	*Their grandson Derek born / Charley's Aunt May dies*
1875	*Their daughter Pamela and Nicholas marry*
1876	*Their granddaughter Frances born*
1877	*Charles retires from prison chaplaincy / Their grandson Jonathan born*
1878	*Ben leaves the scene*
1880	*Their grandson Wilfrid born*
1883	*Their grandson David born*
1885	*Does a locum at Felixstowe*
1886	*Their daughter Elizabeth and William marry*
1890	*Charles retires*

10. Time line of the author's life

These are events when and where they actually happened.

1942   David's parents Sidney and Irene marry

1943   David born at the Anchor, Maulden / He is baptised

1944   He locks his great-grandmother in pantry

1946   His brother Peter born

1947   He moves with parents to Ampthill

1948   He studies at Russell Primary School

1949   His brother Keith born

1950   His Aunt Violet and Clifford marry

1951   David's wife Barbara born / He studies at Bedford Road Church of England School

1954   David's sister Janet born / He studies at Redbourne Secondary School

1956   David confirmed / He becomes server at Saint Andrew's (but not choirboy)

1956   David walks home from Luton / He starts working with his father in butcher's shop

He studies at Luton Technical School / He kisses head girl in Ampthill tunnel

He becomes lifelong supporter of Luton Town Football Club

1957   David pours rubbish over his father's head

He is responsible for maggots in sausage machine

1958   He reads Pilgrim's Progress by John Bunyan

1959   David studies at Kelham

1960   He is injured in privates keeping goal at Kelham

1961   He works in aircraft factory at Coventry

1962   David studies theology at Kelham / He becomes college barber

He makes mess of monks' hair

1963   David becomes football captain / He paints goalposts red and white stripes

1966   David nearly gets expelled / His mother Irene dies / His father Sidney marries Beryl

1967   David ordained deacon

He is curate of Wingerworth, Chesterfield, with Fr Norman Wickham

He founds WASPS (Wingerworth Amateur Soccer Players)

His half- brother and half-sister twins Raymond and Diane born

1969   Susanna has a crush on the curate

He performs Three Little Maids from School with churchwardens

1970   David leads pilgrimage to Oberammergau with Fr Jim Baker / He meets Barbara

He is curate of Greenhill, Sheffield, with Fr Stanley Reynolds

1971   David and Barbara marry / They honeymoon on Isle of Wight

1972   Their daughter Penelope born

1973   David is team vicar at Eckington, Renishaw, Ridgeway, Marsh Lane, Handley in Derbyshire, with Fr Eric Gunn

He is appointed chaplain to 73 Engineer Regiment (V)

1974   Their daughter Sally born

1975   He contracts mumps

1976   Their daughter Emily born / Vicarage catches fire

1978   He is vicar of Saint George Bury St Edmunds

1979   He is appointed chaplain to 5 Royal Anglian Battalion (V)

1980   David is appointed chaplain to 6 Royal Anglian Battalion (V)

He obtains Public Service Vehicle licence

He drives coach full of diocesan clergy to Swanwick conference in Derbyshire

1981   He becomes member of diocesan exorcism team

1982   He marries his sister Janet and Bill

1885   David drives coach on pilgrimage with cathedral choristers to Kevelaer

He is awarded Territorial Decoration

1986   David is vicar of Leiston with Sizewell

He is appointed chaplain of Sizewell A Power Station

1989   He is appointed Rural Dean of Saxmundham

1991   He is awarded Bar to Territorial Decoration

1995   He goes on Grand Tour of Italy with Simon Merrett (Sabbatical)

1996   David is appointed chaplain of Sizwell B Power Station

He is awarded second Bar to Territorial Decoration

1997   David is installed as canon of cathedral / His father Sidney dies

1998   He is vicar of Saint John the Baptist Felixstowe

1999   David is appointed chaplain to two Felixstowe hospitals / He becomes a Rotarian

He is appointed chaplain to Bedfordshire Army Cadet Force

2000   David starts doing locums in Sicily / His uncle Clifford dies

2001   Their daughter Emily and Ben marry / He joins Clergy Correspondence Chess Club

He is awarded Rose to Territorial Decoration

2002   Their daughter Penny and Jonathan marry / He is awarded Queen's Jubilee Medal

2003   Their granddaughter Megan born

2004   Their grandson Charlie born / David's aunt Violet dies / He contracts cellulitis

They move into new vicarage

2005   Their daughter Sally and Dean marry

2006   Their granddaughter Tilly born /

David becomes chairman of diocesan liturgical committee

2007   Their grandson Harrison born

He is appointed Officiating Chaplain to the Military to 23 Parachute Engineer Regiment

2008   Their daughter Emily and Ben divorce

David retires and moves to Sutton Heath, home of Rock Barracks

2010   Their grandson Oliver born

2013   Their grandson Oscar born

2016   Their daughter Emily and Mark marry

11. List of illustrations by Simon Merrett

i)   The Queen's Head inn
ii)   St Andrew's Parish Church
iii)   The Anchor Inn, Maulden
iv)   The Old Sun inn
v)   The Town Pump
vi)   The Moot Hall
vii)   St Mary's Parish Church, Maulden
viii)   Formerly the British School on the Sands
ix)   St Andrew's Hall, formerly the Friends' Meeting House
x)   Methodist Church
xi)   Graveyard of former Wesleyan Chapel
xii)   The White Hart inn
xiii)   Formerly Charles May's drug manufacturing premises
xiv)   The Baptist Church
xv)   Formerly the Royal School of Embroidering Females
xvi)   Formerly the Union Workhouse
xvii)   Formerly the Police House
xviii) Alameda Gates
xix)   Eliza's House
xx)   The Prince of Wales inn
xxi)   Formerly the National School
xxii)   Sign on Oliver Street to the former Foundry
xxiii) The King's Arms Yard
xxiv)   Formerly the Primitive Methodist Church
xxv)   The Town Clock
xxvi)   Formerly the Fire Office
xxvii) Formerly a Hat Factory
xxviii) Formerly the Rectory
xix)   Eliza's Grave

12. Acknowledgements

Foremost I thank my friend, SIMON MERRETT, for his inspired cover design and his exemplary illustrations. If readers become bored with my writings, at least they will have these magnificent sketches to enjoy. Simon and I, with our wives, Sheena and Barbara, enjoyed a stay at the Old Piggery in Haynes, which we used as a base for our perambulations around Ampthill and Maulden to peruse buildings that would become the subjects of the drawings. By studying the sketches it might be inferred that Simon admires noble edifices and that his profession is indeed architecture. The inference would not be wrong.

Writing of the Old Piggery, I thank RACHEL and ROBERT for looking after us well and breakfasting us grandly.

High on my list of thanks is master church crawler, friend and fanatic, ROY TRICKER. Roy examined the text and pointed out numerous errors, most being ecclesiastical anachronisms. Deferring to his knowledge I took note of Roy's wise suggestions and made appropriate alterations. A few points, however, I ignored. For instance, he told me that a bride in the nineteenth century would not have worn a see-through wedding dress. I preferred to keep her in the see-through dress. Roy was concerned about some of my more daring phraseology, mindful that the work might be read by elderly and staid ladies of my former church congregations. Had I not succumbed to his recommendations, the wording of the text might be even more indelicate than it is. Roy tells me that he cannot wait to read my *real* autobiography.

SHEENA, Simon's wife, read the draft. She pointed out that white wedding dresses (not to mention see-through ones) were not in fashion before Queen Victoria. She also informed me that butchers would not have sat on up-ended wire trays, because there were no wire trays at the time.

BARBARA, my wife, was more scathing as a critic. She queried whether I would have used sausage skins. That reminds me: she also queried the use of condoms. She questioned circumcision in a Christian home. And she thought it unlikely that even a husband would be allowed by a midwife to see his wife in the bath after childbirth, let alone the parish priest.

I'm grateful to both wives: Sheena, for her help and support; and Barbara for her patience and understanding.

I thank SHEILA PAGE and CHRIS GREGSON, who have taught me so much about family history. They, together with my neighbour, LORRAINE WEST-FLINT, have helped untangle branches of my family trees.

Simon drew all the illustrations with the exception of the family trees. The author wishes to give a special thanks to the AUTHOR, who himself drew the trees!

Finally, I wish to convey profuse thanks to PEGASUS, the publisher, for their helpful guidance and advice at every stage of production.

All mistakes, in spite of the assistance and advice received, are the author's alone.

13. Bibliography

The Revolution in Tanner's Lane by Mark Rutherford
My Young Memories of Ampthill by Amy Sharpe
My Mother's Memories of Ampthill by Mary Smith
After the Fire by John Lockley
Around Ampthill by Andrew Underwood
Home Rule for Ampthill by Andrew Underwood
The White Hart by Andrew Underwood
The Clock Strikes Five by Charles Matthews
Memoirs of Lord Ullswater [Speaker of H of Commons; delightful vignettes of Ampthill life in 19th Century]; by the Rt Hon James W Lowther, MP
The Smaller English Home of the Later Renaissance 1660-1830
Town and Country by Charles Cooper published 1937
Marlborough by Richard Holmes pp 31-32
Ampthill, Full Steam ahead, Ed Barry Dackombe with Andrew Underwood
Verses written on the Alameda at Ampthill Park by Jeremiah Holmes Wiffen
Scandal in the Church: Dr Edward Drax Free by RB Outhwaite